# Praise for
# THE SUMMER OF
# LOST AND FOUND

"Mary Alice Monroe takes you on a trip to the idyllic sun, sand, and gracious lifestyle of a Southern summer. This season's must-read!"

—Nancy Thayer, *New York Times* bestselling author of *Surfside Sisters*

"Mary Alice Monroe's inspired choice to write about the pandemic *during* the pandemic has paid off in this next installment of her acclaimed Beach House series, which can easily be read as a stand-alone, too. A novel of growing up, saying good-bye to the past, and learning to ask yourself the hard questions, including one of the most vital of all: 'Who do you really want to be?'"

—Kristin Harmel, *New York Times* bestselling author of
*The Forest of Vanishing Stars*

"The latest in Monroe's long-running Beach House series gives dedicated fans a chance to catch up with old friends, and provides enough background on the characters for new readers to enjoy. The intimate island atmosphere keeps the focus on family and romantic relationships, as the characters deal with a global pandemic. Monroe's book acknowledges some of the hardships that real people endured over the past year, addresses loss and change, and finds hope where it's possible, which gives depth to this timely story."

—*Library Journal*

"Not a lot of authors have addressed the pandemic in their fiction, particularly if they write beach books, but South Carolina author Mary Alice Monroe has risen to the challenge in *The Summer of Lost and Found*. . . . Monroe has captured the pandemic months with her characteristic warmth and keen eye for family dynamics. Readers will recognize their own challenges and emotions in this thoughtful examination of a difficult summer."

—*The Augusta Chronicle*

# Praise for
# ON OCEAN BOULEVARD

## Also by Mary Alice Monroe

### BEACH HOUSE SERIES
*Beach House Memories*
*Beach House for Rent*
*Beach House Reunion*
*On Ocean Boulevard*

### LOWCOUNTRY SUMMER SERIES
*The Summer Girls*
*The Summer Wind*
*The Summer's End*
*A Lowcountry Wedding*

### STAND-ALONE NOVELS
*The Summer Guests*
*A Lowcountry Christmas*
*The Butterfly's Daughter*
*Last Light over Carolina*
*Time Is a River*

# Mary Alice Monroe

# the summer *of* lost and found

Gallery Books

New York   London   Toronto   Sydney   New Delhi

# G

Gallery Books
An Imprint of Simon & Schuster, Inc.
1230 Avenue of the Americas
New York, NY 10020

Copyright © 2021 by Mary Alice Monroe
Maps and family tree by Danielle Fabrega

First Gallery Books trade paperback edition May 2022

For information about special discounts for bulk purchases, please contact Simon & Schuster Special Sales at 1-866-506-1949 or business@simonandschuster.com.

The Simon & Schuster Speakers Bureau can bring authors to your live event. For more information or to book an event, contact the Simon & Schuster Speakers Bureau at 1-866-248-3049 or visit our website at www.simonspeakers.com.

Interior design by Davina Mock-Maniscalco

Manufactured in the United States of America

10  9  8  7  6  5  4  3  2

Library of Congress Cataloging-in-Publication Data is available.

ISBN 978-1-9821-4834-8
ISBN 978-1-9821-4835-5 (pbk)
ISBN 978-1-9821-4836-2 (ebook)

Dedicated to my dear friends of Friends & Fiction.
Thanks for the encouragement, the love, and the sprints.

Mary Kay Andrews
Kristin Harmel
Kristy Woodson Harvey
Patti Callahan Henry

Map artwork © Danielle Fabrega of The Town Serif

Artwork © Danielle Fabrega of The Town Serif

# chapter one

*Beware the Ides of March.*
William Shakespeare, *Julius Caesar*

March 2020

HOW COULD THIS happen to her? Again?

Linnea Rutledge drove her vintage gold VW bug across the vast expanse of marshlands on the arching roadway known as the Connector. It was the main route from the mainland to the small island she called home. Below, the tide was low, revealing marsh grass that was just beginning to green at the bottom—one of the lowcountry's first signs of spring. When Linnea reached the apex of the roadway, she caught her first glimpse of the Atlantic Ocean. Today she didn't feel her usual euphoria. Rather, she felt numb.

She crossed onto Isle of Palms and drove the short distance seaward to Ocean Boulevard. Less than a mile more until she reached the quaint house she called home. Primrose Cottage was one of the few remaining 1930s houses on the island. It sat now dwarfed by the luxury mansions that dominated the boulevard.

Pulling into the gravel driveway, hearing the crunch of stone under tires, Linnea climbed from her car and walked swiftly to the front door, struggling with tumultuous thoughts of the injustices of fate. She didn't take in the first signs of wildflowers dotting the dunes or stop to enjoy the heady scent of honeysuckle along the fence. Linnea climbed the stairs with savage purpose, seeking safety. She pushed open the door, then closed it behind her and leaned against it, as one holding back a storm.

Closing her eyes, she panted, mouth open. She'd held herself together by sheer force of will while she gathered her personal photographs and belongings and carried them out in a cardboard box from her cubicle office at the South Carolina Aquarium. Her face muscles ached from hoisting a smile and bidding teary farewells to her fellows. It was a mass exodus of nonessential personnel. The aquarium was closing its doors to the public because of the pandemic.

She collected her breath and opened her eyes. Looking around the dimly lit house, Linnea felt the quiet familiarity embrace her. This was her aunt Cara's beach house, left to Cara by her mother, Linnea's beloved grandmother, Lovie. Linnea had grown up visiting here, becoming part of the group of women who loved the beach, sea turtles, and each other with an abiding devotion. This little beach house had been their sanctuary from whatever buffeted them outside the clapboard walls.

It was her house now, albeit by rental from Aunt Cara. She let her eyes glide across the creamy-white and ocean-blue walls of the small rooms, along the fireplace mantel where sat silver-framed photographs of the Rutledge family that went back generations in Charleston, across the shabby-chic white slipcovered furniture.

Linnea feared she wouldn't be able to stay here any longer. She dug through her purse and pulled her phone to her ear. Within moments, the familiar voice of Cara answered.

"Hello, Sweet-tea. You're home early today."

Linnea loved the nickname her aunt had called her since she was little. "I, uh . . . was let off early. Can you come over? I have to talk to you."

A pause. Then in a more cautious tone, "Of course. I have to get Hope gathered. She has a doctor's appointment. I'll be there in ten."

Linnea tucked her phone away and strode directly to her bedroom. Sunlight poured in across the pine floors and oriental rugs. Her gaze swept the view of the ocean beyond; seeing it, she felt an immediate connection. Bolstered, she unzipped her pencil skirt and laid it on the mahogany four-poster bed that dominated the small bedroom. A simple skirt and crisp blouse constituted her uniform at the South Carolina Aquarium where she worked as the conservation education director. It was a style adopted from Cara.

Linnea had been Cara's assistant at the aquarium. After Cara resigned, the position as education director was offered to her. It was her dream job. Linnea loved teaching and inspiring others, as she had been taught and inspired by the women in her life. Though Linnea emulated Cara's sleek dress at work, at home she changed into her favored vintage look.

She went to the bathroom and, with efficient movements, washed the makeup from her face, then unpinned her blond hair, letting it fall to her shoulders. Scratching her head vigorously, she tried to shake off the tension that had held her taut since the news. Feeling a bit better, she put on cuffed jeans and a worn pink sweater, finally stepping into blush Capezio ballet slippers, a favorite since she'd taken ballet lessons as a girl.

Feeling more comfortable, she went out onto the porch from her bedroom and took in the view of sea and sky. The power of the vista had a calming effect. Then, hearing the crunch of tires on the driveway, Linnea hurried down the deck stairs and rounded the house to the driveway to see Cara's car parked there.

"Thank you for coming!" Linnea called out.

Cara's long legs, encased in black jeans, slid out from the car. She offered a quick wave. "I can only stay a moment. I was on my way out for Hope's physical."

Linnea waited while Cara removed her precocious six-year-old from her car seat. Hope's dark hair was tied in two braids and she wore a blue-gingham smocked dress.

"You look like Dorothy in *The Wizard of Oz*," Linnea said, placing a kiss on Hope's cheek.

"Who's that?" asked Hope.

Linnea looked at Cara with mock indignity. "She doesn't know *The Wizard of Oz*?"

Cara lifted her shoulders. "She's only six. Those evil trees and monkeys . . . I think Baum had older children in mind."

"Oh, please. Let me read it to her. It's a classic." Linnea lowered to meet Hope's eyes. "You're not afraid of witches or scary trees, are you?"

Hope's eyes were round, but she shook her head. "No," she said with a hint of doubt.

Cara laughed. "If she wakes up in the middle of the night, it's on you."

"Oh, she won't," Linnea said, then turned to Hope. "It has a happy ending. Let's read it." Then looking back at Cara, she added, "Even if the Wicked Witch of the West tells me not to."

"Who's that?" asked Hope.

"Later," Linnea answered with a wink. Straightening, she asked Cara, "Want to go to the deck? I have wine? Coffee? Water?"

"Nothing. Thanks. I have to leave in a few minutes." As they began walking to the oceanside deck, Cara's dark eyes focused on Linnea. "So, tell me, what's up?"

Linnea gestured to the patio chairs under the pergola. They sat while Hope hurried through the porch doors into the house to the toy bin that was filled with Hope's playthings. Linnea pulled her hair back into her hands, then let it go with an exhale.

"The aquarium is closed until further notice. I'm furloughed."

Cara's face reflected her shock. "My God. But of course they had to. The coronavirus is shutting down everything. They can't allow people to gather. Still, it's sobering." Always practical, she asked, "How are you fixed financially?"

Linnea shook her head. "You know what my salary is. I'm in trouble."

"Savings?"

"None to speak of. Even with you helping with rent, I'm not sure how long I can keep afloat."

Cara waved her hand. "Forget the rent for now."

Linnea was awash with relief. "Seriously? Are you sure?"

"Don't be silly. These are hard times." She put her hands on Linnea's shoulders. "Back when I was in financial"—she lifted her shoulders and her lips in an ironic smile—"and emotional trouble, my mother welcomed me into this little house, knowing I'd find my way. And I did. And now, it is my turn to offer the same to you. This is what we Rutledge women do. We take care of each other. And other women as well. It's a tough world out there for women, as you've just experienced." She let her hands drop. "So, darling girl, no thanks necessary. This is your legacy. And the purpose of this dear house. With so many blessings, we pay it forward."

Linnea felt the responsibility of her aunt's mandate profoundly. This was a passing of the torch. There were no words, so she remained silent.

Cara said, "Frankly, I'm more worried about the aquarium. How long will they be able to survive with their doors closed? They still have all those animals to feed and house."

"They've kept on a skeleton crew. I know it was a hard decision for Kevin to furlough us."

"He had no choice. Bosses have to make the tough decisions and do what's best for the institution." She sighed then shook her head and said wryly, "Beware the Ides of March."

Linnea looked at her aunt sitting across from her. Always cool and practical, she had a long history in management. She'd left Chicago almost two decades ago to settle in the lowcountry, but even on the island, she maintained her city chic. In jeans and a crisp chambray shirt, she looked elegant. Her hair was cropped short again and framed her face in a style that flattered her cheekbones and dark eyes.

Cara had the dark Rutledge looks of her father, Stratton. Linnea, like her father—Cara's older brother, Palmer—had the softer, petite, blond genes from Grandmother Lovie. As always, Linnea was taken by the way her aunt casually waved her hand in the air as she spoke or raised her fingers to tuck a wayward lock of hair behind her ear. Linnea studied the subtle and refined gestures, wanting to emulate this woman she admired. Cara was not merely elegant or in possession of a razor-sharp intellect, she was generous. Family came first with her. Cara might look like her father, but in this, she was most like her mother, Lovie.

Cara glanced at her watch. "I really must go," she said, rising. "Don't worry, Sweet-tea. Keep the faith. We always pull through somehow, don't we?" She looked over toward the house. "Hope! Time to go, honey."

From inside they heard a wail: "I don't wanna go to the doctor."

Cara met Linnea's eye, smirked, and went to fetch her daughter. Linnea heard a brief complaint before Cara walked out of the house with her daughter's hand firmly in hers.

"Come for dinner Sunday?" Cara asked Linnea as they walked together down the gravel driveway to Cara's car. "I'm hoping David will be home."

"I thought he was back."

Cara's lips tightened as she shook her head. "Not yet. The coronavirus is hitting London hard and he's been trying to get out for days. Flights are packed and there's talk of shutting down the airports."

Linnea heard the worry in her voice. "If anyone can get home, David will." She smiled. "He's like a homing pigeon."

Cara met her eyes with a grateful smile. "He's pretty resourceful." Then she said in a more upbeat tone, "Shrimp and grits sound good?"

"I'll be—" Linnea broke off. Catching a movement from the second-floor window of the carriage house next door, she stopped short, gripping Cara's arm.

"What?"

"There's someone in the carriage house," Linnea said sotto voce.

Cara looked up to the window and broke into a wide grin as she waved. "That's John."

Linnea felt her throat grow dry. "John Peterson?"

Cara laughed and looked at her with amusement. "Of course, John Peterson."

Myriad emotions flooded Linnea. This shock threatened to break the dam of her emotions, already brimming over with worry over being laid off.

"What's *he* doing here?" she demanded, her cry sounding petulant to her own ears.

"He had a conference in the area and stopped to visit his mother. Emmi, of course, was over the moon. She dotes on that boy. While he was here, he got word one of his colleagues in San Francisco tested positive for coronavirus. So, rather than take a chance of infecting others, he put himself into quarantine in his old apartment. He's worried not only about his mother, but about Flo. In her eighties, she's vulnerable. I admire him for that decision."

Linnea's brain was stuck on the fact that John was back. Living next door. She hadn't seen him since their breakup a year earlier. She'd thought he was the love of her life. And then he wasn't.

"Why didn't Emmi tell me he was back?" she asked.

Cara's brows rose. "Why would she? You've made no secret of the fact that you don't want anything to do with John. He is her son. That put her in a tough position."

Linnea crossed her arms. "She could have at least given me fair warning." Her gaze shot up to Cara along with her temper. "Wait. *You* knew. Why didn't you tell me?"

She felt the tension flare and saw the spark of indignation in Cara's eyes, the slight lifting of the chin.

Cara waited to speak, considering her words. "I suppose I could have told you. And might have if I wasn't so preoccupied." She paused. "Excuse me if I'm worried about my husband. The fact is, I just didn't give John's being here much thought."

Linnea swallowed, awash with shame for her show of pique. "I'm sorry. I shouldn't have jumped at you like that. I'm all off-balance, thinking only of myself." She reached out to place a hand on Cara's arm encircling her daughter. "Is there anything I can do for you? Watch Hope for a while? Make you a casserole?"

Cara's shoulders lowered and she quickly shook her head. "Please, no casseroles!" She smiled. "You know what I really need?"

Linnea shook her head.

"A nanny."

Linnea's heart sank. "Oh?"

"I have to get the house ready for David's arrival and Hope is cranky. She hasn't been able to play with anyone since they've closed the school. Not even her cousin Rory. Heather is under lockdown with him and Leslie." She sighed dramatically. "Hope is clinging to me. Honestly, I could use a break to get something done. I'll pay you, of course. And"—she raised a brow—"don't you need a job?"

"I do. And of course I'll be your nanny."

Cara looked skyward. "Thank heaven. I'll take her to the doctor's for her checkup, then could you watch her for a few hours? I want to spread plastic in the hallway, spray things down, get everything ready."

"Just drop her off."

"Thanks. Better go." Cara looked meaningfully at the carriage house window. "Be nice," she said cajolingly, then leaned forward to kiss her.

"How long is John going to be here? Gordon is coming from England in April. I don't think I can bear the battle of the beaux."

Cara raised a brow. "I didn't think John was still in the beau category."

"He's not," Linnea said firmly. "At least not in my mind. But I haven't seen Gordon since he returned to England, what . . ." Linnea did a quick count on her fingers. "Over six months ago. That's a long time to be apart. I don't want my ex hanging around when he finally gets here."

"You and Gordon are still together, right?"

Linnea nodded.

"Then it's only a problem if you still care about John."

Linnea felt a prick of uneasiness. "Right."

Cara looked at her watch. "Really must go. Thanks so much for being Hope's nanny. It's only temporary."

"I'm her aunt. 'Nuff said."

Cara smiled and climbed into the car.

Linnea waved, then stepped back from the Range Rover as it backed out of the driveway. Then, because she couldn't stop herself, she glanced up at the large arched window of the carriage house. In the light of midday, she saw John clearly. His dark auburn hair caught the light but his face was shadowed. In her mind's eye, she could see him smiling his crooked smile.

John lifted his hand in a wave.

Linnea reluctantly raised her hand and gave a halfhearted wiggle of her fingers. Then she turned heel, rolling her eyes, and walked resolutely to the rear deck. Once out of his sight she grabbed her phone and texted her friend Annabelle. She was on the staff of the sea turtle hospital and was also a victim of this morning's layoffs at the aquarium.

Can you come over? Must commiserate. I have wine.

She went indoors to pull out two wineglasses. As she set them on the counter, her phone pinged with a return text.

On my way.

———

LINNEA SETTLED BACK into the wicker chair, tucked her feet up, and crossed her arms. The large wood deck extended seaward from the house over the wild dunes of the Rutledge property. Most of the yards on Ocean Boulevard had been manicured with grass and plantings to resemble mainland lawns. Her grandmother had adamantly refused to alter the natural landscape so their property was a riotous collection of wild grasses, plants, and flowers. Across the road, a large lot was held in conservation, allowing the sand dunes to roll on unimpeded to the beach. It was a rare view on the developed island.

Looking at the sea, Linnea realized how grateful she was for the friends in her life. She remembered what her Grandmother Lovie had told her: *In life you'll have many acquaintances. But consider yourself lucky to have one or two true friends.*

Linnea had always been popular in school. She'd had a dozen girls she'd called friends. But none of them had gone in the same direction she had after graduation. Some were married with children; some had moved elsewhere. Linnea had been part of the latter group. When she'd returned home from California last year, she found she had less in common with her old friends. It had been hard to realize how friendships shifted over the years. She'd made new friends—Pandora James and Annabelle Chalmers. No two women could be more different. They were like oil and water and didn't get along. Still, a tenuous, new friendship had developed.

Pandora was high style, gorgeous, fun, and flamboyant. She was in graduate school for engineering in England and, Covid permitting, planned to fly back to her grandmother's beach house on Sullivan's Island for the summer.

Annabelle was a local girl. She and Linnea had attended the same private high school in Charleston but had never been friends. Linnea was part of the South of Broad elite society of old Charleston. She and her friends had hung in the same circles since the nursery and seemed destined to continue throughout their lifetimes. In contrast, Anna was a scholarship student who lived with her mother in a poorer part of the city. She'd never blended in with the popular group at Porter-Gaud. Though she and Linnea had had a rocky start last summer, over the past year working together at the aquarium they'd experienced a tidal shift in their relationship. Annabelle's habitual resentment of Linnea's privilege had ebbed, and in turn, Linnea's ability to open up, as a true friend must do, began to flow.

Linnea heard the crunch of Annabelle's car pulling up in the driveway. She got up to go greet her but hesitated at the edge of the deck. She sighed with annoyance. She didn't want to get tangled up with John again. Once burned/twice shy and all that. Instead of walking out on the driveway where John could see her from his window, Linnea crossed her arms as she waited for her friend to arrive. *This could make for an annoying few weeks*, she thought. When was John to hightail it back to his beloved California?

13

"Just go," she muttered. Then lifted her frown to a smile as Annabelle's face appeared from around the corner.

"I come bearing wine!" Annabelle called out as she climbed the deck stairs, a bottle of red in one hand, a bottle of white in the other. Her long red hair hung straight past her shoulders and on her ears she wore large gold loop earrings. She was dressed, as usual, in jeans and a black T-shirt that read Save the Seabirds.

"Bless your heart!" Linnea called back, grinning. They walked together into the house in search of wineglasses and a corkscrew.

"Red or white?" Annabelle asked, corkscrew in hand.

"Today we're going to need both."

Annabelle chuckled in her low-throated fashion. "I hear you."

Linnea watched with awe as Annabelle twisted off the capsule around the neck of the bottle. She made it look so easy.

"How do you do that?" Linnea asked. "I'm pitiful trying to scrape that wrapper off."

"Comes with practice," Annabelle replied smugly. "Perks of being a bartender. Interesting fact: the original capsule was wax. Each bottle had to be dipped in wax to seal the end to prevent mold growth. The next innovation was lead. No surprise, that didn't work out, for obvious reasons, but it took them till the 1980s to switch to these polylam ones."

"So, if you collect old wines . . ." she said, thinking of her father.

"Yep. They still have those lead capsules."

"That explains a lot," Linnea said with a laugh. She gratefully took the offered glass of white wine. "I'm sorry, but I'm going to be tacky and add ice cubes. I can't drink warm chardonnay."

Annabelle shuddered. "I'll put this bottle in the fridge—and pour myself a Malbec." She worked on opening the new bottle as Linnea plopped ice cubes in her wineglass. "So, let me guess—you got laid off too?"

Linnea said with a groan, "*Again.* I can't believe I'm back here."

"At least we weren't fired."

"We're not getting paid. . . ."

Annabelle frowned while pouring out her wine. "Jeez, I hope it's not for too long."

"No one knows. That's the scariest part. It could be a while." Linnea brought her glass to her lips. "If the aquarium gets in trouble, people will have to be let go permanently."

Annabelle's finely arched brows narrowed deeper and she took a long sip of wine.

"Let's sit outside," Linnea suggested, hoping the fresh air would lift the sudden drop in mood.

Annabelle grabbed the bottle of wine and followed her. "How are you holding up?"

"Same as you, I expect."

Annabelle settled in the chair recently vacated by Cara. She crossed her long legs. "Not quite the same." Leaning back in her chair she tossed out, "I'm guessing your family will help you out."

Linnea paused to sip rather than rise to the bait, recognizing Annabelle's knee-jerk reaction to the wealth difference between their families. "They'll try, I'm sure," she replied in an even tone, then sidestepped. "Seriously, are you okay, money-wise?"

Annabelle's shoulders lowered as she stared into her glass. She exhaled loudly and shook her head. "No. I'm worried."

"I am too. I have zero savings."

"Savings?" Annabelle snorted. "What's that? I was barely making rent with my extra bartending job. Thank God for catering gigs. That's how I ate most weekends. It's so damn expensive living in the city—hell, even *near* the city—that there's no hope of putting money away. I don't know how I'm going to make next month's rent."

"I'm guessing you won't be bartending much, will you?"

"Nada. Zip. Restaurants are closed. No one is having events."

Linnea looked at her friend's face. Annabelle's normally serious expression had a deeper edge bordering on desperation.

"Can you move home?" she asked.

"Good God, no. My mother's remarried to this creep," she said with a hint of disgust. "Who knows how long this one will last?" She rolled her eyes. "I can't go there."

Linnea licked her lips as a thought played in her mind. Part of her balked at the idea. But the other part, the one that made her think of Aunt Cara as inspiration, won out. In a rush, the words came pouring out.

"I have an extra room here, and Cara is giving me a break on the rent until this virus thing blows over. Seems only right to pay it forward." She paused. "You can move in here with me if you want. You wouldn't have to pay rent. But we'd split utilities and food. That way we'd help each other out. What do you think?"

Annabelle's eyes went wide. "Are you serious?"

"Never more serious."

Annabelle put her glass down on the table, resting her hand there as though to steady herself. Relief flooded her face and she replied, "Yes."

Linnea smiled and felt that gush of joy born of one woman helping another. She lifted her glass. "Well, then . . . here's to being roommates."

Anabelle's face lit up. She lifted her glass, and they clinked in the air. "Roommates!"

Linnea sipped her chardonnay, then settled back in her chair. As she swirled the glass in her hand the ice cubes clinked, and she wondered if this was the best of ideas . . . or the worst.

# chapter two

*She would dig deep to find the strength.*
*Wasn't that what women did?*

CARA STOOD AT the front window staring up at the sky. Thunder-clouds roiled and rumbled. A major storm front was moving in that promised a downpour, possible flooding. Worse still, the leaves on the palm trees across the street were shaking in a frenzy. Never a good sign when flights were due in. Last she'd checked, planes were still landing at Charleston International Airport.

She glanced at her watch and her lips tightened. David's plane from London had been delayed, again. He'd texted from Heathrow Airport that he was boarding the plane. She'd purchased fresh flowers, gone to Simmons Seafood for shrimp, and prepared his favorite din-ner of shrimp and grits. Wine was chilling in the fridge.

She tapped her fingers against the window glass. *Where is he?*

———————

"I LOVE BEING outdoors when a storm is approaching," Julia Rutledge said, tucking her arm into her husband's and moving closer. Small and trim, she fit comfortably beside Palmer's five foot ten height.

"Me too," Palmer said, patting his wife's hand. "But we'd best hustle. That storm's coming in fast."

The wind gusted, punctuating his comment, sending her usually carefully coiffed hair flapping wildly about her head. A hat would be useless in this gale. Julia felt the cool moisture against her face and breathed deep. It was a refreshing respite from the past week's unseasonably warm weather. It was only March and yet it'd felt like June. She lifted her chin and sniffed the air. Her senses were assailed with the sweet ozone scent that heralded the storm.

They walked along the shoreline where the sand was firm. The beach was deserted—neither man nor beast dared the storm. The tide was high. On Sullivan's Island the dunes were low; the maritime shrubs formed a protective barrier against any incoming waves. Their beach path wasn't too far now. She thought they might make it home before a drenching.

"Speaking of hustling home," she said, leaning into Palmer, "what about our son? It sounds like it's pandemonium at Oxford. Do you think the university will cancel classes?"

"I expect they will. Any day now."

"What's he going to do? How will he get home?" Her blue eyes flashed as her worry quick-shifted into panic. "Palmer, you should get him a ticket. *Today*. I want my baby home. I don't want him sick with that coronavirus in a foreign country."

"You sound like a mother hen," Palmer said, patting her hand. "First of all, he's not in some third-world country. He's in England. They're getting a firm hold on this thing. And second . . ." He turned his head to give her a warning look. "Don't forget, Cooper is a grown man now. A junior in college. You can't baby him. He'll let us know what he needs."

"But how will *he* know?" She was in no mood to leave her son's safety up to chance, or even up to the university's decision whether to close the college. "He might be twenty-one, but he's not an experienced traveler." She squeezed Palmer's arm. "Wait, that gives me an idea. We should call David. He's there now. Cooper can fly out with him."

"David's already on a plane out of London."

"Already?" She exhaled with disappointment. "Well, phooey. See what I mean about an experienced traveler? He got out."

"Honey, Oxford hasn't canceled classes yet. He's not going to be stranded. They'll have a plan. They're British, after all." He looked up at the sky. "I don't know about us, though. We're the ones in trouble. We'd best pick up the pace. Come on, girl!"

He released her arm and they hustled along the sand as thunder rumbled louder, closer. Julia pumped her arms as her maternal adrenaline kicked in.

"What airport will he be allowed to fly into?" Julia asked, mulling this over. "The news channels are so vague. No one seems to know what's happening. Can't you just buy him a ticket and bring him back now?"

"Like I said, we have to trust our son."

She cast him a suspicious glance. He was stalling. When Palmer wanted something done, he plowed forward like a bull in the harness.

"He may have to fly first-class to get out. Do you have the money for his ticket?" she asked.

Palmer didn't reply, but his lips set in a grim line.

Julia felt a now familiar flutter of fear in her gut. She didn't mean to embarrass him, but the question had to be asked. Money was always tight, but lately he'd been closemouthed about how tight. That usually meant trouble.

"I have money set aside from my business," she offered. "Mrs. James is scheduled to return in April when her house is finished. She owes me a pretty penny." She chewed her lips. "But with flights from the UK suspended, who knows when she will be allowed to fly in? I won't get paid in full until her final approval."

"I'm fine."

Julia walked beside her husband, keenly aware of the shift in dynamics between them. Palmer, like his father before him, had a firm grasp on the family finances. The men did not "bother" their wives with figures. Yet after Palmer had gone bankrupt and the family sold off their holdings and Julia had begun her decorating business, she had experienced a heady sense of empowerment. Julia danced on the head of a pin—trying to give Palmer his respect, while rejecting her role as the little woman. Julia no longer trusted Palmer's business acumen, or his remaining sober. She was beginning to rely on herself.

"Palmer, I don't want to wait until it's too late. Let's look for a ticket for Cooper when we get home. It will be expensive, given the lack of time." She licked her lips, knowing any offer of hers to help finances would come as an insult to her traditional husband. "We could pool our resources."

"I'll buy him the damn ticket." Palmer's face was as clouded as the sky.

She felt slapped. They hurried a few more steps in a tense silence, squinting as the intensifying wind tossed sand in their faces. Julia turned to study his face. It was set, and she didn't like the worry she saw in the new lines carved around his eyes. Worry lines, her mother had called them. Julia wasn't trying to be mean-spirited. But she had to ask.

"Palmer . . . are we okay?" When he didn't reply, she asked in a softer voice, "Will we weather this storm?"

She felt the tension lower between them.

"I should be able to finish this house project," Palmer said in a serious tone. "I need to get the house on the market right quick. But truth be told, who knows what the market will be like in this pandemic? Spring's our busiest time, but everyone's staying home. No one is looking to buy. But who knows this summer?"

Julia decided to be forthcoming and not protect him from the truth. "I was notified there may be delivery delays on the appliances."

Palmer swung his head to look at her, then cursed under his

breath. He ducked his head as wind gusted, then made the turn to-ward the dunes and forged ahead. He looked dejected, with his head down and shoulders slumped. Julia said a quick prayer that he wouldn't fall off the wagon. He'd been sober for ten months. When they reached the beach path, he waited for her to catch up. His mama had trained him well.

"Don't worry, Palmer. We'll just have to take it day by day," she of-fered, forcing her voice to sound upbeat.

"I reckon." He didn't sound convinced.

"We've weathered worse."

Palmer's chuckle was a welcome sound. He glanced her way, his eyes gleaming with appreciation of her support. "We have. And we pull though."

"We always do."

"We just have to tighten our belts," he cautioned.

Julia knew that experience all too well. "I went shopping today. I just got the essentials, because they're warning of shortages. Lord help us, you should've seen the crowds at Harris Teeter. And the shelves were nearly empty! I couldn't get toilet paper! People are panicking, hoarding." She rattled off the long list of food items she'd purchased as provisions. "This virus is making people act like a hurricane's coming."

"It's an economic hurricane."

As they approached the white 1940s beach house, Julia's thoughts went, as they always did, to what she would do to its exterior, if only they had the money. She'd never loved this beach house the way Cara loved hers. That little cottage had such charm. She'd had fun helping Cara decorate that one. But this one . . .

Julia frowned, approaching the flat-faced, unremarkable house. Palmer had purchased it twenty years earlier—one of his friend-to-friend deals that he couldn't pass up. Charleston was a small town that way, especially for the tight group that lived South of Broad. Someone had died and the beachfront house was available for a song. Palmer had told Julia with his usual bravado that beachfront property was always a good investment. It didn't matter about the house, he said—one day they'd sell the place, or tear it down and she could build a spanking-new house, one she could design.

Julia had never cared much about beach houses. She was a Charleston girl, born and bred. When his father passed, Stratton had left the great house on Tradd Street to his only son, rather than to his wife, and Julia and Palmer had moved into the Rutledge House with their children, Linnea and Cooper. Palmer had considered it his duty to take care of his mother, and as for Julia, she'd doted on Olivia.

Palmer had rented out the Sullivan's Island beach house every summer after buying it, needing the income. The arrangement suited them. A few weeks on the island for vacation was enough for Julia. She had always planned to sell the house one day and use the money to purchase one of the more attractive cottages that she coveted.

Then the Charleston export/import business that had been in the Rutledge family for generations had gone bankrupt under Palmer's watch. Her world had flipped. They'd had to sell the family house on

Tradd Street, as well as the hunting lodge, and were forced to retreat to the beach house. Palmer didn't seem to mind much. The arrangement kept him in the game with plans to build a spec house. Palmer was always looking for a quick way to make his fortune. Linnea had left for California and Cooper for college.

It was harder on Julia. She'd loved living in Charleston. Loved the beautiful house on Tradd. She'd decorated each room with loving care, believing one day she'd pass it on to Cooper or Linnea. That was never going to happen. . . .

She felt the first drop of rain, cold and wet on her face.

"Hurry up, woman!"

They took off at a trot, reaching the house just as the sky opened up.

"We made it just in time," Palmer declared, wiping the wet from his face with meaty palms.

Julia looked around, taking in the unadorned clapboard house. *Ugly as ever*, she thought, shaking the rain from her hair. There were times it pained her just to look at it. She turned her back on the sparse, sandy grass and the leggy azaleas.

Palmer punched in the key code and pushed open the front door, stepping aside. Julia hurried indoors just as thunder cracked above them.

"Sweet Jesus!" Julia exclaimed, hand on heart. "That one was right over us."

The rain was coming down in torrents and the wind gusted as clouds raced over the island. Julia slipped out of her windbreaker and shook it over the tile, then hung it on the coatrack. She pushed her damp blond hair from her face and let her gaze sweep the large, open, and airy room, checking that the windows were closed.

For as ugly as the outside of the house was, the inside was a charmer. It had taken a solid hissy fit for Palmer to give her the funds to redo the cottage, but she'd refused to move into the rabbit-warren rooms unless he'd agreed. Julia had gutted the house and done to it what she'd dreamed of doing for twenty years. Her motto was *good-bye, box!* The small rooms were gone, and the ceiling soared, opening the space to light and air from the ocean visible beyond their property. Expansive space and white walls with vibrant splashes of color were Julia's signature décor. On a shoestring budget, she'd transformed the interior of the shabby, blah house into one she could be proud of. She couldn't afford to change the outside—yet—but the inside was home.

And it had made all the difference.

CARA STARED OUT as gray sheets of rain pounded the earth in a steady drumbeat. Thunder clapped right overhead, sending Hope running to wrap her arms around Cara's legs. The wind pushed the water in sheets down the streets and shook the fronds of the palm trees into a frenzy. She chewed her lip, hoping David hadn't been caught in the deluge. The streets of Charleston were notorious for flooding. There'd likely be a photo in tomorrow's *Post and Courier* of people trudging through water or floating in a canoe down some street.

She tensed at the sight of a long black car inching its way through the waterlogged road toward the house. Its windshield wipers were madly sweeping off water and the lights cut a swath through the darkness. When the car pulled into her driveway, Cara's heart jumped.

"He's home!" she exclaimed. Hope squealed at her heels as she raced to the front door and pulled it open. The wind whipped against her face, moist and chilled. She gripped Hope's hand, restraining her, and put one foot out onto the covered porch. She wanted to rush down the stairs into David's arms. Hope clung to her hand as they watched the car door open and David's familiar shape emerge, no raincoat or umbrella. He slammed the door and sprinted up the stairs to the porch.

Hope rushed forward, but David extended a hand to ward her off. "Stay back, Moonpie. Come on, girls. Let's get inside."

Unsure of what was happening, Cara ushered Hope into the dry house. David followed, closing the door. But instead of drawing near, he created a six-foot distance between them. Rivulets of water slid from his thick salt-and-pepper hair down his broad forehead, to a face chalky from fatigue. He wiped the water from his face, then removed his drenched jacket. He looked around helplessly for a place to put it.

"Just drop it on the floor," Cara said. She searched his face, wondering why he didn't grasp her in a hug, kiss her soundly, as he always did when returning from a trip. "David, are you ill?"

David wiped away a shock of wet hair from his forehead. "I don't think so . . . God, I hope not. But I don't want to take any chances," he told her, his eyes boring into hers. "Not with my girls. It was a packed flight. Damn airline lost my luggage."

"Oh no," Cara said, understanding now his delay.

David shook his head. "I put in a claim." He glanced at Hope clinging to Cara's leg with a look of confusion on her face. "Sorry I can't hug you, pumpkin," he told her gently. "Daddy wants to. You know I do. But I might have a nasty germ and I don't want you to catch it. Okay?"

Hope nodded, but Cara wasn't sure how much of that she understood. "Where's my present?" Hope asked coyly.

"Daddy doesn't always have to bring you a present," Cara admonished.

Her face was crestfallen. "But he always does when he comes home from a trip."

"True," David said, then lowered so he could look into Hope's face. "The airline lost my luggage. But it will get here, soon . . . I hope. And you know what? Your present is in that suitcase."

Hope frowned and turned, giving him the cold shoulder.

Cara chuckled wryly. "I don't think our daughter understands the concept of delayed gratification."

David tried to laugh, but he was so tired it was little more than a smile and a nod of the head. "No gift—no hug. Hey, I get it."

Taking in the chalkiness of his skin, the droop of his shoulders, Cara grew serious. "How bad was it in London?"

David's smile fell. "Bad. Cases are rising. I got a message when I landed. A colleague in London tested positive."

Cara felt her stomach fall. "Oh no."

"That's why I've got to be extra careful. I have to go straight into quarantine," he said soberly. "In fact, I shouldn't be talking to you now," he added, stepping farther away.

"Quarantine? What does that mean?" She'd heard the word tossed around, but there were no guidelines.

"To start, we have to keep away from each other, completely, for two weeks."

Cara blew out a stream of air. "Okay, we can do that. You stay in the master bedroom," she added, beginning to realize what quarantine would entail. "I'll bring you meals, mail . . . anything you want."

"We'll work out some system." David tried to sound positive.

"Can't you get a test? Maybe at the hospital?"

"There are no tests. I called my doctor and he said quarantine was the best thing to do. And wash hands. A lot."

"I looked up the CDC guidelines online. We're already hand-washing."

"We have to do more. Eliminate going out, unless necessary."

"We can do that. I'm just so glad you're home."

David shook his head. "I'm sorry. It's better if I stay away, as in completely away, from you and Hope. No need to panic. It was a long flight, and a big push to get out of London. That's probably why I'm so exhausted. But I don't want to take any chances. Not with you two. I'm going to our room—alone. You'll feel better staying with Hope in the other wing. I won't leave the suite. I can't be in the kitchen, either. I hate to ask you to serve me, but it's safer for you to bring me trays of food and leave them outside the room. Then wash your hands immediately after."

"Of course. Two weeks isn't that long. Do you really think it's necessary?"

"Absolutely. This thing is spreading like wildfire. I don't even want to be this close to you without a mask."

Cara looked at her daughter and felt her chest constrict. "Hope is compromised because of the measles."

David's gaze sparked with worry. "You should take her farther from me. I'm going into the bedroom now to shower off. And I'll crash." He wiped his face again, and Cara could see that the hours of stress had taken a toll. He looked haggard, and she felt a sudden shiver of fear that he had contracted the coronavirus.

"Off you go," she said to David and, taking Hope's hand, hurried her off into the bathroom in the other wing, where they both thoroughly washed their hands.

"Is Daddy sick?" Hope asked, her dark eyes round with worry.

"I hope not," she replied. "We'll have to wait and see. But we can't go near Daddy until he says he's better, okay? Promise?"

Hope's face clouded but she agreed. "I promise."

———————

IT WAS A sleepless night. Cara had settled in the guest room with Hope in her own room across the hall, while David slept in their bedroom on the other side of the house. Though they all were together again under the same roof, Cara felt very alone.

The night cloaked the room. She had left the porch doors wide open, allowing the cool night air to waft through the bedroom and whisk across her skin. The storm had raced off to sea, as storms often did when they traveled from the mainland, over the barrier islands to the ocean. David had been in Europe on business frequently all fall and winter, and she was accustomed to sleeping alone. But tonight, knowing he was so near, she longed to feel his arms around her. She would not share his bed again for at least two weeks, or longer if, God forbid, he had caught the virus.

The threat of another serious illness on the heels of Hope's measles had her trembling in anxiety. Cara was no stranger to sorrow. What woman was as she approached sixty years of age? Life, she knew, was like the tides. They rushed in, filling the marshes to the brim, then retreated, revealing the dark mud.

She brought the sheet over her shoulders. No one really knew what this virus was capable of, only that the elderly were the most vulnerable. David was nearing sixty-five, and he'd been in London, which already had cases skyrocketing. Cara closed her eyes tight. *Please, God, do not take another husband from me. I could not bear it.*

Her restless thoughts drove her from her bed. She glanced at her phone—3 a.m.—and sighed. Her usual wake-up time. Too early to get up, yet impossible to fall back asleep. She'd read once that one should give up the fight and embrace the early hours. Do something and wait for sleep to return. Cara pushed back the covers, rose from her bed, and stepped out into the steely gray of early morning. The moon was waning. In the darkness, she heard the ocean crashing against the shoreline, fierce, aftermath of the storm.

Countless stars formed constellations and her thoughts turned to her first husband. *Brett could name them,* she thought. They used to lie next to each other on the beach and he'd stretch his arm toward the sky and point out the constellations: "There's Hydra, Leo, Cancer."

Cara brought her hand to her forehead, frowning. Why did her former husband come to mind while she was worrying about her current one? Crossing her arms tightly around herself, she sighed deeply, awash in memories. She'd never forget Brett. Never wanted to. He was the love of her life. The one man who had taken hold of her heart and dragged her, kicking and screaming, away from her life of determined isolation and loneliness and into love. She'd come home to Isle of Palms for her mother. She'd stayed for him.

There were nights, like tonight, she could hear his voice so clearly. His presence was palpable.

Cara wiped away the moisture welling in her eyes. Scents assailed her—salt, honeysuckle, rain—punctuating the memories that were coming on strong.

*Damn fate,* she cursed. How much more death did she have to face? She'd lost Brett. Her mother, Lovie. Last year she'd nearly lost Hope. Not again, she vowed. She would not sit idly by and let illness strike her family again.

Cara was not one to sit in a corner and wait. Her mind began clicking off possible solutions. The threat of coronavirus was real—she accepted that. But she needed to know more. At first light, she'd research how to effectively handle quarantines and, if necessary, how to minimize the contagion and prevent it from spreading. The Centers for Disease Control website advised everyone to wash their hands and practice social distancing. But she had more to learn, and she had to learn it fast. If David was sick . . .

Her gaze traveled across the pool to her master bedroom on the other wing of the house. The doors were open there too. She could see the big four-poster bed through the screen. Her heart thumped with love for her David. It felt so odd, so wrong not to be lying beside him. She hoped David was sleeping well, and that all that ailed him was exhaustion. He needed all his strength to fight off any virus. She wouldn't let him down. She would dig deep to find the strength. Wasn't that what women did? She'd nursed her mother. She could take care of him too.

She turned to look back at the guest room she'd moved into. Just across the hall was Hope's room. Maternal resolve fluttered in her heart. Hope was the one she had to worry about most. Her bout with the measles the previous summer had taken its toll, leaving Hope immunocompromised. Cara would never forget how close she'd come to losing her, and the months of watching her little girl valiantly fight to regain strength. Hope was healthy again, but if she caught the coronavirus, she'd be highly vulnerable. Of course she had to keep Hope away from David. But was that good enough? Could Hope stay here in this house? With David?

Cara began pacing and brought her hands to her face as a solution took root. It would break her heart to separate from her daughter for two weeks, but what choice did she have? Cara stopped walking. Hope had to leave the house. The answer was simple. Tomorrow, she'd make plans. There'd be pushback, but she had to be strong for all of them.

Cara brought her fingers to her head and scratched vigorously—then, dropping her arms, felt sleepiness ebb slowly through her body. Her eyelids felt heavy. Her decision made, she could finally go to sleep.

Tomorrow, she would call Linnea.

———

LINNEA OPENED THE front door to find Cara, wearing her mask, half-hidden by a large bouquet of flowers.

"Cara! What a surprise. Come in!"

"Is this a bad time?" Cara asked.

Linnea tightened her pink robe at the waist, embarrassed to be caught still in her pajamas at 10 a.m. Cara looked positively chipper in black jeans, a jacket over her tee, and white tennis shoes.

"It's never a bad time to see you." Linnea stepped aside, giving Cara a wide berth to enter. "I'm feeling like I'm in limbo. I can't go to work, and I can't go shopping or to a restaurant. I'm not used to being stuck at home. So, believe me, seeing you is a treat." She laughed shortly with self-deprecation. "If in my pajamas."

"I know it's early and I didn't call. I barely slept last night." Cara stretched out her arms. "These are for you."

Linnea accepted them, surprised by the gesture. "What did I do to deserve these? I should be giving *you* flowers. You're the one who bailed me out."

"I'm about to ask you to bail me out too."

Linnea paused, then said, "Want some coffee?"

Cara shook her head. "I'd love some, but I can't stay. Hope is in the car. I can't leave her home because David isn't feeling well. He's in quarantine."

Linnea felt her blood drain and knew a moment's fear for her own well-being. "Is it the coronavirus?"

"We don't know for sure. There are no tests and the doctor told him to go into quarantine, just in case. Don't worry, he kept his distance from the moment he arrived home and went straight into our room and closed the door. He's going to stay in the master bedroom and I'll stay in the guest room on the other side of the house."

Cara paused to take a breath, and Linnea readied herself for the *but* that she knew was coming.

"But . . . and here comes the ask," Cara said. "I'm worried about Hope. She's at risk because of the measles last year. I've been up all night thinking about this, and I called her pediatrician this morning, just to make sure I'm not being an alarmist. She agrees that we should take extra precautions for Hope. So . . ." Cara took a breath. "Would you please consider letting Hope live with you for the two weeks that David is in quarantine?"

Linnea hadn't expected this, and it took a moment to process. "You mean, I'd take care of Hope and you'll be living at your house?"

"Yes. Just across the street. I don't want her in the same house as

David. The virus is contagious, and even being careful, if he ends up having it, the risk is too great for her. I'll pay you, of course."

A moment's hesitation gave way to her willingness to support her aunt, who, after all, had just forgiven her rent payments. "I'll do it, of course," Linnea said. "But before we agree, you should know . . . I took your message about paying it forward to heart. You remember Annabelle?"

"Of course."

"She was furloughed, too." Hearing Cara's sigh encouraged her with her news. "She's in worse shape than I am financially. She can't pay rent and without family to fall back on, that leaves her pretty much homeless. So," Linnea took a breath, "I offered to let her stay here as my roommate. Rent free. Plus she can help with my expenses."

"I see." Cara considered this. "Good decision."

Linnea smiled with relief. "But what about Hope staying here? Are you concerned?"

"I'll have to insist that you practice precaution. Annabelle will have to wear a mask for the first ten days when she's in the same room with Hope, just to be sure. If she agrees to that, I have no problem at all."

"I'm sure she will."

"Good, that's settled, except for what I pay you."

"Oh, you don't have to pay me. The rent and all . . ."

"I insist. Please, don't argue that with me." Cara smiled. "I believe you need a job?"

Linnea smirked at the obvious.

Cara continued, "I'll pay for groceries, supply anything you need. And I'll come by to play with her and give you a break."

"It will be fun," Linnea said. "When do you want to start?"

Cara took a breath, then said, "Today?"

# chapter three

*Spring revealed her glory in the lowcountry.*
*The world might be in chaos, but the season of rebirth rolled in regardless.*

THE GRAVEL CRUNCHED beneath the tires as Linnea pulled the Gold Bug into the driveway. Stepping out of the little gold Volkswagen Beetle, she took a moment to look around the property. Spring revealed her glory in the lowcountry. The world might be in chaos, but the season of rebirth rolled in regardless. She found the consistency of nature reassuring. The sweet scent of honeysuckle wafted past, and looking over to her neighbor's yard, she saw it growing wildly on Emmi's fence. It brought back memories of Easter egg hunts here with Grandmama Lovie. A smile played on her lips as she closed the car door. *Hope will love that,* she thought. She wanted the little girl to be happy at the beach house, as her mother had been. She'd spent the morning cleaning the pink bedroom and shopping for special foods that Cara said Hope might enjoy.

A tapping caught her attention; curious, she followed the sound to Emmi's carriage house, letting her gaze travel higher to the second-floor window. It was tall and in the Moorish style, more a door than a window. Linnea's heart stopped and she froze at the sight of a tall young man standing at the window. There was an awkward pause as she stood, limp-armed, staring up at him.

Seeing that he'd caught her attention, he waved.

On automatic pilot, she raised her hand in halfhearted acknowledgment—then spun on her heel and walked directly to the front trunk of the VW, her head bent with purpose.

The small trunk was crammed with brown paper bags filled with groceries. She loaded each arm with a bag and headed straight to the side door into the kitchen, not looking back at the carriage house window. She plopped the bags on the kitchen counter, then returned to the car for the second load, eyes to the ground. Once again came the insistent tapping at the window, but this time she pretended she didn't hear it. When she reached the car, however, she heard a sharp whistle and looked up, startled.

John had pushed open the large windows. They divided in half vertically, giving her a full view from hip to head. His dark auburn hair was longer than she remembered and fell over the collar of his open chambray shirt. She couldn't see his eyes from this distance, but she knew that devilish spark in the green would be there. John gestured for her to come closer.

Linnea pointed to the grocery bags, then shook her head.

John darted his hand out, lifting a finger to indicate she should wait a minute. He disappeared from the window.

Linnea's lips tightened in impatience. What was she doing, standing here waiting on him? *Him?* No, she wouldn't, she decided. She ducked in to grab hold of the remaining grocery bags when another whistle pierced the air. She straightened and looked over her shoulder. John was back at the window; he lifted his hand and, to her surprise, released a paper airplane. Linnea watched the pointed missile catch a breeze and fly gracefully across the lawn, over the shrubs, to crash-land on her driveway pebbles a few feet away. He smiled, obviously pleased with himself.

Linnea did not smile. She stared at the little white paper plane in the driveway. One of the wings was bent from the landing. With a frustrated sigh, she walked toward it, under his watchful gaze, and picked it up. The plane was made from white computer paper, tightly folded. She lifted it in the air to show John she had it, then walked back to the car. She wouldn't give him the satisfaction of reading it in front of him. She tossed the paper plane into a bag, then hoisted the two remaining bags, using her elbow to close the trunk. It fell into place with a loud, rusty squeak. She heard him shout her name, but she pretended she didn't, striding at a determined pace into the house without a backward glance.

She set the paper bags on the counter, then lowered her head. Her shoulders ached, not from carrying the bags but from the tension of dealing with John. She wondered again what he was doing on Isle of Palms. She reached into the bag and drew out the paper airplane, smirking as she opened the neat, tight folds. It was so like John to create a toy. He was childlike in so many ways. His spontaneity. His quick wit. His love of a good time. It was both his charm, and his flaw. He was Peter Pan who never wanted to grow up.

She unfurled the paper and immediately recognized his bold print.

Linnea-
Can we talk?
John

The memory of their last argument a year ago surged through her, bringing the shame, hurt, and humiliation hurtling back.

————

THEY'D BEEN LIVING together in John's San Francisco condo for nearly two years. When Linnea was out of work, she tried desperately to make herself useful to John since she could no longer pay rent. She'd cleaned the condo, did the shopping and the cooking, ran errands, but no matter how hard she tried, John grew increasingly morose and testy. It came to a head one evening in April as the rain streaked against the tall, stark windows of the modern space. It was more a bachelor pad in feel than a home with his furnishings, all leather and wood. Even now, a year since the breakup, John's words reverberated in her brain as clear as when he'd spoken them.

"I'm just not ready," John said.

"What does that even mean?" Linnea had asked. "Ready for what?"

"I'm not sure," John said, raking his hair with frustration. "It's just, things have changed since your layoff. I work from home. And . . . no offense, but you're here all the time."

"I live here!"

"And I'm the one paying all the bills. It's—it's like we're married."

She felt slapped. Shame swept over her. "You know I'm not happy that I can't contribute to the rent. I'm looking for work. I try to be helpful."

"Yeah, I know," he said, pacing the floor. "That's what I mean. You're more like a wife than a girlfriend."

She felt her blood chill. "Is that so bad?"

John stopped pacing, his face blank. "Is that what you want?"

She swallowed hard. She hadn't anticipated the conversation going in this direction. Wasn't prepared. She stumbled through her answer. "I . . . I don't *not* want it. I mean, not right now. But someday, sure. Isn't that where we're headed?"

He looked like a deer in the headlights.

"John?" she said.

"Linnea, I've never lied to you. I told you, before you left South Carolina, that I wasn't ready for marriage. I might never be."

She stiffened. "I'm not asking you to marry me."

"No, I know that. But . . . it *feels* like we are married. We're setting up a life together."

"That's called living together."

He scratched his scalp, a sure sign he was in discomfort. "I don't know, Linnea. . . ."

She did. The whole scene was too domestic for him. "You told me to come to California with you," she said accusingly.

John went very still. "I cared for you. I wanted you to be happy. You were trapped out there and I wanted to offer you a place to stay while you started your new job."

"Not as a roommate!" she shouted back at him, angry now. He was twisting things around. "That wasn't the deal." Her voice broke. "You told me you loved me."

"I did. I do." His voice was so low she barely heard him.

She stared at him, arms limp at her sides. All the things she wanted to tell him, all her fears and worries, her dreams and hopes, froze in her throat. From the start this arrangement had been fraught with uncertainty. He'd been honest with her. He'd told her he wasn't ready to commit. And she'd accepted that. For two years she'd been careful to give him his space, never complaining when he went out with his friends, leaving her at home. She'd tried to be cavalier and went out with her girlfriends too. She never pressed him to declare his love, though he was always affectionate and generous. Yet all their intentions not to crowd each other, not to be under any obligation or commitment, not to make declarations of love, had left them in a limbo of discontent. Linnea having lost her job, becoming a dependent, had forced them out of complacency.

She searched his face for some sign, some signal of his feelings. "John, if you love me, what's the problem?"

John shook his head. "The problem is. . . like I said, it feels like we're married."

"And you don't like that." It wasn't a question.

"I don't know. I feel a little suffocated, ya know? My shoulders hurt like hell from the stress."

She took a minute to steady her breath as fear sent her heart pounding. "These are just bad days. Financially," she hastened to add.

He didn't respond.

"Come on, John. Talk to me."

"I'm just not ready to go to the next level. Okay? I said it."

"Will you ever be ready?"

John looked away.

She closed her eyes tight for a moment, but saw all clearly. "You had no problem living together when things were good. But," she added with a bitter laugh, "when one bad thing happens, when I lose my job, suddenly the thought of taking care of me, of assuming any responsibility for me, is too much for you to handle?" She snorted. "You're a real jerk."

He didn't reply.

She felt herself crumble inside and took a deep breath. "I followed you to California, even though my family thought it was a terrible idea! That awful fight with my father? He thought it was crazy for us to move in together. But I told him I knew you and I could make it, because I believed in us."

"It's not that I've stopped believing," John said. He raked his hair with his fingers. "I don't know. Maybe . . . we just need a break. Take some time to get our heads together."

"A break?"

"Some time apart. To see how we really feel."

She huffed in disbelief. "Where would I go?"

"Home?" he offered.

She looked at him, standing wide-legged in jeans with his fingers tucked into his pockets, his button-down shirt wrinkled and hanging out, his dark hair disheveled. A final snapshot. With that one word, Linnea knew it was over.

---

LINNEA SHOOK THE memory away, looked at the note, and felt anger surge. *Oh, hell no!*

She crumpled the paper and tossed it toward the garbage bin, missing it. The paper ball rolled to the corner. Linnea rested her face in her palms. "Shit, shit, shit . . ." Once again John Peterson was sending her into a tailspin. She'd thought she'd gotten over him. She'd ignored his texts and e-mails for a year. Refused his phone calls. Not a word had passed between them. And now he was back living next door and her foolish heart was betraying her.

She straightened and went to retrieve the crumpled paper. Smoothing it out, she read his words again. *Can we talk?*

She brought the wrinkled paper to her nose and breathed in. There was no scent.

*Words* . . . she thought, crumpling the paper again. John was good at words. This time, when she tossed the ball it went into the trash.

Linnea put the frozen food and milk in the fridge, leaving the rest of the groceries on the counter for later. She hurried out of the house and furtively looked up at the window. John was not in sight.

She crossed the driveway with a determined gait, passed through the white picket gate into Emmi's garden. If she turned right, she'd head to the carriage house. Turn left, she'd head toward Emmi's kitchen door. It was a path that young Rutledge girls had traveled for generations.

Big pots overflowing with purple and yellow pansies greeted her on either side of the brightly painted blue door. John's mother, Emmaline Baker Peterson, opened the door promptly. Emmi was Cara's lifelong friend. When she'd divorced, she moved in with Flo next door to Cara. Emmi was a force of nature, full figured with red hair too bright for natural, pulled back into a loose ponytail. Her unmade-up face broke into her signature Carly Simon grin of recognition.

"Linnea! What a surprise! Come in!"

"I'd better not," Linnea said, taking a step back. "We're not supposed to go into each other's houses. Especially with Flo's advanced age." Her lips twitched. "And yours."

Emmi skewered her with a faux scowl. "Oh, Lord, I keep forgetting. I haven't got used to all that yet. You're right, of course. I—I don't have a mask. I meant to get one."

"That's okay. I don't have one yet either. I thought I'd sew some up. I'll make you a few. Flo, too."

"Why, aren't you precious. Thank you, I'd love that. Tell you what—let's sit outside. We can keep a distance and it's a beautiful day."

Linnea followed Emmi into the garden. She was right—it was a beautiful day, and her large, impressive garden was abloom with azaleas taking center stage. The green shoots of perennials were peeping through the earth with the promise of beauty yet to come.

"Oh, Emmi, everything is so beautiful."

Emmi grinned with pride. When she'd purchased the house from Florence Prescott ten years earlier, she'd completely redecorated it from the ground up in the shabby-chic style she loved. Flo had never cared about decorating or gardening back in the day when she was working. If it was clean and functional, that was good enough for her.

"I had a lot of energy after my divorce and I needed to funnel it somewhere useful. This house was a lifesaver. Once I got the inside done, I turned my focus to the garden. It was a sorry mess. No offense to Flo, bless her heart."

"Not like the mayhem of wildflowers that cover the dunes around Primrose Cottage."

"Which is a look I also admire," said Emmi. "Lovie and I used to argue about my garden. She never wanted anything cultivated. Said I should only have indigenous plants, as nature intended." She shrugged.

"As does Cara. And me." She lifted one shoulder. "I guess it runs in the family. But it doesn't mean I don't appreciate your beautiful garden."

"It doesn't come easy when you're digging in sand, I can tell you.

Nothing cultivated lasts long. In truth, your grandmother was right. But I'm an old dog and all that."

As she followed, Linnea couldn't help but notice that, under Emmi's plain green tunic top, a riotous pattern of flowers and rhinestones covered the rear of her jeans. No matter that Emmi ordered all the new fashions for the women's department of the local Belk department store—when it came to her own clothing, Emmi loved her "doodads and sparklers," as she called all the colorful stitched designs, beads, and rhinestones.

Emmi led them to the black iron patio set, and they took care to settle on the bright coral cushions at far opposite sides of the table.

"I think I can guess why you're here," Emmi opened.

"John," said Linnea.

Emmi nodded, her green eyes sparkling with joy. "You could've knocked me over with a feather when he just showed up at my door. That boy likes surprises."

"I'll say. When did he arrive? I hadn't heard a peep."

"You mean to say he didn't tell you he was coming?"

Linnea looked at her hands and shook her head. "He wouldn't."

Emmi looked at her, one brow raised. "That's sad to hear." She skipped a beat. "I told him to tell you he was coming."

"He might have. I, uh . . ." Linnea tucked a lock of hair behind her ear. "I haven't answered his texts."

Emmi paused and digested that. Linnea felt a slight chill enter the space between them. Talking about a breakup with the ex's mother was, by definition, awkward.

"Well," Emmi said crisply, "I'll start from the beginning. There was this conference for one of his clients in Myrtle Beach. John flew in to make a presentation. I gather it was successful," she added with a mother's pride. "He's really good at public speaking. So, being so close and all, he surprised me and Flo with a visit. No sooner did he arrive when he got a text from a friend saying he'd caught that virus that's going around."

"The coronavirus," Linnea said, sitting straighter.

"That's it," Emmi said with a quick nod. "You know John. He made a decision right quick to isolate himself. He went straight to the carriage house. There's no getting a test because there are no tests to be had. John instructed me to scour the house with antibacterial soap, which I did. I'm in that dangerous demographic, you know. And especially Flo, at eighty-nine—everything is a worry. We're being super careful. John's been holed up in the carriage house ever since. I bring him meals; he orders food in." She sighed. "We're trying our best. It's all so confusing."

Linnea was grateful that Emmi didn't cast aspersions for her not answering John's texts. "When did he arrive?"

"Why . . ." Emmi paused to count on her fingers. "Can't have been more than four days. He's not budged from that room, and he won't until another week has passed. You know how he is when he has his mind made up."

"Yes," Linnea replied, and clenched her hands in her lap. "Does he have any symptoms?"

"He says he doesn't. But he's worried he could carry the germs.

What's that called when they don't have the symptoms but they do carry it?"

"Asymptomatic."

"That's right. He wants to stay in quarantine the full two weeks."

"And then he'll leave?"

Emmi's brows rose. "I don't know. That's up to him."

Linnea frowned. "You mean he might stay longer?"

"I hope he does."

She saw Emmi stiffen slightly and heard the subtle shift in tone. Of course she'd want him to stay as long as possible. What mother wouldn't? And the last thing Linnea wanted was to get into an argument with John's mother. She loved Emmi and valued their relationship. She wouldn't allow John to ruin that.

"Is that a problem for you?" Emmi asked directly.

"It's just . . . he's trying to make contact with me."

"Well, why not? You're still friends, aren't you?"

Linnea shook her head and looked at her hands clutched in her lap. She heard the loud buzzing of a bee near her ears. "No, Emmi. We're not."

Emmi shifted in her seat, clearly uncomfortable.

It was time to go. Linnea looked up and said earnestly, "I hope he's well. Thanks for bringing me up to speed."

"You don't have to rush off."

"I left groceries on the counter," Linnea replied. She rose and turned to leave, then stopped. It had to be said. "Listen," she said, resting her hand on the back of the iron chair for support. "Could you do me a favor? If you see John, or talk to him through the door, could you ask him not to try to contact me? I'd rather he didn't."

Emmi's smile fell to a frown. "Now, isn't that going a bit too far? He's just being friendly."

Linnea shook her head. She didn't want to talk to his mother about this. "There's nothing left for him to say. He was quite clear when I left California that he didn't want me in his life."

"Oh, honey, are you sure? That's not what he tells me."

Linnea put her hand to her forehead. The pain felt fresh, threatening tears. She straightened her spine and drew in a long breath. "Emmi, he bought my plane ticket home. One-way. That message was pretty clear to me."

Emmi's face was pained. "I'm so sorry. I didn't know."

"Don't be. It really isn't any of your business. I shouldn't have told you now. Emmi, I don't want this to come between us, okay?" Linnea sighed. "I wouldn't have said anything if he hadn't come back. But he did, and here we are. So please, tell him for me . . . I already heard all he has to say. He can do whatever he wants. But I don't want to talk to him." She lifted her chin. "I've moved on."

"I haven't."

At the sound of John's voice, Linnea swung around toward the garden gate.

# chapter four

*Listen, there's a hell of a good universe next door, let's go.*

e. e. cummings

LINNEA STARED, ANNOYED by the dizzying sensations that always accompanied the sight of him.

The first time she'd seen John Peterson was when she was prepubescent and he briefly made an appearance at Cara and Grandmama Lovie's Fourth of July party. He and his brother, James, Emmi's sons, had made a command appearance. All she remembered was some cute, tall, and very rude teenager who had stayed long enough to do family service, wolf down food, and make a hasty exit.

When she'd spied him on the beach some ten years later, she was a woman, and he was a man. A handsome surfer, all tanned muscles and salt-stiffed hair. He'd grabbed her wayward surfboard, offered her one of his signature crooked smiles, and she was done for. It had been a long time since she'd met someone who sparked an immediate attraction. She'd spent the rest of the summer reeling him in. He was a tough fish to angle, too. She knew from the start that John was heading back to California, that he was, as Cara liked to say, a lone swimmer. But there'd always been a line between them—indefinable but very real . . . very strong. She'd thought she'd at last severed it, but seeing him standing in front of her she felt the strong tug again and was furious at her traitorous body for the response. Her mind screamed for her to cut and run.

"How long have you been standing there?" Linnea demanded.

"Not long. Just long enough to hear that you've gotten over me." His forced smile was sad.

His voice, so familiar, reverberated through her. She'd recognize it in a crowded room. The faint Southern accent was still there despite his years on the West Coast. She lifted her chin, bolstering her confidence. "Then I think you've heard all I have to say."

"Linnea . . ." John began, taking one step forward with his arm extended. Then he stopped, keeping his distance. They both knew it was because of the virus. He dropped his arm. "Hear me out."

She looked away and shrugged as though to say *no big deal*.

Emmi awkwardly cleared her throat and said, "I'm going inside." She passed them with her eyes downward, making a hasty exit.

"Will you talk to me?" John asked. "Please."

Linnea looked at him again. His forehead was creased over pleading eyes. She put her arms around herself in a protective gesture, took a deep breath.

"Just a few minutes," John said. When she didn't reply, he added, "You can give me a few minutes, can't you?"

She waited, saw his hands clench at his thighs—then said, "Let's go out to the driveway." She gave a barely perceptible nod toward Emmi.

John followed her out of the garden into the driveway so they could talk in private. When they stopped, he said, "Linnea, it's been a hard year. I've missed you." He lifted his shoulders. "I could stand here for hours and tell you all the ways I've missed you."

"John . . ." she said on a breath. "Just don't." Hearing all this pained her. Linnea had worked so hard to forget. She shook her head. "It's too late."

"I tried calling you. Writing you. Texting." He paused, then cracked a half-smile. "Didn't you get my paper airplane?"

She wasn't in the mood to laugh.

He paused and raised his eyes to the brilliant blue sky. "Look, I know I messed things up. Big-time. It's like that old saying, *you don't know what you've got till it's gone*." He paused then said, "I'm sorry, Linnea."

He fell quiet and looked at her, waiting for some reply.

Linnea considered her words. She wouldn't give him the satisfaction of knowing how he'd devastated her. "I appreciate you telling me all this. It helps, oddly enough. For what it's worth, I had a pretty tough year myself." She looked at her nails. "But there's another old saying. *Time heals all wounds*. I'm okay now. Really." She looked at him squarely. "I'm fine."

She began walking toward her door. She was eager to leave. Needed to leave. She stopped when she felt his hand on her arm. She swung her head around to glare at him.

John raised his hands and stepped farther back. "I'm six feet away. You're safe."

She looked into his eyes and wondered if he'd intended the double entendre. Did she ever feel safe with him?

"So . . . Are we friends at least?"

"I suppose it wouldn't be the worst thing," she replied without returning his smile.

"Hey, I'll take it," John said, smiling. "It's a start."

"Don't misunderstand," Linnea said coolly. "I'm with someone else."

Her words wiped the smile from his face, replaced by stunned surprise. As she turned and walked back to the cottage, she couldn't deny she was glad to see it.

———————

"TIME TO SAY good-bye to Daddy."

Cara stood at her bedroom door with Hope. She rested her hand upon the wood. "Honey, are you there?"

"I'm here," came the familiar voice of her husband.

"Daddy!" exclaimed Hope. "I'm going to stay with Linnea for a few days."

"Oh, that's a treat," came David's voice through the door.

Cara imagined him standing there, hand on the wood like hers, feeling the same mixed emotions about this farewell. Seeing her daughter's enthusiasm, she knew the child didn't understand what was really going on.

"Open the door, Daddy."

"He can't, sweetheart," Cara said. "It's the germs, remember?"

Hope nodded, but her face revealed both puzzlement and frustration.

"Good-bye Hope," David called out. "I'll call you every day. We can FaceTime. You're going to have a lot of fun with Linnea."

"Okay," Hope said in a wavering voice. Suddenly she began to grasp she was leaving home.

"Time to go!" Cara exclaimed cheerily. "I'll be back soon," she told David. "Do you need anything?"

"I'm good." He cleared his throat. "Just take care of Hope."

She leaned forward, her gold band catching the light against the wood, and kissed the door. "I will."

———

LINNEA WALKED FROM room to room of the beach house, turning on lights. The sky was overcast, making the day seem gloomy. She wanted the house to look cheery when Hope arrived.

As she bent to turn on the lamp in the living room, she caught the scent of Murphy Oil Soap and lemony furniture wax. She'd scrubbed and polished every inch of the cottage so it would be spanking clean for Hope. No germs welcome here. Cara was Linnea's landlord as well as her aunt. She'd been so generous, and Linnea was glad to have this opportunity to do something for her.

On the coffee table she spied the new games she'd purchased to play with Hope: Monopoly Junior, Zingo!, Simon, Candy Land, and Chutes and Ladders. She and Cooper had loved board games growing up, and she had to admit she looked forward to playing again. She walked down the hall to Hope's bedroom.

*What a history this one room had*, she thought, entering. This had originally been Cara's bedroom, where she'd spent summers growing up. When Cara had returned at forty years of age to stay with her mother, she'd slept once again in this room. Then after her mother died, Cara moved into the master bedroom and in time, this became Hope's room—all pink with white nursery furnishings. Now they lived across the street in their large home on Ocean Boulevard, but the pink walls of this room remained. Instead of nursery furniture, Cara's old black-iron double bed was back. And now Hope was returning to visit. Cara had bought a new coverlet with a ruffled hem and shams covered with pink kisses and hearts.

She let her fingers glide over the black metal bed. This had once been Linnea's room too, when she'd visited her grandmother and later, when she'd lived here with Cara. Oh the memories . . .

Across the hall a second bedroom faced the ocean. This had once been her daddy's bedroom, back when he and Cara were the children. Years later, when Grandmama Lovie had left Charleston and moved back into the beach house, she'd hired Toy Sooner as her live-in caretaker. After Lovie's passing, Toy married and became a Legare and had a house of her own. In a few weeks, this room would belong to Annabelle.

Linnea closed the door of Hope's room and walked past the black-framed photographs on the wall, showing generations of family members frolicking on the beach, having barbecue at the cottage, gathered in groups with smiles. There had been many wonderful memories in this house for the Rutledge clan. Looking at the faces, she could name them all.

Stepping into the living room, where yellow pools of light spilled out on the muted colors of the oriental carpet, she thought how she'd always felt safe in this house. More so than in the grand house on Tradd Street in Charleston. This cottage had been a sanctuary for three generations of Rutledge women, and their friends as well. She wondered if Annabelle would feel the magic when she moved in. Linnea wanted to carry on the legacy of the beach house. To be the support and inspiration to others that Cara and her grandmother had been.

The beach house wasn't very different today from when her grandmother lived in it. A respect for the original design of the house had endured the generations. The only change was when Cara and Brett had enclosed the seaward screened porch into a three seasons room and extended the deck. She'd refreshed the paint, changed fabrics, but the cottage remained intact. As Cara liked to say, why mess with perfection?

Linnea went to pour some apple juice for Hope when she heard a quick knock on the porch door.

"Hello?" came Cara's voice.

"In here!" Linnea was all smiles, eager to make Hope feel welcome. She picked up the new Barbie doll she'd bought as she turned to greet them.

Hope spied it immediately. "For me?" exclaimed the little girl, her dark-brown eyes lighting up even as her hands reached out. At six, she loved presents.

Linnea caught Cara's eye and mouthed a *thank you* for the suggestion.

Cara handed Hope a manila envelope. "It's all the things you need to know for Hope." She began to rattle off items using her fingers. "Her doctor's phone number, her favorite foods, the foods she hates, her favorite games, TV shows, her routine. Anything I could think of to help you. But of course, just call me if you have any questions at all."

Linnea pulled out two pages of typed notes. "I can't imagine you've left anything out," she said with a wry smile.

"It's tough without her going to school. The days get long, believe me," she added with a roll of the eyes, then sighed. "Two weeks seems forever. I may not make it. I've never been away that long before. Not even when she went to the hospital. I slept in her room." Cara clasped her hands tight as though to keep them from shaking. "I would stay here with her, except I have to take care of David."

Linnea had never seen Cara so vulnerable. "We'll be fine," she said reassuringly. "And you're just across the street if I need you."

Cara's watery eyes brightened. Support, friendship, hope . . . these were a woman's lifelines. "I'll stop by to see her, of course."

"Is that a good idea?" asked Linnea with trepidation.

Cara's smile fell. "Why not?"

"I mean, you'll be in close quarters with someone who might have the virus. That means you could be a carrier too."

"Oh no, I don't think so," Cara said dismissively. "First of all, he probably doesn't have the virus. This is precautionary. Second, I won't have any contact with David. I even wear gloves when I bring him food and wash the dishes, collect his laundry. And I spray the house with disinfectant all the time. I order groceries in, so I won't have exposure. It'll be fine."

Linnea had her doubts. If Cara felt that secure, why was she bringing Hope to her house at all? she wanted to argue. Cara was usually very level-headed and was obviously having a hard time with the separation.

"We'll be fine, won't we, Hope?" Linnea asked, turning to smile at the little girl. Hope glanced up and returned the smile before focusing again on her new doll. "Now, off you go. Deal with your patient." She leaned in to kiss Cara's cheek, then caught herself. "Oops, no! We don't do that anymore."

Cara shook her head with a sad smile. "We'll get through this."

"We always do."

———————

LINNEA GLANCED AT her watch, feeling the need for a glass of wine. Yep, it was almost 5 p.m. She was sitting on the living room floor across a game board from Hope, who was lying on her belly, ignoring the game, obviously as bored as she was. Next to them was a scattered pile of games that they'd already played. Lunch had been a disaster. Nothing Linnea prepared was like Hope's mother's—therefore rejected. Hope had settled for plain bread and butter and a glass of water. Linnea put her head in her palm. *My God, I'm feeding the child bread and water!*

The afternoon had gone smoothly enough. But now the games were done, they both were bored, and the dreaded dinner hour was approaching. Linnea wanted nothing more than for Cara to come by and pick up Hope. Babysitting was done, thank you! How was she going to manage ten to fourteen days?

"I think we're done with the games for the day, don't you? How about I make us some dinner?"

Hope didn't look at her. She appeared dejected and tired as she started picking up the red, blue, green, and yellow game pieces. "I want to go home."

"I know you do, honey. And you will. As soon as your daddy gets better."

"I want to go home," she said, this time louder with a tremor in her voice.

Linnea took a deep breath, then climbed to her feet. They needed a change of scenery, some fresh air, before the child had a meltdown. "Let's go outside and take a walk," she suggested in a cheery voice. "What do you say?"

Hope looked up at her, frowning. "No."

"Come on," she cajoled. She reached out her hand. "It'll be fun."

Seeming unconvinced, Hope took hold of Linnea's hand and allowed herself to be tugged to her feet.

They slipped into shoes and sweaters, since it was unusually chilly. Linnea gently herded the child out the door into the waning light. The sun was lowering, cooling the air even more. Immediately Hope took off in the direction of the beach—and home. Linnea did some fast thinking.

"This way! There's something I want to show you."

Hope stopped and pointed to her house. "No, there."

"I have to show you something. You're going to love it. Hurry, now." She wiggled her fingers in a *come on*, even as her mind scrambled to think of what she could possibly show that a six-year-old would find amusing.

The azaleas were aflame, honeysuckle filled the air with its cloying scent, and the dunes surrounding the house were sprouting with buds of wildflowers. These were spring glories that she thrilled to—but would a child? No, she thought with a sigh. Linnea searched the natural landscape, and as she did, it dawned on her that she had to see the outdoors with new eyes—with the eyes of a child—filled with awe and wonder.

Her gaze swept the nooks and crannies along the base of the house. Where was an anole? A green tree frog? She searched the thick shrubs for a bird's nest. A flash of red in the sky drew her attention to the live oak tree in Emmi's yard. A cardinal! They nested here as early as March. She heard the high-pitched calls, which sounded like the male was saying, *kiss me, kiss me.*

"Hope, come see!" Linnea gestured again, and smiled with relief when Hope walked toward her. She held her hand as they approached the tree and checked out their scarlet visitor. Suddenly, she heard a loud, insistent knocking on a window. The cardinal flew off. Linnea rolled her eyes and, looking up, saw John standing at the tall window.

"Who's that?" asked Hope, staring up.

Before she could answer, John pushed open the double window and shouted out, "Hello!"

Hope, curious, stepped forward and waved back with exuberance.

John called out something, but from where they stood, they couldn't understand. Linnea cupped her hand to her ear and shook her head. John put up a finger in the universal *just a minute* sign and disappeared.

Hope turned to look at her. "Where did he go?"

Linnea shrugged. But she could guess. Sure enough, a moment later John returned to the window and waved again. Then he pointed to Hope with one hand, and with the other released a paper airplane.

The plane sailed through the air, avoiding the large live oak and crossing over the fence. Enchanted, Hope squealed with delight and took off after it. Linnea had to laugh at the sight. Hope scampered across the scrubby dunes in front of the cottage and, arms high in the air, managed to catch the plane. She was beaming, proud of herself. Linnea hurried to her side.

"Let's see what he has to say," she said. "You can unfold the airplane."

"But I'll break it!"

"It's okay. He'll make another." *I'm sure*, Linnea thought. "Inside I think he wrote a message, just for you. Open it!"

Hope carefully unfolded the paper, her pink tongue worrying her lip. Linnea watched, realizing that this was the child's first paper airplane. She looked up at John and smiled her gratitude that he'd given Hope something to be happy about.

Hope spread the paper flat and slowly read out the words. "*HELLO. MY NAME IS JOHN. WHAT IS YOURS?*" She turned toward the window and shouted, "My name is Hope!"

John put his hand to his ear and shook his head.

"He can't hear you, honey."

"Can I send him an airplane?"

"It will be hard to fly an airplane up to the second-floor window." She tapped her lips. "I know. How about we write him a note and leave it for him in a special place?"

"Okay!" Hope was all into the game. "How will he know where to find it?"

"I'll tell his mama. Miss Emmi."

Hope nodded with enthusiasm. Then she asked, "Miss Emmi is John's mother?"

"She is."

"Can we write him a note now?"

"I don't see why not."

Hope turned and waved to John again. She cupped her mouth and yelled, "I am writing you a note. You have to find it!"

John whistled and surprised them by holding up another paper airplane. He stood wide-legged, the window gaping open before him *Don't fall*, Linnea thought, unbidden. This time, he pointed the airplane directly at Linnea, head bent in concentration as he took aim. She imagined his green eyes, intensely focused. Then, with a quick movement, he released it.

Hope squealed with delight. This plane traveled farther than the first, in a direct line over the fence toward Linnea. Hope was after it like a dog on the hunt, arms out, crying, "I got it!" She lurched for it, but the little paper plane sailed past her grasp and landed gracefully on the gravel a few feet away from Linnea's feet. She smiled as she watched Hope pounce on it.

"Can I open it?" she called back.

"Knock yourself out."

Hope's pudgy fingers struggled to unfold the paper plane against the gravel. The folds were neat and tight, and Linnea thought how typical it was of John to be so precise. In a flash, she remembered watching his intense concentration when he constructed his architectural models. It was the last hobby she'd ever suspected the lowcountry surfer dude would have. John's mind was a wonder—brilliant in computer programming, inventive, creative. His outward behavior was loose and relaxed. But his mind . . . It was as if he could harness a tornado of ideas into a powerful laser focus, in both his work and his hobby. He'd showed off his models in his condo on glass shelves like the works of art they were—the Eiffel Tower, the Chrysler Building, and his first, a train depot. Each had taken years to build. And now, she thought with a laugh, paper airplanes.

Hope had the paper spread out on the pebbles. She looked up with a frustrated expression. "I can't read it."

"Let me take a look." Linnea reached out for the wrinkled paper. Smoothing it, she read the words.

*Listen, there's a hell of a good universe next door, let's go.*

"What's it say?" Hope asked.

"It's a quote," she said softly, feeling the impact of the words. "From a poet I especially like, e. e. cummings."

It was a phrase she and John had often said to each other when they were living next door to one another, that first summer they'd fallen in love. She slipped back in memory to the many hazy, sultry hours she'd spent lying in his bed in the loft next door, the walls surreal, painted in a Van Gogh swirl of stars and planets and sea animals by Flo's mother, Miranda Prescott. They'd talked, made love, read poetry. They'd taken turns reading aloud the lines of e. e. cummings, W. H. Auden, Rumi, Mary Oliver, and Marjory Wentworth, the South Carolina poet laureate. Linnea sighed, lost in the memory.

Hope sidled close and leaned against her. "Read it."

Linnea blinked, coming back. "Please . . ." she prompted.

"Please," Hope replied, chastened.

"*Listen, there's a good universe next door, let's go,*" she paraphrased, leaving out the word *hell*. She felt a softening in her heart and looked up at the window. John was standing there across the garden, watching her.

Neither moved to wave.

"What does that mean?" asked Hope.

"I think," she replied, "it means he wants to be my friend."

"*I* want to be his friend," Hope said with a pout.

Linnea laughed softly. "You can be his friend too. Let's go inside and write him a note telling him just that." Taking Hope's hand, she walked back toward the cottage, letting Hope's enthusiastic wave and calls of "Bye!" suffice for them both.

———

THE FOLLOWING MORNING was warmer, and Emmi's garden perked up. The cheery red azaleas competed with bursts of yellow daffodils. The air was heady with the scent of honeysuckle along the fence.

"Where should we leave the note?" asked Hope.

Linnea held the child's hand as they searched Emmi's garden for the right spot to put Hope's note for John.

"The flowerpot?" suggested Linnea, pointing to the potted blooms at the base of the stairs to John's loft.

Hope ignored that suggestion. Releasing Linnea's hand, she wandered through the small yard in front of the carriage house, eyes peeled.

Both the house and the carriage house were painted a soft coral with sea-blue trim. Back when Flo owned it, her mother, Miranda, had used the carriage house as her art studio. She'd died when Linnea was still young, but she remembered the bohemian artist. Everyone had loved her. Miranda lived to shock the neighborhood. Emmi and Cara still regaled them with stories of running to the studio during summer afternoons for hours of dress-up and painting lessons. Miranda had passed of Alzheimer's disease, and now Flo—opposite from her mother in every other way—was going down the same path.

The live oak tree that sprawled across the front yard drooped its heavy limbs low to the earth in a gesture of lazy welcome. Something shiny, tucked in the notch of the tree where a limb met the trunk, caught Linnea's eye.

"What's that?" called out Hope, spotting it too. She took off for the tree. It was easy climbing for a child. She scampered up and across the low-lying limb, then higher, on a beeline for the shiny object. Linnea was right behind her. Reaching way up, Hope grabbed hold of a paper airplane and a small tin box. She crouched on the limb, hunching over the tin like a bird mantling its prey.

"Come down," called Linnea.

"Okay." Hope placed her own note to John up in the notch of the tree, then scooted down to show Linnea her loot.

"It's candy!" Hope exclaimed, holding up the box. "Will you open it?"

Linnea took the tin and said, "What does the note say?"

Hope unfolded the airplane, then handed the paper to Linnea. "It's long. Read it."

"Please," Linnea prompted.

"Please," Hope responded, taking the tin back from Linnea and examining it. Inside were colored candies that looked like Skittles.

Linnea smiled. "It's another poem. This one is by A. A. Milne." She read aloud.

*"When I was One,*
*I had just begun.*
*When I was Two,*
*I was nearly new.*
*When I was Three*
*I was hardly me.*
*When I was Four,*
*I was not much more.*
*When I was Five,*
*I was just alive.*
*But now I am Six, I'm as clever as clever.*
*So I think I'll be six now for ever and ever."*

Hope put her hand over her mouth and giggled. "I can be six forever!" Then more seriously, she said, "I like being six."

Linnea joined in her laughter, thinking how wonderful it was that a child had no real sense of time. She wondered if living in the present wasn't the wiser course after all.

------

THE WI-FI CONNECTION to Gordon Carr in Oxford, England, was poor that evening. They had to ditch their usual FaceTime and instead used the phone only. Their long-distance relationship had evolved, at least in her mind, from a boiling summer affair to a simmering, confusing relationship. They'd had a connection from the moment they met. Maybe it was because she was on the rebound, but Linnea had jumped into that relationship—and his bed—without qualms. They'd shared an idyllic summer.

And then Gordon was gone.

She'd hoped to visit Gordon in England sometime over the spring, but the coronavirus had effectively quashed any hope of that. In the flush of their good-bye at summer's end, they'd planned to talk on the phone at least once a week, but that goal had proved elusive as well. Gordon's erratic schedule working two jobs—one as a professor at Oxford University and the other as a researcher in the field of marine biology—made regularly scheduled calls difficult. Gordon was in the publish-or-perish period of his life when he needed to make his mark in the world.

In the months that passed, Linnea had discovered she was not good at long-distance relationships. She needed to feel the comfort of an arm around her, to hear a laugh shared just between the two of them, to see that telling, knowing glance across the room that made her blood race. Even video chats were no match for the power of the senses.

Truth was, she'd been so consumed by her new job at the South Carolina Aquarium, she didn't miss dating. Linnea, too, was in her career-building stage of life. She'd found her dream job. In fact, when they spoke, both she and Gordon often said how lucky they were to love their jobs. She felt like they understood each other. And she wondered if they were becoming in fact more best friends than lovers.

Still, as the months passed, they held tight to the promise that Gordon would return to South Carolina in April to resume his research on marine animals. All would be well when they were together again, she hoped.

But again, the pandemic threatened. No one knew for certain how long the restrictions would last. Linnea held the phone closer, wishing she could see Gordon's face. He had such expressive eyes. She needed to get John out of her head and see Gordon tonight. Gordon's eyes were blue, not green. His hair was red, not dark auburn.

Linnea had the phone against her ear while her call to Gordon rang. She stood at the kitchen stove boiling water. According to the files Cara had left her, plain noodles with butter was a favorite dish of Hope's. She glanced across the room into the three-seasons porch and saw Hope sprawled on the floor with her crayons, coloring a picture for John. The game had distracted her from homesickness.

"Hello!" Linnea said into the phone.

"At last. I thought we'd never get a connection tonight. How are you?"

Linnea told Gordon all that had transpired since their last phone call. "The virus is becoming real. We're waiting to see if David caught it, so Hope is staying here with me while he quarantines."

"You're a nanny now?" he asked, amused.

"More than a nanny. This is full-time care. Poor Hope, I think the separation from her mother is coming hard on her. She's homesick."

"You said she's six?"

"Yes."

"Tender age. I was sent to boarding school at eight. I sympathize with her." Linnea couldn't imagine sending her child away so young.

"They've closed the schools, so she's home all the time. That's a lot of disruption."

"We're under bloody lockdown here," Gordon said, frustration ringing in his voice. "The university will be canceling classes for the rest of the year." He snorted. "They're taking their bloody time announcing it."

Linnea added the noodles to the boiling water. She loved Gordon's accent, and had to smile when he used British swearwords. "I'm worried about Cooper. Are the foreigners being sent home?"

"I'm sure they will be. He should make plans to leave now. While he can. It's chaos at the airports."

Linnea felt a chill and made a mental note to call her mother. "You'll keep an eye out for him?"

"I will," Gordon said with a reassuring emphasis. "He knows he just has to call."

"If the university is shutting down, can't you come here with him? You'll be early, but at least you'll be here."

"Truth is, Linnea . . ." He paused. "I'm not sure what this means about my trip to Charleston. At all."

"Why?" She stopped moving. "Are they canceling the research project?"

"No. At least, I hope not." He sighed, again with exasperation. "I don't think so, but one never knows these days, does one? Actually, it's more a matter of my being able to enter your country. They're shutting everyone out. Slamming the door tight."

"Starting when?"

"Effective immediately."

"Oh, Gordon," she said, suddenly filled with dismay. She'd been pinning her hopes on his arrival. Counting the days. "It's been forever since I've seen you."

"I know. I feel the same. I'm doing everything I can to get there, pulling every string, tapping every connection. Don't give up hope. But I doubt it will be early April as planned. The sodding virus has pushed everything back."

Linnea turned and reached for her glass of wine. She took a bracing sip. "Please tell me you'll find a way."

His voice lowered and she heard a faint tremor. "Linnea, you know I'll do everything in my power to get to you. I miss you."

"Gordon . . ." She felt a sudden urge to tell him that John had returned. That he was sending her thoughts hurtling back in time to when they were a couple. To confess she felt on shaky ground—her mind screamed no, but her body's memory lit up at the sight of him.

But no, she couldn't tell Gordon that John was back next door. Not when Gordon couldn't come back to Charleston himself. It would be unfair to create a sense of competition when there was none.

"Yes?"

She held the phone close to her cheek. "I miss you too."

# chapter five

*We're in this together.*

April

CARA PUT HER hand against the smooth wood of the bedroom door.

"You have a fever?" she asked, forcing her voice out. It felt like her chest was constricting. She leaned closer, setting her lips close to the door. This wall of wood separated her from the man she loved.

"Yeah," he replied despondently, then coughed. "It could be a cold," he offered. "I have a headache, and I usually get those when a cold is coming. I was out in all that rain. . . ."

"David . . ."

"Don't worry."

"Of course I'm worried."

"I only told you because . . . well . . . you should know about the fever. Just in case." He didn't need to say the word. "I'll call and let the doctor know."

"There's nothing she can do. There are no Covid-19 tests available." She clenched her hand into a fist of frustration. "The last time I talked to the doctor she said the best thing to do was to keep you quarantined. Get lots of sleep. Drink fluids. Do you have enough water?"

"I'm floating in water," he said.

She imagined him smiling. "I'll go to the store to get more chicken for soup."

"You shouldn't be going out. You've been in contact with me. The virus is very contagious."

"I've been careful."

"We should be more than careful. You can have food delivered."

"But . . ." Her daughter's face came to mind. "What about Hope?"

There was a long pause. "Under the circumstances, with my fever . . . I don't think you should see her."

"For how long?" Her voice rose.

"Until I'm well."

"But, David," she sputtered, "how long will that be?"

Another long silence. "I don't know."

She felt anger rise against him. *No*, she wanted to scream. *This is terrible. I won't do it.* Cara dropped her face into her palms. Then she lifted her head and took a calming breath. He must be worried too, all alone in that bedroom. She wouldn't shut him out, the way she had when Hope had the measles. They were married now.

"We'll get through this," she told him, meaning it. "We're in this together."

———————

HOPE THREW THE peanut butter and jelly sandwich on the floor. "It's yucky! I won't eat it!" She glared at Linnea, blaming her for the terrible food. Then she burst into fresh tears.

Linnea stared at the child for a moment, holding her breath, then turned heel and stomped into the kitchen. She clutched the counter and counted to ten. How could she screw up a PB&J? She'd even cut off the crusts. The sandwich was the third dish she'd prepared for Hope's lunch. A plate of chicken nuggets sat abandoned, and beside that a bowl of mac and cheese. She was ready to blow her stack and scream what her mother used to say to her when she'd refused food: *Go to your room and stay there till you're really hungry!*

The three days since Cara had told them that she couldn't be physically close to Hope had been a nightmare. At first, Cara had tried to come to the house and talk to Hope from outside the sliding glass porch doors, the way family members were doing for elderly relatives in retirement homes. It didn't take Freud to tell them that wasn't going to work for a child. Predictably, Hope cried and begged, throwing herself against the glass, to go outside with her mother. FaceTime at bedtime was equally bad. Just when Linnea had Hope quietly engaged in a bedtime story, Cara called to say good night. Again, predictably, Hope began howling for her mother.

Linnea finally had to tell Cara to *please* just stay away. Any contact with her came hard on Hope. Not to mention on Linnea. For Hope, seeing her mother, especially at bedtime, was like ripping off a Band-Aid repeatedly. Cara had wept but agreed. At least temporarily. No one knew what the time line was for David's illness or how long Cara could hold out. Every night, Linnea prayed for his speedy recovery.

Linnea looked out at the dining table and saw Hope slumped over with her head lying on her arms. Her heart went out to the little girl. This *was* hard on Hope. She didn't understand why her mother couldn't visit her. Her daddy was sick, not her mommy. She was confused and a little scared. Linnea needed to remember that during the histrionics. Who was the grown-up here, after all? Did she want to look back at these weeks as a chore, or as a special time shared?

She released the counter and took a cleansing breath.

"Hope?"

No response.

Linnea walked into the dining area, ignoring the peanut butter sandwich lying on the floor. "Hope?" she asked as she gently smoothed the hair, damp from sweat and tears, from her face. "I have an idea." Linnea lowered beside the chair so her face was near Hope's. "Let's make eating time fun. Like a game."

Hope turned her head. Linnea was sorry to see that her dark lashes were wet and her brown eyes rimmed red.

"How?"

The question gave Linnea courage. "I was thinking. Why should I decide what you eat for lunch? Or dinner? Why don't we decide together? We could make a spinning wheel of your favorite foods. You could spin it, and where it lands will be what food you get to eat that day. Like . . ." She made a show of tapping her cheek in thought. "Let's say you spin the wheel and it lands on chicken nuggets. Then you get to have chicken nuggets. If it lands on pizza, you get pizza. See how it works?"

Hope smiled with interest, then said, "But you don't make it like Mommy does."

"Right," Linnea said. "You'll have to help me. Show me how to do it the way you like it."

"Me? I can cook?"

"Do you want to?"

Hope thought about that a moment. "Yes."

"Okay, then. And you know what? Not only will we cook together, when I go online to order the food, you can help me. That will be fun, won't it?"

The little girl beamed with anticipation. "I help my mommy shop."

"Okay. Let's go shopping right now. On the computer! And later, we can make the game board. I'll have to figure out a way to make the spinning board."

"Ooh! We have one at school."

"Good, then you can help me. Now, for today's lunch, do you think we can fix up any of these?" Linnea gestured to the items on the table.

Hope scrunched her nose and shook her head resolutely.

"I was going to make myself a banana smoothie. Do you want one?"

Her eyes lit up. "Yes, please."

Linnea smiled and thought that maybe this was going to be okay after all.

————

EACH DAY FOR the next week, Linnea and Hope walked to the oak tree in front of John's carriage house with all the excitement of an egg hunt. And John never disappointed. It was the highlight of Hope's day. It was a simple game, but one that encouraged a child's wonder and awe. John had left a pack of Wrigley's Doublemint gum, two shiny pennies, and a roll of gray twine. Linnea thought the gifts a bit random, but Hope treasured them because they came from John. The man loomed large in her imagination.

"Can we go now?" Hope called out from the kitchen table.

It was a struggle to contain Hope until she finished her breakfast.

"Wash your hands," Linnea said.

She helped the little girl climb up on the chair by the sink to wash her hands. Today Hope was leaving John a gift. Linnea had dug through her drawers and pulled out a supply of travel soaps and shampoos that Hope thought would make great gifts.

Hope sprinted out the kitchen door to race to the oak tree. Linnea followed at leisure. By the time she arrived, Hope was already scrambling up the tree like a squirrel. Looking up at the window, she saw John standing there. He waved. Linnea waved back, not feeling the awkwardness she'd felt the first few mornings.

"What did you find today?" Linnea called.

Hope turned and, with wide eyes, showed her what looked like two sculptures. Linnea went to take them from her hands so Hope could climb to the ground. On close inspection, the figurines were roughly carved from soap.

"It's a boy and a girl," said Hope.

Something about the gift niggled a memory in Linnea's mind. Suddenly she laughed out loud and swung her head to look at John. He was grinning.

"What's so funny?" asked Hope, retrieving her precious soap sculptures.

"Well," Linnea began, trying to figure out how to explain it to a child, "John and I have a favorite book. It's called *To Kill a Mockingbird*. I just figured out that some of the gifts John left you in the tree were the same as a neighbor put in a tree for the two children in the novel. Jem and Scout."

"Oh." Hope didn't seem particularly interested in that fact. But in Linnea's mind, John shot higher in her regard.

---

THE HOUSE THAT Palmer Rutledge was building was well situated near a small creek that meandered lazily through the thick marsh. The tide was high. The water glistened. Linnea looked out over the waving, greening grass under a wide sky and thought she could gaze at this bucolic view every day for the rest of her life and never get bored. While beach views were thrilling, the real change of seasons, the mysteries of wildlife, were found in the salt marsh. The marsh was crawling with fiddler crabs, snails, worms finding food and shelter. It was a cornucopia of exploration for a child of any age.

Hope shot off to stand at the edge of the marsh. She scooted low and began investigating something with a broken stick that had caught her eye.

Shifting her gaze, Linnea took in the house her father was building. It was more modest in size than the last one he'd built on Isle of Palms—the house on Ocean Boulevard that Cara and David lived in now. This one was more quaint than grand, a traditional lowcountry house with a wide, covered front porch, gabled windows, and a tin roof. It sat prettily on a slightly raised hill overlooking the open expanse. She felt pride swelling in her chest. Once again, her father's sense of symmetry and Southern flair were evident in the telling details. She turned back toward the marsh to check on Hope.

"So, little girl," came her father's booming voice from behind her. "What do you think?"

She spun back around to see his broad frame striding toward her from the house, the blueprints in his hand. Not far behind him came her mother.

Palmer Rutledge was approaching his sixtieth birthday, and in the last few years she'd witnessed his aging. He'd had to loosen his belt notch a few times, his hair was thinning, and what there was had as much gray as blond now. Palmer was a conservative dresser, even on the construction site, in khakis and his ever-present polo shirt. He believed that clothes spoke of his position as the boss. He was building this house on spec, as he had the house before. Each project was a roll of the dice. He had to do well, or once again slide into bankruptcy. With the stakes so high, both she and her mother worried about his stress levels, lest he slip off the wagon and turn to drink.

"It's great, Daddy," Linnea exclaimed. He reached out for her as he approached, but she held out her hands. "No hugging," she warned.

He stopped abruptly, his smile falling.

"We can elbow-bump." She poked out her elbow.

"Hell, you mean I can't hug my own daughter?" Palmer blustered.

"Daddy, you're not even wearing a mask."

"I can't wear a mask out here when I'm working. Can't breathe in the damn thing. Besides, I heard it was okay if I was outside."

"If you stay six feet away. Thus, no hugging."

"I hate this damn corona stuff," Palmer said with an angry sweep of his hand. "We don't even know if those masks work."

Her mother walked up and put a calming hand on her husband's shoulder. "We've got to do what we've got to do." She looked at Linnea. "Hey, baby."

Linnea was proud to see her mother wearing a mask—then smiled at how the soft blue tie-dye was color-coordinated with her blue blouse over tan pants. Julia was as conservative a dresser as her father. They were a matched set, like the china spaniels sitting on her mother's mantel. Linnea had rebelled, albeit gently, against her parents' social conformity in most areas of her life, choosing to study environmental science rather than business, pursuing her career rather than a husband. At the aquarium, Linnea modeled her classic sleek attire after her aunt Cara's. But at home, where she could be herself, she went vintage. Her grandmother Lovie's clothes were treasures in her closet.

As different as she was from her parents, however, she knew there were many areas of overlay. Family meant everything to them. They were happy only when their feet were planted in the low-country, preferably near Charleston, where their ancestors had founded the city. The coastal landscape shaped their lives. Saltwater ran in their veins.

Yet Linnea didn't rest on nostalgia. She was passionate about educating people on how to protect the landscape they loved, about endangered habitats and species, about critical issues facing them because of climate change. And her prime target student was her father.

Despite loving the land, Palmer fell into that group who believed the wetlands would always be there, that climate change was sometimes confused with normal climate cycles, that a wall alone could protect the city from flooding. As long as he could make his dollar, all was well with the world. They'd had some pretty explosive arguments, especially when Linnea had left Charleston and moved with John to San Francisco. But they'd weathered that storm, as they had countless hurricanes. She was home again. Love had prevailed.

And she worried about them, because both her parents were in the more at-risk demographic for the pandemic. Since they came out to the construction site every day with the other construction workers, they had to be doubly careful.

"Hey, Mama," Linnea said. "The house looks wonderful. It's got the Rutledge stamp of style."

Palmer beamed and turned to look again at the house. "I told you my daughter had an eye. Yes, indeed. It's coming along nicely."

"I love it," Julia said. Then, looking at Palmer, "I wouldn't mind moving into it myself."

"Let's not beat that ol' horse again," Palmer said.

"We might get more for the beach house," Julia countered.

Palmer ignored that, and it was just as well. Everyone knew Julia was right. This house, as pretty as it was, set in Mount Pleasant would never fetch more on the market than a beachfront house on Sullivan's Island. It went without saying that the beach house, no matter how much her mother hated it, was their ace in the hole financially.

"Have you had any delays?" Linnea asked, referring to the virus. "The news said everything was getting backed up."

"Nope, knock on wood," Palmer replied, tapping his head with humor. "I've got a right good team. They show up."

"Well, that's not entirely true," Julia said. "There are delays on deliveries of the appliances. And the lighting fixtures, the bathrooms. Pretty much everything I need to install." She gave her husband a look of encouragement. "But we've got time for all that."

They heard a short squeal, and all turned to see Hope holding a green anole by its tail at the marsh edge. Then, with a spasm, the little lizard leaped from her hand, leaving its tail in Hope's fingers. She screamed, shaking her hands, as the anole fled back into the marsh.

Linnea hurried to her side. "It's all right."

Hope's face twisted in distress. "I killed it," she cried.

Linnea's heart went out to the child and she hugged her. "No, you didn't. That's a special way the lizards escape. If another animal bites it, they can lose their tail and run away. It will grow back."

"It will?"

"Yes."

"Oh." Hope wiped her eyes, mollified, still working it out in her mind. "Where did it go?"

Linnea's lips twitched. "The anole or the tail?"

"The anole."

"Someplace in the marsh to rest."

"Oh. Okay." Hope picked up her stick and walked off in search of more critters.

As Linnea walked back to her parents, she called out, "Don't get your shoes muddy, hear?"

"Honey, that's like telling a child not to breathe. Mark my words, you'll be washing those sneakers tonight." Her mother turned back and looked at Linnea with a bemused expression. "Look at you, being so motherly. I don't mind saying, it looks good on you. You know, I was your age when you were born."

"Don't get your hopes up, Mama," Linnea said with a short laugh. "I don't even have a boyfriend."

"What about Gordon?" Julia asked.

Linnea swallowed her sigh. Her mother's not-so-secret goal in life was to see her only daughter married. "He's still in the picture. But"—she shrugged—"he just told me that he might not be able to get into the country in April. Apparently, we're not letting the Brits in. And by the way," she said with more urgency, "I came to tell you.

He warned we should get Cooper out as soon as possible. It's chaos at the airports."

Julia looked back at her husband with a pleased smile. "Your daddy was on it like a tick on a dog," she said, reaching out to pat his shoulder. "Weren't you, honey? Cooper's on a plane home tomorrow."

"Really! Oh, Daddy, good for you. I have to say, that's a relief. I asked Gordon to look out for him, but it seems you've got it all taken care of. Mama, be sure to tell Cooper to wear a mask."

"He's a big boy."

"He's a *boy*. 'Nuff said. Really, Mama, all those people crammed into an airplane . . . Look what's happened with David."

"How is David?" Julia asked, all concern.

"You heard he's sick, right?"

"What? No!"

Palmer stepped closer. "Not that coronavirus?" The worry in his voice rang clear. Palmer liked David. They occasionally hunted together, went fishing. They were brothers-in-law. But most of all, David was an investor in Palmer's company.

"I think so," said Linnea. "Cara said he's got a fever and headache and a cough. I mean, that's the trinity of symptoms. But there's no test available, so we don't know for sure. He's staying in strict quarantine, of course. Cara's feeding him chicken soup by the gallon. She's giving her instapot a workout."

Palmer shook his head. "Damn, that's bad luck."

"That's why I'm concerned about Cooper. He'll have to go into quarantine when he gets home." Then with worry, "Mama, you and

Daddy will be careful, won't you? With him living with you and all. He might be a carrier too. Spray the house every day with antibacterial soap. Wear a mask if he's in the same room."

"I know, honey," Julia said reproachfully.

"Take this seriously, Mama. John's in quarantine at Emmi's, but at least he's staying in the carriage house. Cooper's going to be living right in the house with you."

"What's that?" Julia latched on to that comment. "John is back in town? *John Peterson?*"

*Now the cat's out of the bag*, Linnea thought. Anything remotely connected to Linnea's love life was of top interest to her mother. John had never been her parents' choice of a proper suitor. Her mother had always considered John a rival to her earlier beau, who came from one of Charleston's historic families. The two families had been planning their wedding since they were in diapers. Her parents both felt justified in their opinion of John once he'd lured their daughter clear across the country to California, of all places.

"He's been back for almost two weeks now."

"No one mentioned that to me." Julia appeared miffed.

"Nor to me. Imagine my surprise," Linnea said wryly.

"He's got that coronavirus too?" asked her father.

Linnea shook her head. "I don't think so. He didn't have any symptoms, like David."

"What's he doing back here?" Palmer asked, his displeasure clear in his voice.

"He'd come to see his mother for a visit when he learned a colleague had it, so he quarantined himself, just in case. Especially with his mother and Flo there. And he didn't want to fly as a potential carrier. I thought that was very responsible of him."

His father frowned at the compliment. "When's he going back?"

"I have no idea," Linnea replied honestly. "We barely talk."

Julia thought this over. "With David sick, how long will you be taking care of Hope?"

Linnea puffed out air. "I don't know. As long as it takes. But I'll say this—thank heavens for John. He and Hope have been playing this game of leaving notes and gifts for each other. Hope has to go out and hunt for them every morning. She can't see him, but he's very much a presence. I swear, it's like having Boo Radley living next door."

Julia shook her head with amusement. "What would Cara have done if you were working?"

"Called you, I suppose." She raised her brows. "By the way, I would really appreciate some relief time. I'm on twenty-four/seven and I don't mind admitting, I'm not up to the task. This motherhood thing is exhausting."

Julia laughed lightly, looking a bit too much like the Cheshire Cat for Linnea's liking. "Tell me about it," she replied airily. Then, more seriously, "I'm sorry, honey, but *I'm* the working girl now. My phone is ringing off the hook. Women are suddenly finding themselves stuck at home with time on their hands. Everyone wants to redecorate."

"But *I* need you." Her voice sounded disturbingly like Hope's at the moment.

"You're the one who encouraged me to hang out my shingle," Julia reminded her. "I'm a viable businesswoman now, and like it or not, I'm no longer free."

Linnea sighed loudly for effect, then turned in desperation to look at her father.

"Don't look at me," Palmer said, backstepping.

"Well, thanks a lot, you two." She looked over her shoulder at Hope, who, naturally, was standing ankle-deep in the mud. Linnea squelched a groan. Where she was going to find the strength?

---

THE FOLLOWING MORNING, an answer to her prayer arrived. Or so Linnea thought.

"Hello! Anybody home?"

At the sound of her mother's voice, Hope sprang to her feet and hurried to the back porch door, calling out, "Mama!" Linnea, in the kitchen cleaning up the breakfast dishes, had the bright thought that Cara was here to announce all was well on Ocean Boulevard. She grabbed a towel and swiftly walked to the porch, drying her hands, smiling widely.

Her smile fell when she arrived to see Cara holding the sliding door firmly closed to just a few inches so that Hope wouldn't escape. Hope was jumping up and down in excitement at seeing her mother. Or rather at . . . Linnea looked closer. Were her eyes deceiving her? There on the patio, in a pink crate beside Cara's legs, was a puppy.

Her mouth went dry and she could only stare, slack-jawed, at Cara, who seemed to think all this joyous chaos was wonderful.

"Hope, you must be still," Cara said in her firm voice. "No loud noises or jumping up and down. You'll scare the puppy."

"But I'm so excited," Hope exclaimed, trying to hold her body still by clenching her hands tight together at her chest. "Is the puppy for me?"

"Of course, it's for you," Cara said, her face aglow with love for her child.

"Uh, Cara?" Linnea said, finding her voice. "I don't believe you mentioned anything about a puppy?"

"I know. I'm sorry. It was an impulse thing. So rare for me. But you told me how sad Hope was, how she cried herself to sleep, and I just thought that, well, a puppy to take care of and love might be just what she needs to focus her attention on something sweet and happy."

"Wait." Linnea stepped closer. "You want the puppy to live *here*?"

"Of course! What do *I* need a puppy for? I have a sick patient to take care of. The puppy is for Hope!"

Linnea wanted to scream, but she struggled to keep her voice calm. "And I have your little girl to take care of. And it's a lot," she added.

Cara's smile fell and her shoulders straightened. "I'm sorry to hear my daughter is such a handful."

*Oh no, now she's mad.* "Let's not have this conversation right now,"

Linnea said, glancing meaningfully toward Hope. Fortunately, the child's focus was completely absorbed by the puppy in the crate and she wasn't paying attention to the women.

Cara's face altered to reveal chagrin. "You're right. I'm sorry. I should have asked you."

"Do you have your mask?"

"Yes, of course. In my purse."

"It's awkward to talk through this glass. If you put it on, we can sit outside on the deck and talk about it." Then she added, "Would you like a cup of coffee?"

"No, I'm good. I shouldn't stay long. I've got the patient, and, as you pointed out, we need to be careful." Cara turned to Hope. "Listen to me carefully. If I open this door, you cannot hug me or touch me because I might have germs on me. Do you understand?"

Hope, at six, was barely able to contain her disappointment. Her face fell. "But can I touch the puppy?"

Cara smiled. "Yes, you can touch the puppy. First let me put this little fence up so you have a place to play. We don't want the puppy to run away." She put her finger in the air. "Hold on."

As Cara set about her task, Linnea reached out to the nearby table and grabbed her own face mask. Slipping it on, she watched Cara scurry about the deck. She hadn't seen her aunt in nearly two weeks. She was wearing fitted faded jeans and a black form-fitting jacket, looking sleek even in her casual clothes. She looked like she'd lost a little weight, Linnea noticed with a twinge of resentment. With all the cooking she'd been doing with Hope, Linnea worried she'd put on a few pounds.

Now in April, the weather continued its cool snap, but the sun was shining. Cara was quick at spreading out the black metal fencing on the deck to form a play circle. She dug into one of her many large bags and pulled out doggy play pads and laid these inside the circle, then tossed in two stuffed animal toys, a package of Nylabones, and a bag of treats. When all was settled, Cara slipped her face mask on, spread some hand sanitizer on her hands, and returned to the sliding door.

"All ready!" she said in a cheery tone.

Linnea couldn't restrain Hope. The child tugged at the door along with her mother until it slid open enough for her to wiggle through. In seconds' time she was at the dog crate, peering through the grate. Cara immediately stepped away, creating a distance. Linnea pushed the sliding door all the way open and joined them on the deck, going straight to join Hope at the dog crate.

Her heart melted. Inside the crate sat the sweetest little brown and white puppy she'd ever seen. It had soft, shaggy hair and the biggest, most luminous brown eyes. They gazed up at Linnea now as the puppy scratched at the grate, whining to get out.

"Can the puppy come out?" Hope asked in a pleading tone.

"Yes," Cara answered. "Linnea, I don't dare come closer. Could you take the puppy out and carry her to the pen? Hope, darling, you'll have to let Linnea help you in. There's a little gate"—she pointed—"right there. It lets her in and out without having to climb over the fence."

Linnea bent low and opened the metal hinge on the pink crate. As soon as she reached in, the puppy climbed into her hands, scrambled up her chest, and began stretching to reach her face, trying to lick it. She could feel the puppy trembling, so soft and little.

"Oh, she is a pretty thing."

"Isn't she?" Cara called from across the deck. "I have to admit, I fell in love with her."

"Easy to see why. What kind of a dog is she?"

"A Cavalier King Charles spaniel. A Blenheim—that's the brown and white. Cavaliers are a child-friendly breed, very sweet-tempered, not biters, and love to cuddle," Cara said in the manner of someone who had done her research.

"What's not to like?" Linnea asked as the puppy nuzzled her neck.

"I think they'll be fast friends."

Linnea laughed as the puppy returned to licking her face. "She certainly is friendly."

"Let *me* hold her," cried Hope insistently, reaching up.

Linnea carefully set the puppy into the confined area. Immediately it leaped up against the fencing and whined to be picked up again. Linnea helped Hope inside the pen. Immediately she pounced on the puppy.

"Gentle!" Cara called out.

Linnea spent a few minutes inside the enclosure getting child and puppy settled with toys and bones. Once she felt the puppy was safe, she went to the wicker table and sat in a chair a distance away from Cara. She looked at her aunt and saw her dark eyes watching her. Waiting.

"So," Linnea began. "A puppy."

Cara had the grace to laugh. It sounded muffled behind her white face mask. She put her hand to her forehead. "I know. I must be losing my mind. It seemed such a good idea at the time. And I'm having a hard time not seeing Hope. Very hard."

"I know."

"I'm sorry. I seem to have created a problem where I meant to solve one," she began.

This was more in character, and Linnea was relieved. Cara had always been level-headed and forthcoming. She came straight to the point and didn't relish surprises. Which was why this puppy showing up on Linnea's doorstep had thrown her. She relaxed and listened more openly.

"I've been so worried about Hope," Cara continued. "I started doing research on how to help children through difficult times, and when I read about a pet, I recalled how Hope has been begging me for a puppy. You know me. I did due diligence—I studied breeds, their size and temperament. Hours and hours. I warn you, looking at dogs on the Internet is sliding down a rabbit hole. And if I'm honest, I think Cavaliers are the sweetest breed. Look at her eyes!" She turned to watch the interaction between Hope and the puppy. Hope was clasping the puppy in what looked like a choke hold. "Not so tight, honey," Cara called out.

Cara leaned back against the cushion. "So, I called my friend who is a breeder, just to see what she might have down the pipeline. I swear, I was thinking the future. She told me she had a litter right now! I went over to see them, and, oh, Linnea, she had all these beautiful puppies. Some Blenheim, some tricolor. It was a puppy love fest. I went hoping to get on her waiting list. But when she learned of our situation, about David being sick and Hope separated from us, she bumped me up the queue and let me have the dog. It was like a gift from the universe. I said yes. How could I not? I bought a crate, the recommended puppy food, and a few toys." Cara leaned forward intently. "Linnea, I'll get anything else you feel you need. I promise."

"Among all those preparations, you didn't think to call *me*? To ask if it was okay?"

"It all went so fast. And to be honest, I didn't think you'd mind."

"Cara, I love puppies. Who doesn't? But I've got my hands full trying to keep Hope distracted and not homesick."

"Exactly! Enter the puppy. I bought the puppy to give her a focus. And it won't be much longer."

Linnea cocked her head in interest. "Really? Is David better?"

"So much better. The headache and fever are mostly gone. Only at night it spikes. So, we're still in it, but we're hoping we're close to the end. As soon as the fever is gone, we're out of the woods."

"I'm so glad!"

Linnea saw Cara's relief, even as she saw how the past few weeks had etched fatigue on her pale face, and how the usual brightness in her eyes was dimmed with worry. Linnea imagined that was how she herself must've looked when she'd arrived home from California the year before, without a job, kicked out by John, and with no place to land. Back then, she'd been every bit as scared as Cara was now. And who had come to her rescue? Cara. Remembering this, her answer came easily.

"Hey, I love puppies. We'll be fine."

"Oh, *thank you*. I won't forget this."

"There's nothing more to say. We're family. We're in this together." She turned and looked at the puppy, who was pressed against the fence again, her large brown eyes locked onto Linnea. "I guess that now includes you."

# chapter six

*The number of coronavirus cases worldwide passed one million.*

APRIL IN SOUTH Carolina was a wonder. Driving over the massive Ravenel Bridge, the link between the Charleston Peninsula and points north, Cooper Rutledge looked into a sky so brilliant a blue it hurt his travel-weary eyes. Below, Charleston Harbor was bustling. Mammoth container ships were docked, one after another, looking like a child's toy set from this height. The Cooper River, for which he'd been named, opened to a sea that mirrored the sky, crystalline and infinite. As the hired car descended from the bridge, Robert Browning's words, *Oh, to be in England, now that April's there*, played in his mind.

He loved the lowcountry. It was his home. But he loved England too. He was sorry to be chased out of Oxford by some bloody pandemic. At Oxford University, the name Rutledge held no weight. His family's history was puny compared to those of royal lineage. He rather enjoyed being a nobody. The expectations of him were based solely on his own ability, his own efforts and dreams. What those dreams might be was still a work in progress. But at least he was sniffing along the right track. He felt the prize drawing near.

He was doing well in his classes. Very well, in fact, which was also a new experience for him. Cooper had always skated on the perimeter of his abilities. Teachers used words like "full of promise," or "he isn't working up to his potential." The truth was, Cooper hadn't cared about school. He'd much preferred to drink with his pals, hunt at private lodges, play football, drive his truck, and spend time with a lady friend. He'd studied just hard enough to pass. He was the only son of Palmer Rutledge, heir of the Charleston Import Export Company. Why did he have to study? Work hard? He was destined to step into his father's shoes to head up the company, as Rutledge sons had done for generations.

Cooper brought his hands to his eyes and gently rubbed them. That was no longer his destiny. Under his father's stewardship, the company had gone belly-up, and with it the carefully constructed path that Cooper was intended to follow.

It had been the making of him. When all hell broke loose the summer he'd graduated from high school, Cooper finally broke free of the chains of expectations. From his father's demands. It was hard-won, true. He pinched the bridge of his nose. He didn't like to think about those times, or his near miss with death. It often felt like that was another lifetime ago. Another person.

Somehow, with his sister's support, Cooper had escaped to the University of South Carolina in Columbia. Granted, not far from home, but far enough. He was out from under his father's roof. By the time he got to college, he'd had his fill of drink and drugs. It took a lot of rehab and therapy to realize he preferred to be sober. For the first time in his academic life, Cooper had actually applied himself. He studied. He attended classes. He excelled. So much so, he was recommended for a junior year abroad at Oxford for international business.

He'd loved every minute there. The private tutorials gave him no room to bullshit or dodge questions. He'd learned to come prepared to think and speak his mind. And he'd loved the British way of speaking clearly, intelligently, relishing the use of the English language in all its intricacies and history. Many Brits remembered poems at a moment's notice. Cooper had started reading poetry and the classics, just to keep up. He'd looked forward to the rest of his term there, perhaps trying to arrange another year, or at the very least a summer.

The black car made its way through the town of Mount Pleasant. Through the darkened windows he saw how the city had changed just in the past year. It seemed apartments and houses had sprouted up on every square inch of land, edging farther into the boggy wetlands. As he crossed the vast marshland from the mainland onto Sullivan's Island, he adjusted his seat and rubbed his face, waking more. He felt his blood stir at being so close to home. It had been a manic few days of arranging for his ticket to the States, then throwing whatever he had into his luggage in record time. There was a mass exodus of Americans; classes were closed, and everyone was worried about getting out.

The transatlantic flight had been packed, and few people made any effort to wear a mask. Sitting in coach toward the rear of the plane, his legs pinched almost against his chest, was one of the few times he'd regretted being over six feet tall. But he was home at last.

Home. Cooper leaned forward, resting his elbows on his knees as he looked out the window. The car drove along the oak-lined streets of the island, past quaint cottages that had survived a century of storms. He knew these streets like the back of his hand, had raced his bicycle along the rutted roads and, later, roared past in his truck filled with hootin' and hollerin' friends. He had mixed emotions where he saw the changes. This was no longer the sleepy neighborhood he'd grown up in. No longer shabby-chic. The impressive new houses, each worth millions, were decidedly upscale.

His lips curved upward as the car pulled into the driveway. Then there was his family's house. It looked just as he'd remembered—the overgrown shrubs; the scrubby lawn, more sand than grass; the ancient oak drooping enormous cragged limbs to the earth; the white, plain-fronted house on pilings. His mother was right, he thought as he pushed the dark hair from his broad forehead. It was an ugly house. And he was glad of it. Something had not changed.

The driver parked and the engine quieted. He felt his heart constrict at the prospect of walking into his parents' house. At twenty-one, he was once again a kid living with mom and dad. He released a heavy sigh. It hadn't worked out well the last time. Cooper closed his eyes at the memory. His overdose at eighteen had broken the family; but it had proved their redemption and the first step toward rebuilding. They'd all made strides forward since that summer after his grad-uation. He'd gone off to college, Linnea had left for California, and his father had gotten sober. Since he'd left, they'd had a tenuous peace. Cooper hadn't spent more than two weeks under their roof. God help him now.

He pushed open the car door. Brown wing-tip shoes stepped on the sandy soil as he emerged from the car. His tan suit pants were creased, his white button-down was wrinkled, and he smelled of stale food. He'd dressed formally, in the British style, a signal to his parents that he wasn't a boy any longer. That he'd changed.

Lifting his arms over his head, he stretched, breathing in the salt-tinged air, moist and refreshing. The front door of the house flung open. Looking up, he saw a blur of pink. Heard his mother's voice.

"He's here!"

———

LINNEA ALWAYS FELT a surge of goodwill when she walked through the gate into Emmi's garden. Gardening had become a bond shared between Emmi and Flo since they'd shared the house, and it served as an inexpensive intervention that kept Flo occupied as her dementia progressed.

Hope enjoyed the garden too, Linnea thought as she spied Hope on her knees digging in a patch of earth. The puppy was deliriously happy digging nearby, spraying dirt. Both little girls would need a bath tonight. Emmi had been her salvation the past week, cheerfully volun-teering to babysit a few hours in the mornings while they gardened.

Emmi had set aside a small plot just for Hope so she could have her very own garden and allowed her to choose what she planted.

Linnea slipped on her mask and entered the enclosed garden, making a beeline for Hope. "What have you got there?" she asked the little girl, curious to know what she'd chosen.

Hope turned, her face blooming with color when she saw Linnea. She rose and rushed to Linnea, wrapping her arms around her legs, making her love the child even more. Something had changed in the past week between them, a connection that went beyond their being cousins, or even caretaker and child. Linnea wasn't sure if Cara had been right and it was the puppy, or perhaps it was due to Hope's time outdoors in the garden, or their cooking together, or the hide-and-seek game of notes with John, or a combination of all, but Hope had blossomed from the recalcitrant, listless child into the sweet, bubbly one she'd remembered. Her homesickness had abated, replaced with a joy for life that lifted the spirits of all she encountered.

Hope sneezed and wiped her nose, leaving a muddy smear on her face. Linnea's inner alarm went off. That was the fifth time she'd sneezed today. Linnea tightened her lips in concern—could she be coming down with a cold? She'd not enforced mask wearing outdoors for Hope, given her age, but the sneezing gave her second thoughts. Especially when Flo was in the area. She glanced toward the old woman staring at the rosebuds.

"How are you today, Flo?" she asked, walking to her side.

Flo swung her head and looked at Linnea. After a moment she offered a quick smile of recognition. "Good. Roses coming up."

"I hope it's a good year."

"No black spot," Flo declared.

"That's good."

"Maybe. Insects a problem." She shook her head and looked at Linnea, her once bright blue eyes faded now. "If it's not one thing, it's another." Without another word, Flo walked away.

Linnea watched her stooped form, the hesitancy of her steps, and recalled the upright, strong stride of the woman she'd once been. Florence Prescott's wisdom had guided them all for decades. It was hard to watch her diminish.

In contrast, Hope flitted from plant to plant like a butterfly. Linnea walked over and asked her questions about the plants, listening intently, giving the child her full attention. Hope pointed out, in a voice bubbling with excitement, each seed and flower she'd planted. The child's garden was a mishmash of a few potted annuals—colorful zinnias and marigolds—and two crooked rows of radishes, spinach, and lettuce seeds. Linnea took a photo of the little finger indentations in the tilled soil for Cara.

Emmi came closer, beaming with pride. "She's a natural." In a lower voice, she added, "Those are seeds that grow fast for impatient children."

"And look!" Hope called out, running to the flagstone patio on the opposite side of the garden. "A pond!"

Emmi's voice rose with excitement to match the child's. "We're building a small koi pond. I've always wanted one, and John offered to build it for me. It's a work in progress."

Linnea saw the kidney-shaped hole dug into the ground, and beside it, liner and equipment. Listening to Emmi describe the project, Linnea couldn't tell which thrilled her more—the fact that she was getting a pond, or that her son was building it for her.

"How's John doing?" she asked.

"Why don't you ask him yourself?" asked Emmi.

Linnea's heart began to pound and she searched the garden. "Why? Is he out here?"

"He was, earlier this morning."

"He's out of quarantine?"

"At last. What a relief he didn't have any symptoms. Not like poor David. We have him in our prayers."

"Poor Hope. She's anxious to get home. Who knows how long it will be now?"

"And Cooper! Doesn't he get home today?"

"Yes, thank God. Daddy got him a seat on the earliest plane he could. He's gone directly into quarantine at home, so I can't see him. But I received a text that the package has been delivered." She chuckled. "Mama is over the moon, as you can imagine. She's been baking and cooking for days. I'm hoping she'll bring leftovers here."

"So, the Rutledge family is back together."

"Yes, if we can ever gather in a room together again," Linnea said wryly.

The sound of a car pulling in, followed by two short beeps of the horn, had them turning their heads.

"You've got company," said Emmi, looking over her shoulder into Linnea's driveway.

"That must be Annabelle. She's moving into the house today." Linnea felt spurred to movement. "Do me a favor? Corral that puppy in her crate. I've got to welcome her."

"Child, I can't keep up with your goings-on!" Emmi called after her as she hurried out of the garden.

"You're here!" Linnea called out when she saw Annabelle climb from her Subaru. Her tall, lanky figure was clad in somber brown pants that clung to her long legs, a black T-shirt under a torn jeans jacket, and brown ankle boots. A far cry from the denim shorts and 1940s-era red-and-white-checked shirt that Linnea had on. Annabelle's red hair was bound up in a messy bun and, her hands filled with a pot of trailing vine, she kicked the door shut with her boot. The door of the old green car creaked loudly and didn't quite close.

Annabelle turned at the sound of her voice and peered at Linnea through large aviator sunglasses. "Ready or not, here I come."

"Welcome," she called, hands out to assist her friend. From the corner of her eye she spied Hope running from the garden.

"Incoming," Annabelle said wryly as she handed the plant to Linnea.

Hope careened to a stop beside Linnea and looked at Annabelle in a proprietary way. "Who are you?"

Annabelle, Linnea quickly discovered, treated children as she did adults. She crossed her arms, gave Hope a cool once-over, and replied, "I'm Annabelle. Who are you?"

Hope lifted her chin. "I'm Hope Rutledge-Wyatt. I live here."

"As a matter of fact, I've come to live here too," Annabelle replied in a serious tone.

"Oh. Then you must be Linnea's friend. From the aquarium."

"I am." Annabelle pointed to Hope's cheek. "You've got a little something there."

Hope reached up and only smeared more dirt on her face. "Here?"

Annabelle smirked. "Yeah. Nailed it."

"Let's bring all your stuff in," Linnea said. Stepping closer, she peered into the car. There was a bag of groceries, a potted fig tree and a few other small plants, and a single carry-on bag. "Is this all you have?"

"There's also a bunch of stuff in the trunk," Annabelle said, walking toward it. She pushed a button and lifted the lid. Inside was one very large, very old suitcase, an open basket filled with shoes, another filled with makeup, and a large black plastic bag stuffed to bursting. It looked like she'd tossed everything she had into baskets and bags.

"I put my furniture and stuff in storage," Annabelle continued. "I don't have much, but I like what I have and wanted to keep it. I figured I won't need a lot here." She hoisted the suitcase out of the trunk with a grunt and let it slide to the ground with a thump. "It weighs a ton, I'm afraid. No, don't you try," Annabelle said, shooing away Hope's hand. "I can barely lift it. Think you can handle one of the baskets?"

"Let me help," John called out. He approached from next door dressed in his usual jeans and T-shirt and wearing a face mask. In his hands, he carried a bird feeder.

Linnea swung her head at the sound of his voice, feeling suddenly tongue-tied.

Hope clapped her hands in surprised joy. "John!" she called out, rushing toward him. "You came out of your house! Are you all better now? Did you get my pictures? And my notes?"

He held out his hands to ward her off. "Hold on, sweetheart. Best not to get too close."

Hope stood rigid, scowling, and said in a disappointed tone, "I thought you were better."

"I am," he replied in his easy manner, not the least put off by her mercurial emotions. "Quarantine's over, but best to keep a social distance, right?" He lowered to talk with Hope, still at a distance. "Thank you for all your notes and gifts. I really liked getting them."

Hope melted and got all flirty once again. "I got your notes too. And the candy. And your poems. Linnea read them to me."

He glanced up at Linnea and their eyes met. "Did she?"

Hope pointed to the bird feeder. "Is that for me?"

"Who else? I thought since we're all looking out windows"—he looked up at Linnea and winked—"why not have something to look at? Other than me, of course."

Linnea made an unladylike snort.

John reached out to poke Hope's tummy and she squealed with laughter. "I thought we'd let Linnea tell us where to put it, and I have a big bag of birdseed." He looked again at Linnea. "What do you say, Lin?"

He'd called her by her nickname. The name sounded sweet on her ears. She lifted her shoulders. "I think it's a lovely idea. Hope, we'll write down the names of all the different birds that come to our window." Looking again at John, her face softened. "Thank you, John. That was thoughtful."

"I remember how much you love watching birds."

"Tell me a poem now," Hope demanded.

"I don't know, kiddo. You caught me off guard."

"Please, John?" Hope begged with hands together.

Linnea laughed at her brazen flirting.

"Well, here goes," John said, then made a show of clearing his throat.

"There once was a girl who moped
She sighed and her shoulders sloped
Till an airplane came flying
And she stopped her crying
And said, 'That plane gives me hope!'"

Hope clapped her hands. "That's my name!"

"Uh, I don't think e. e. cummings has anything to worry about," chided Linnea.

John set the bird feeder on the ground beside the front steps, then walked closer to Annabelle. "Hey, I'm John," he said, and extended his elbow. "I'm guessing you're Annabelle."

Laughing, Annabelle bumped elbows with him in the new 2020 greeting. "You can call me Anna."

"*Anna?*" Linnea asked, her gaze askance.

"I've decided to shorten it. I've never felt like an Annabelle. It's too"—she speared Linnea with a look—"like a Southern belle. I'm a woman from the South, and that is not the same thing."

"No," Linnea agreed with a laugh.

Anna shrugged. "I figure if 2020 could change my life, then I could change my name. It's Anna now. Straight, simple, like me."

"Well, *Anna,*" John said with exaggeration, "may I carry one of your suitcases in?"

Linnea watched as John, in his inimitable fashion, immediately broke down Anna's chilly wall. He had her laughing about something, and she readily stepped back and allowed him to hoist the enormous suitcase with enviable ease.

"Back room?" John asked Linnea as he passed.

"Yes. Let me get the door." Linnea sprang into action and hurried ahead of him, up the stairs to push wide the front door while juggling the potted plant. "Follow me. She'll be in Palmer's room."

She walked into the seaward bedroom. The walls were paneled with pecky cypress and a door opened out to the deck with a view of the ocean. The coastal décor, rich with texture, was fit for a man or a woman. The furniture was vintage: a curved wicker headboard on the full bed, Palmer's old painted wood dresser, and the small wooden desk under the window where, years back, Toy had studied for her GED under Lovie's tutelage.

Linnea set the potted plant on the desk and turned to see John taking in the room.

He said, "It's funny in a cool way how you still refer to the bedroom as your dad's."

"It's the way it's always been," she replied. "Back when Grandmama Lovie lived here, these were Cara's and Palmer's rooms." She pointed to the bedroom across the hall, currently occupied by Hope. "They shared the bathroom. Years later when Cara returned to the island, she stayed in her old room while Toy Sooner, who was pregnant, stayed here in Palmer's old room. I don't mind telling you it annoyed him to no end."

"Why would he care?"

"He didn't want Lovie out here in the first place, then to find out an unwed mother was her caretaker—well, you know my father. Always worried about what other people might think. Anyway, Grandmama Lovie had her own way, and it was the best thing that ever happened to Toy. Changed her life . . . Now it's Annabelle's turn."

"Anna's . . ." they said at the same time, then laughed.

"This sweet cottage has welcomed many visitors in its time," Linnea said wistfully.

"Which way?" called Anna's voice from the front door.

"Here!" shouted Linnea, and hurried from the room. John followed, pausing to scan one of the many black-framed family photographs.

"Hey, that's the Fourth of July party." John drew closer, then pointed and laughed. "Is that you?"

Linnea knew the photograph he was looking at, had looked at it many times the summer they'd dated. It was the Fourth of July party when they'd first met. Well, in truth, John didn't remember her, but she'd sure remembered the handsome Peterson brothers in their prime, all bronzed from surfing. They'd breezed through the party as a courtesy to their mother, wolfed down burgers and shrimp, and headed straight back out without talking to anyone. Emmi had been furious.

Linnea went to his side and peered at the photo. He was pointing to the skinny, gawky preteen in pigtails tied with red, white, and blue ribbons.

"Yes, that's me."

"Adorable." He turned, his face inches from hers. "As always."

A noise at the door had her jumping back. "Annabelle, let me help you," she called, and hurried down the hall. "I mean, Anna. It's going to take time to get that right."

"Coming through!" Anna called out, hoisting the large black plastic bag. "Goddamn, this is heavy."

"I'd better take it," John said, grabbing hold of the twisted end of the plastic. "If it drops one more time, I think it's going to burst." He lifted it with relative ease and carried it down the hall into the bedroom.

"Nice guy," Anna said, sotto voce. "Is that John, as in your ex? I thought he was in California."

"*Was* is the operative word."

"He's come back? For how long?"

Linnea shrugged. "Who knows?"

Anna's eyes brightened and she said in her low voice, "Well, hello, neighbor."

"Let's grab the rest of your things," Linnea said with a smirk. "I have to check on Hope."

"What is the deal with Hope?" Anna asked as they walked down the front stairs. "I thought she was going to be gone when I arrived."

"Change of plans," Linnea informed her. "David's not one hundred percent yet, so Hope has to stay until he gets the all-clear. Which should be any day. And," she added, stopping at the bottom of the stairs to make the point, "we have to be extra careful around her. You'll have to wear a mask when you're in the same room with her."

"I've been living alone for the past few weeks. I'm, like, perpetually quarantined."

"Have you gone shopping?"

"Yeah, sure, but I wore a mask."

"Just to be safe, please do it. I promised Cara we would. And she's our landlord, by the way."

"Fine. But tell the little rug rat to stay out of my room."

Linnea smirked. "You'll want to keep your door shut anyway. We have a puppy too!"

Anna's brows rose with obvious delight. "You're kidding. Where is it?"

"Next door in the garden. I'm going to fetch her now. You finish unloading your stuff and we'll all meet in the living room."

"Puppies. Cute guy next door. Things are looking up, Rutledge," Anna said, and headed toward the car.

———————

WHEN ALL ANNA'S things were settled in her room, Hope and the puppy had been washed and changed, and Linnea had served beers and sweet tea, she gathered Anna, John, and Hope in the living room to establish ground rules for the house. Hope sat on the floor playing with a wood puzzle. John sat on one of the two upholstered chairs, a beer bottle in hand, a mask on his face, while Anna slouched in the other, texting on her phone, sans mask. Cuddling the puppy in her lap on the sofa, Linnea looked around the room and realized it was the first time a group had gathered in her house in several weeks. She adjusted her face mask.

"Since we're all here . . ." she began—then waited. Anna was still texting. "Anna?"

Anna lifted one finger to indicate *wait one minute*. She finished her text, then lifted her head, alert. "I'll all ears, boss."

"I'm glad we're all here, but before we begin, Anna, could you put on your mask?"

"But we all live here. Doesn't that make us a pod?" She looked at John. "Well, not you. But still."

"But *still*," John said, then pointed to his mask, "I'm wearing a mask."

"Why are you even here?" Anna asked him. "You don't live here." She looked at Linnea, a question burning in her eyes.

"Hope and John have this hide-and-seek game going on, and we spend a lot of time together in Emmi's garden. I thought it was a good idea for us all to be on the same page for rules regarding Covid. And, Anna, I thought we'd discussed this." She looked meaningfully at Hope.

"Fine." Anna rose and went to her room.

"Where'd she go?" asked Hope.

"To get her mask," Linnea said. "In fact, Hope, when we are all together inside, I want you to wear your mask too. Especially since you might be catching a cold. Can you get it, please?"

"Okay." Hope climbed to her feet and scampered off to her room.

Linnea looked to John and asked in a soft, strained voice, "What's the big deal?"

John just shrugged, then looked over his shoulder as Anna returned wearing a mask in a camo design. She plopped back into her chair, then pointed with both hands to her mask in a gesture of *okay now?* In contrast, Hope reappeared wearing a pink polka-dot mask, one of many adorable masks Cara had delivered, and settled back on the floor, happy to be included in the group of grown-ups.

Linnea strove for the positive. "I know these are strange times and we're all trying to learn how to deal with the new normal, but I want us to think how we can make this time special. Unique. I'm not trying to be a Pollyanna, but it seems to me we can either see this time as an opportunity to do things we wouldn't otherwise have had time to do. Or"—she shrugged—"we moan about it and feel miserable. I vote for the former."

"Sounds like a plan," John said.

Anna huffed a short laugh. "Sorry, but it still sounds a bit Polly-anna to me."

Linnea groaned inwardly and hoped again she hadn't made a mistake inviting Annabelle, Anna, or whatever name she chose to use, to move in. What was going on with her? She'd seemed so eager to move in. Sometimes Anna could be negative, but she had shown she could be supportive if she chose. She'd been a real ally at the aquarium, standing by her when Linnea initiated new programs. Linnea had hoped this would be a time for bonding. But now . . .

"Thank you," Linnea said in a chilly tone.

Anna shook her head. "Hey, I'm joking. I'm all for being positive." She mock power-punched the sky. "Woo-hoo."

Linnea took a breath and met John's eyes. The green sparkled with mirth and he barely perceptibly lifted his bottle in support.

"Okay, then, let's get down to the rules."

"What's your puppy's name?" asked Anna out of the blue.

"What?" Linnea shifted gears.

"She doesn't have a name," said Hope.

"We haven't given her a name yet," Linnea explained, stroking the puppy asleep in her lap. "Hope can't quite make up her mind, can you?"

Hope shook her head, her gaze fixed on her puzzle.

"What names do you like?" John asked her.

Hope straightened, taking John's question seriously. "I like Moonpie, because my daddy calls me that on account of I love the moon.

We always watch the full moon together." She turned to Linnea. "When is the full moon?"

"Next week. I put it on the calendar."

"Moonpie is a great name," said Anna.

Linnea said, "But it's Hope's special name from her daddy. I don't think the dog should take it. She also likes Maggie and Gigi, don't you?"

"I guess." Hope shrugged and said in a bit of a whine, "But I love the moon."

John leaned forward, elbows on his knees. "Your name in Spanish is Esperanza, right?"

Linnea knew that Hope's biological mother had named her Esperanza, and that at adoption, Cara had given her the name Hope in honor of her Spanish name.

"Uh-huh," Hope told him. "Esperanza means hope."

"Well," John continued, "*moon* in Spanish is *luna*. You could call the dog Luna. Then you'd both have a Spanish name too."

"Luuuunaaaa." Hope rolled the name in her mouth, testing it. She brightened. "I like that name!"

Linnea swallowed her smile, thinking Hope would like any name John suggested. She looked at the brown and white dog in her lap, thought of her luminous eyes, and said, "I do too. It's perfect, and easy for the puppy to learn. What do you think, Esperanza? Should we call her Luna?"

"Yes, that's her name! Luna!" Hope promptly scrambled to her feet and climbed up onto the sofa. She reached out and dragged the sleeping puppy into her lap.

"Careful now," Linnea said, worried about her rough handling of the puppy. Hope didn't know better, and Linnea had grown inordinately fond of Luna and thus protective.

As the adults conducted a serious discussion of the house rules, Hope began sneezing and her red-rimmed eyes watered. Anna made a joke of leaning farther back in her chair, away from germs.

Linnea didn't laugh. Growing alert, she studied Hope's reaction. The sneezing, the watery eyes, the nasal congestion . . . they all got worse when she was near the puppy.

"I wonder if she doesn't have a cold after all, but allergies." She looked at John. "The first night I put the puppy in her bedroom, she started sneezing. I thought it was a cold. The puppy whined and cried, so naturally I moved her into my room instead. Hope didn't get any worse, but she was still sneezing—and now that I think about it, the sneezing and watery eyes began when the dog came into the house." She paused, reality dawning. Linnea looked at Hope and said, "Oh no. I think you might be allergic to the dog."

"I'm not 'lergic," Hope said with a quivering lip, and held the dog tighter.

"You'd better put *keep the dog away from Hope* on your list of house rules," said Anna.

Linnea shot her a look. "That's not helpful."

"But it's the truth," Anna said, lifting her hands.

John got up and walked to Hope's side. "May I see Luna?"

Hope nodded as she rubbed her eyes.

John stooped to gently pick up the puppy and cradled it in his arms. Luna, yet another female besotted with John, began licking his face. She looked so small against his large frame. He moved away from Hope to the perimeter of the room and settled the pup in his arms.

"The way I see it, we established some important ground rules tonight," John said in an even voice, but his look toward Anna was loaded with meaning. "We all wear masks near Hope. And to that point, wash hands a lot and practice social distancing. Basically, follow the CDC ruling. Lest we forget, the number of cases worldwide passed one million. Anna, you really should stay secluded in your room for the next two weeks. You just moved in, and even if you've pretty much stayed home, you don't know if you're a carrier and I don't think you want to put Hope in jeopardy."

Anna's eyes widened, but she nodded in agreement. "Yeah, fine. I'll stick close to my room for the next two weeks."

"Thank you," Linnea said, meaning it. "Then we're agreed. And I will call Cara immediately and let her know about Luna. Until we get your mama's verdict, honey," she said, directing this comment to Hope, "I'm afraid you have to stay away from Luna. I think she's making you sneeze."

Hope was crestfallen. "I'm sorry!"

"Oh no, honey. It's not your fault." Linnea's heart went out to her. She was still so young. She thought that somehow she'd made the puppy sick. Linnea wrapped her arms around the child, who had begun to cry.

"I hate germs," Hope wailed.

"We all do, honey," she said, looking up at John for support. "But we'll be okay. And so will Luna. You'll see."

"On that note," John said, "I'd say this meeting is adjourned."

# chapter seven

*Sometimes a touch, a hug, the feel of an encircling arm—more than*
*words—had the power to restore one's faith that all would be well.*

ACROSS THE STREET on Ocean Boulevard Cara sat alone on the white
suede Chesterfield sofa in her living room leafing idly though *Charles-*
*ton* magazine. Out the large plate-glass windows, the sky was ominous.
Gray clouds hovered over a turbulent gray ocean littered with white-
capped waves. It would be dark soon, she thought. The end of another
day. A wave of loneliness swept over her. So many days without David
and Hope. She wondered again how she had lived so many years alone.

When she'd left Charleston at age eighteen, she'd been hell-bent
on heading anywhere north to start her life, as far away from her abu-
sive father as she could get. She'd thought when she left town, it
would be for college. She was academic, had excelled at school and ex-
tracurricular activities, and rarely dated. She had her dream ahead of

her like a carrot in front of a mule. When she'd received her acceptance from Boston University, she was elated. She'd succeeded!

Or so she'd thought. Her success was what had started that last, desperate argument with her father. Stratton Rutledge had reared up, stomped his foot down and thrust his chin out, and laid out his rejection of her dreams—of her—in a final challenge.

Cara closed her eyes and shuddered, alone on the sofa, the whole scene coming back to her, vivid and real, even after nearly forty years. She brought the cashmere throw up around her shoulders as the memory played itself out.

She was just eighteen, and the family was sitting in the dining room, their favorite battleground. During family dinner conversations at the long, polished table, her mother had usually sat quietly, or moved silently from kitchen to dining room to serve. Only when asked a direct question did she participate in the debates that usually raged over some point no one could remember or even cared about. For Cara and her father, these arguments were all about firing shots and winning. For her mother and, to a lesser degree, Palmer, it was about dodging the bullets. They thought she was so strong. What they'd never understood was that, for Cara, firing back was a means of survival.

That evening, her father was drunk again. Her mother sat at the opposite end of the dining table, her eyes cast down at her plate as Cara and her father argued about her choice of college. Palmer was frozen across the table from her, begging her with his eyes to just be quiet, to go along and not cause trouble. But Cara had been accepted to Boston University, her dream college. Her number-one choice. She was not backing down.

"This is where I want to go," she'd shouted back at him when he'd refused to send her. "I worked hard, real hard, for four years. I got straight As, glowing letters of recommendation. I earned this, Daddy." She'd set her jaw, not knowing she was a mirror of her father. "I'm going!"

Stratton Rutledge, patriarch, favorite son, husband, father, the man who sat at the head of the table, planted his elbows on the gleaming wood and pointed his finger at the young female who dared challenge his authority.

"Who the hell do you think you are, little girl?" her father had roared. "You'll do as I say. And if you step one foot out of this town—out of this house—that'll tear it between us, you hear? You are not going north, and that's final. I'll not tolerate this arrogance. Especially not from some blunt-mouthed teenage girl who won't act like the lady she's been bred to be. You're an embarrassment to your mama. And to me. Where do you think you're going? Come back here! Caretta Rutledge! You leave and you'll not get one dollar, not one stick of furniture, not so much as a nod of the head when you pass on the street with me, hear?"

If that had been the end of it, just another drunken episode, her life might have been different. But Cara had shown her independence. She'd risen from the table, glared at him, and, without another word, walked out of the dining room.

She hadn't expected him to follow her. In a drunken rage, he'd struck her down as she tried to escape up the stairs. Howling with fury, he hit her, again and again, as her mother and brother watched, frozen in terror in the front hall. Cara still remembered his lips, tight with a line of spittle. His eyes, glazed red with fury. The slap of his hand across her face. Yet she did not remember the pain. It was as though she were numb, unable to feel. What she remembered most clearly as the blows came was staring at her mother, meeting her gaze in a silent challenge: *Why aren't you stopping him?*

By dawn, she'd left the house, her family, Charleston, all she knew, to head to any point north. It was an act of survival. She'd ended up in Chicago with nothing but the clothes in her suitcase and a few thousand dollars in her bank account. A cousin living there had let her crash in her apartment. Once her bruises healed, Cara went out in search of a job. She was hired as a receptionist for an advertising firm. She worked during the day and took college classes at night. It had taken seven years, but she got her bachelor's degree and, in the following years, rose up the ladder to become one of the youngest executives at the firm.

At forty, Cara had achieved all she had set out to do when she'd left her family that horrid night. And in the blink of an eye—or rather, a financial shift of power—she'd lost it all. She was summarily fired. There was a particular kind of humiliation associated with being escorted out of the building by an armed guard.

Staring out the window of her Chicago condo at a stormy Lake Michigan, with her mother's letter begging her to come home for a visit in her hand, Cara had the cold realization that in all those years focusing on work and success, she had forgotten to live. Gazing at the threatening water, she'd faced the fact that she had no real friends, no relationship, and, at forty, no children.

Cara had never felt so utterly alone. Used up. Depleted. Picking herself up, she went where most children went when the world kicked them to the ground—home. Her father was dead, opening the door in her mind to reconciliation with her mother. Once again, her life had changed, and she had to start over. It wasn't easy. She'd spent the past twenty years carefully crafting her world and her response to it. Her mother had named her Caretta after the loggerhead sea turtles she adored. Cara had always hated it, choosing to be called Cara. Yet she'd adopted the signature lone-swimmer lifestyle of the turtle for which she'd been named.

Back in the lowcountry, settling into her mother's beach house, Cara had learned in small increments, year after year, to give up her life as a lone swimmer and instead to join a family that not only welcomed but loved her. She'd opened herself to love and, to her great surprise, found it in Brett Beauchamps. Her first husband had been the love of her life, and for ten years they had been happy. Their one serious hurdle had been their inability to have children, though they'd tried one in vitro effort after another. The harsh reality that confronted her was that she'd simply waited too long. And then Brett was gone. Once again, Cara was alone.

And once again, she'd picked herself up from the ground, leaving town once more. Broken, Cara couldn't bear to stay where once she'd found happiness. She'd loaded up her car and this time headed for

Chattanooga, Tennessee, a town filled with welcoming people, great art, a heart for environmental protection, and a world-class aquarium. She'd started again, day after day making the effort to craft a new life at age fifty. And then, when least expected, another miracle had happened. Cara found hope in the form of the infant she'd prayed for and had given up believing would ever happen for her. A little girl named Esperanza was made available to her for adoption, and Cara, shaking in her boots at the thought of being a mother at age fifty, doubting her abilities, took a leap of faith and said yes.

Cara had returned home with her baby girl, back to the beach house that had always been a sanctuary for Rutledge women. This new journey had not been easy either—but by now, she didn't expect it to be. Cara was older and wiser. She had a better résumé. She found work, support from her family and friends. She also found love again. Another miracle.

But it seemed fate was not yet finished testing her.

The wind gusted, shaking the palm fronds outside the house, tossing cushions off the porch furniture to points unknown. Cara rubbed her arms and rose from the sofa, chasing away the memories. She felt a wave of despondency that put her feet in motion. She had to move, pace, cast away the worries as chilling and fierce as the wind outdoors. She had thought she was safe at last. She'd married, moved into this beautiful house. Foolishly, she thought she could let down her guard and just be. She was grateful, even humble, thinking she'd been given so much happiness and, too, wealth with David, that she wanted to share it with the next generation of family who were struggling, as she had struggled. Playing matriarch was one of the greatest satisfactions she'd ever known.

Her lips trembled. And now, again, illness threatened all she held dear. First, her mother. Then Brett. And now . . . David was in the other room, and though he was getting better, they were still awaiting the all-clear. She missed her daughter. Hope was just across the street, yet she could be a thousand miles away, for all that Cara could not visit her.

As well, tonight Cara had received a phone call from Linnea reporting that Hope was sneezing and coughing, likely allergic to the dog. Cara brought her hand to her forehead. What an idiot she was to have bought the dog. She should have waited until Hope came home, should have made sure that all was well before impulsively buying a puppy with as much forethought as she would a stuffed animal. What if the allergies compromised Hope's breathing? Her lungs were still recovering from the serious pneumonia she got from the measles.

Worry overwhelmed her. She wanted her baby home again. In her arms. She felt the lump thickening in her throat, water pooling in her eyes. Try as she might to hold it in, the tears trickled down her cheeks. Defeated, Cara put her face in her hands and let go a gush of tears. Crying was a testament to how low she'd fallen. Cara hated to cry, was embarrassed to reveal that weakness. But cry she did. Great, blubbering sobs, like a baby. She couldn't stop.

Suddenly she felt arms encircle her. Cara choked back a cry and, looking up, saw David's face, so close to hers for the first time in nearly a month. Her gaze devoured him, though she was still in shock.

His face was pale though not sickly. His eyes were no longer glazed with fever but alert and full of concern. She sniffed and slowly reached up to wipe her eyes, then moved her hand to cup his jaw, rough with the beginnings of a pepper-and-salt beard.

"David," she managed to get out, barely coherent, "what . . ."

He brought his hand to the back of her head and guided it to rest against his shoulder. He smelled fresh and soapy, like he'd just emerged from a shower.

"My darling, don't cry."

The feel of his hand against her skin brought her to a place of security, safety, contentment. Cara closed her eyes and let her body melt against his. Sometimes a touch, a hug, the feel of an encircling arm—more than words—had the power to restore one's faith that all would be well.

She moved her head back to look at his face again, sure her own was blotched and swollen. She stared at him in wonder. "But what are you doing out of your room?"

David took a tissue from his pocket and gently dabbed at her face. Cara reached up to take it and quickly wiped her eyes and nose, then, feeling more composed, looked again at his face. "Tell me."

"It's been twenty-four hours since my last fever. And that was a low-grade fever."

"I know. But you didn't tell me your fever was gone."

"I didn't want to get your hopes up." He smiled. "My symptoms are gone. I feel stronger, clearheaded. No headaches."

"I can't believe it," she breathed out.

"I only wish I had flowers to give you, to thank you for being so good to me these past weeks. You held this family together. Cara Rutledge-Wyatt, you are the strongest woman I know. I don't like to see you cry. Unless they're tears of joy."

Cara felt a fresh batch of tears building up. "Now, *these* are tears of joy. I can't believe you're standing here in front of me. Real flesh-and-blood *you*."

Then, for the first time, and it still felt somehow illicit, David lowered his mouth to meet hers. The kiss was tender and brief. More a connection than passion. It was, she thought, perfect.

"Let's get Hope," David said.

She laughed, and the sound of it filled the room. "David, be serious. It's late and she's probably getting ready for bed. Let's fix up something to eat, have our first meal together in ages, and catch up. Then tomorrow morning, first thing, we will pick up our little girl."

"And the dog?"

Cara laughed again, and patted his chest with affection. "That's a long story."

---

DAVID LOADED THE last of Hope's belongings into the back of his Range Rover. All with the notable exception of the puppy. A spring storm was rolling in, kicking sand into the air and sending their hair fluttering about their heads.

Cara said, "I'm sorry to leave you with the dog."

"Not at all! I'm thrilled to keep her. I'm just sorry it didn't work out for Hope. And you. You fell in love with her too," Linnea said.

"I'm so happy to have my daughter back, and David well again." Cara glanced over to where her husband was buckling Hope into her car seat. "Nothing else matters. Besides, I can always try another breed, one that is hypoallergenic." She paused and said wryly, "*Someday*. At the moment, Hope doesn't seem very upset to be leaving Luna behind."

"She never really bonded. The dog kept jumping up on her, licking her face. She didn't like that."

"Perhaps"—Cara wiggled her brows in amusement—"you were right. She was too young for a pet."

"As long as you're sure." Linnea's smile was wistful. "I don't think I could give Luna back if she stays."

"She's all yours."

"Really?" Linnea was taken aback. The pricy, pedigreed dog was an extravagant gift. "I was hoping for maybe a discounted price. That I could pay off in time."

"Don't be silly." Cara put up her hand. "And if you try to thank me, I'll change my mind."

Linnea put her hands to her cheeks. "Sorry. I have to. Thank you!"

"I'll have the papers signed over to you. Sometimes life has a way of sorting things out for the best. I was trying to think of a gift to give you for all your care of Hope, and one materialized all on its own."

"I confess, I've grown quite attached to Luna."

They smiled at each other, aunt and niece, but more, two friends who could count on one another when the chips were down. That, Linnea knew, was the true gift.

Linnea looked at Cara in her cherry-red wind jacket, her dark, glossy hair held back by a navy and white scarf, her freshly scrubbed, smashing face. So strong. Vital. Another gust of wind sent Cara hurrying around to the passenger door.

"Take care, Sweet-tea!" she called, then climbed in.

A moment later the great engine sparked to life, and Linnea stepped forward to tap on the car's back window. She gave a final wave at Hope. The girl sat beaming in the backseat, thrilled to be going home. She returned a quick wave before turning her head to look up one last time at John's second-floor window. Just in case.

---

THREE DAYS LATER, the weather shifted again. A blustery wind rattled the windows, sending the palm fronds scratching at the windows. Both she and Anna had retired to their rooms after an early dinner of comforting lentil soup, Gouda cheese, and chunks of sourdough bread. Linnea was exhausted. No child to feed or put to bed or worry about. Bliss. Linnea nestled in the big four-poster bed under the down comforter with Luna cuddled beside her. The puppy was always at her side now, seemingly relieved to no longer have to dodge the grasp of a six-year-old.

In her lap was her phone, waiting for Gordon's call. Also, another letter from John. Although Hope was gone, John had continued leaving poetry for Linnea in her mailbox. They saw each other from time to time, waved, asked about each other's health, commented on the weather and other such banalities. But in these letters, John's poetry selections spoke of stronger, more passionate feelings. She reread the poem from Hafiz.

*Don't surrender your loneliness*
*So quickly.*
*Let it cut more deep.*
*Let it ferment and season you*
*As few human*
*Or even divine ingredients can.*
*Something missing in my heart tonight*
*Has made my eyes so soft,*
*My voice*
*So tender,*
*My need of God*
*Absolutely*
*Clear.*

She thought she knew everything about John. They'd shared poetry when they'd dated. But in San Francisco, he'd gotten too caught up in his own world of work, going out for business meals to which she wasn't invited. Perhaps, too, once living together, rather than getting closer, he had put up a wall to keep a part of himself—the tender, vulnerable part—separate.

The phone rang, and her thoughts quickly shifted gears. Picking up her phone, she saw Gordon's name pop up. *Must get John out of my head*, she ordered herself as she sat up straighter. Luna rose and looked at her, alert, as if questioning what had happened to their serene evening. Linnea smoothed her hair, put a smile on her face, and pushed the accept button for FaceTime.

"Gordon!" she exclaimed when she saw his face appear on the screen. His red hair was longer, unkempt, curls trailing down the sides of his chiseled face. He looked tired; there was a five-o'clock shadow around his jaw. It was near midnight in England. Gordon never called at any particular time; so much depended on his teaching schedule or if he was out doing research. Recently he'd been conducting studies on gray seals along the Cornish coastline.

"Linnea. Are you in bed?" he asked, amused. "It's only seven o'clock there."

She smiled, loving his accent, his face. She leaned back against the pillows. "It's a blustery night and I thought I'd cuddle up in bed."

"Sounds inviting."

"Too bad you're not here."

Gordon offered one of his crooked smiles, the one that melted her every time she saw it. It always made her think he knew some private joke he was going to share with her.

"I wish I were. God, seeing you lying there, alone in bed . . ." He paused. "Not fair. Shouldn't be allowed by international law."

"Should I get up?" she teased. "Move to the kitchen?"

"No. I've got the bed in my mind. Don't ruin it."

"I hope you're not going to suggest we get naughty," she said.

"I wasn't going to . . . but if you insist."

"No!" she said, then laughed and reached again for her cup of tea. "Besides, I'd need something much stronger than this glass of herbal tea."

"No, it's not a good idea," Gordon agreed. "One reason being it's bloody freezing here. The wet seems to go right to the skin. The seals . . ." He laughed. "They've got that blubber to keep them warm. If I could invent a self-generating heating system like they have, I'd be rich."

"What's the station you're staying at like? Warm, I hope."

"It's primitive. There's this ancient heater and a wood-burning stove that seems to be letting cold air in more than warming anything. I'm stuck in the middle of nowhere—and it's rained every day. I can't keep my sodding socks dry," he added before taking another swallow of his drink. "It was warmer on the boat. And let me tell you, the wind was brutal."

"Poor baby."

He snorted and shook his head. "I really do miss you, Lin. Miss being in bed with you. Brings back memories. Lots of memories."

She looked at her tea and smiled, remembering too.

He asked, "So, if we're not going to be talking dirty to one another, what do you want to talk about?"

"Your work. I'm always fascinated. What are you learning?"

He smiled at her answer. She knew that their shared passion for marine life was one of the bonds that united them.

"Well," he began, collecting his thoughts. "We're trying to follow up on last year's study. . . ."

She listened closely. The previous summer, Gordon had come to Charleston to continue research on the landmark study he'd participated in along the Cornish coast. They had examined fifty animals, from ten species of dolphins, seals, and whales and found microplastics in them all.

"We need to know how the fish are getting the microplastics," he said. "Is it directly from the water or from their prey? This would mean that the plastics are transferred through the food chain."

"If the fish eat the plastic and we eat the fish . . ."

"That's right," he confirmed. "We've documented that even the deepest-dwelling marine organisms have plastic in their stomachs." He sighed. "It's a concern."

She hid her smile. Gordon, like most scientists she'd met, was a master of understatement. Linnea thrilled to his intellect and his hands-on knowledge of what was really happening in the environmental world they both cared so much about. She leaned forward a bit, absorbed by what he was telling her.

"Anyway," Gordon said in a tone that implied he didn't want to talk about work anymore, "that's what's happening here on our coast. Tell me what's going on in your life on the beautiful Isle of Palms. I want to hear that the sun is shining and it's warm."

She laughed. "Sorry. It's not much different here. Chilly and blustery."

"Bugger."

"My thoughts exactly. But it should turn by the weekend. Sunny skies on the way."

"Bliss. Go on, tell me more."

"Well," she said, puffing out a plume of air. She set the tea mug back on her nightstand. "How long has it been since we talked. Three weeks?"

"Sorry. This virus has thrown a spanner in the works. I was closing up shop at the university when the opportunity to join this project came up. No one expected me to be free."

"That's a great opportunity, Gordon. I understand. Truly."

"And I've been on a boat the past week. No reception."

"Do you get seasick?"

He shook his head. "I'm one of the lucky ones. But there were some days out there when the sea got pretty choppy."

"I'd die. I get so seasick on choppy water."

"Enough about bad weather. I have plenty of that. Tell me what's new," Gordon prodded. "I want to hear every tiny detail."

Linnea leaned back against the pillow. Luna seized the opportunity to climb up her chest and begin licking her face.

"Well, *that's* something new," Gordon said, leaning forward to peer into the phone. "When did you get a dog? And tell it to stop licking your face. That's my job."

"Try telling Luna that," she said with a laugh, moving the puppy to her side. Pushing back a fallen lock of hair, she began telling him about all that had transpired the previous few weeks.

"And I thought I was busy," he said. "I'm sorry to hear David was sick. Was it coronavirus?"

"We don't know for sure, but he had all the symptoms."

"We don't know much about it, so Cara is smart to take care with Hope." He swirled his drink and asked, "How was it being a nanny?"

"Whatever they're paid, it's not enough," she quipped. She heard him laugh and it made her feel lighter inside. This was what she was hoping for tonight. "It's so hard. You never really get a break. And, for the record, I was more than a nanny—I was the stand-in mommy. We're talking twenty-four/seven. Tears, histrionics, food fights, defiance . . . I survived it all. And I love Hope! Imagine if I didn't." She shook her head. "The puppy was my prize at the end."

"Do you think so?" he asked doubtfully. "Have you ever had a puppy before? They can be a lot of work. Like a baby with a tail. How did you end up keeping the dog?"

She laughed, thinking how spot-on he was. "Turns out Hope is allergic. So, lucky me, I got to keep Luna. I'm besotted. She's the sweetest dog. You're going to love her." She paused and said more seriously, "But children? It was an eye-opener. Honestly, there were days I didn't think I ever wanted to have children."

"But you do?" he asked, a subtle shift in his tone. "Want to have children."

She suddenly felt her humor slip away. She'd been gabbing away with lighthearted banter, and suddenly there was this serious question. "Uh, sure. I guess. Someday." She took a breath. "Do you?"

"Yes. Absolutely. An army of them. Six boys and three girls."

"What?" She laughed, hoping he was joking. "Boyfriend, you are barking up the wrong tree."

He laughed. "I love your American sayings. So vivid. Well, then, I'd settle for an heir and a spare."

"Much more reasonable," she said, glad to have tiptoed past that subject. "I was fortunate to have some help. There were times I was at my wits' end. Cara couldn't even come by to visit, and poor Hope was so homesick. But John's been great." The moment she said the words, she knew she'd made a mistake. Gordon's eyes sharpened and he had that worried furrow in his brow. She wished she could take the words back.

"John? John who?"

She cringed. Linnea tried to make her voice sound casual. "John Peterson."

His brow rose even as his voice lowered. "Ah. Your old boyfriend John Peterson?"

"Yes," she answered as though it were nothing. "He was visiting his mother—she lives next door," she reminded him.

"I remember. And you just . . . ran into him?"

"Well, sort of. When he arrived, he learned that a colleague of his tested positive for the virus. So rather than try to fly back to California, he went up into the carriage house and straight into quarantine."

Gordon mulled this over, while Linnea stroked Luna's soft coat.

"So, if he was up in the carriage house in quarantine," Gordon began, "how was it he was such a help?"

Linnea curled her toes in tension. "Paper airplanes," she replied with a light laugh.

Gordon didn't laugh. She watched him reach out and grab his glass, filled with a brown liquid she was quite sure was scotch. He took a long sip. "How's that?"

"Oh, Gordon, it's a long story."

"I have a lot of time."

She took a breath and forced a smile. "Oh, it's all very innocent. John saw Hope and me from that tall window up on the second floor, you remember . . ."

"Yes. Moroccan. Exotic. I remember. Go on."

"Well, he saw us, whistled, and when we looked up, he flew a paper airplane down to Hope. She was enchanted. It's hard to believe she'd never seen a paper airplane before. Another generation." She laughed and thought it sounded too high. "She started sending him notes, and he sent notes back, then little gifts. It went on for a while. It was very sweet and totally distracted Hope from being homesick." She smiled. "See? Paper airplanes."

"Ask him how he is at origami. Now, that takes talent."

She laughed. "It was very nice of him."

"Is he well now? From the virus?"

"He never contracted it, thank heavens. Or if he did, he was a silent carrier. But the quarantine is over."

"Oh, good. Glad to hear it. Hallelujah." He took another sip.

Linnea reached for her cup of tea, wishing now it was a glass of wine.

"So, now that he's cheered everybody up with his paper airplanes, is he still there or did he go back to California?"

"No, he's still here."

"Really. Still there. That's good. That's perfect. Is he planning on making dirigibles next? Maybe a nice big zeppelin?"

"I have no idea," she replied, glad she could be honest. She looked around the room, at the white curtains, her perfume bottles on the mahogany dresser, at Luna sleeping again curled up beside her hip.

"I have some good news and some bad news," Gordon said.

"Oh?"

"Which should I tell you first?"

She always hated being asked this question. Really, what did it matter? She was going to hear both anyway. "Surprise me."

Gordon scratched behind his ear with a curious smile on his face, like he knew she was deliberately giving him a hard time. "Okay. The good news first. My research project in South Carolina is arranging for me to continue my work on a limited basis, providing, of course, I follow strict protocols."

"Oh, Gordon, that's wonderful! That means you're coming back?"

He smiled and it lit up his face. "I only just learned today. I couldn't wait to get off that floating nausea machine and call you."

"When do you arrive?"

"That's the bad news."

"Oh no."

His face was somber. "Maybe as soon as two weeks."

"What?" Her face brightened. "You're wicked. That's amazing. Wonderful! However did you manage it?"

"Well, it seems there's this amazing loophole. It's called the fiancé visa."

Linnea froze, a lump in her throat.

Gordon laughed and put up his hand in mock surrender. "I'm joking." He laughed again. "I guess that joke fell flat. In fact, looking deeper into it, I found it would take six to nine months to even get that visa."

Linnea feigned a laugh, but inside she was in shock. *What? He really looked into it?*

"I found a workaround for the visa," Gordon continued. "I could fly to another country like Costa Rica for fourteen days. They haven't been hit with the virus yet and the US is still allowing travel from there. So, I've made a plan to meet with Leatherback Trust. I have some business I can do there. That means I can be in Charleston in maybe less than two weeks, give or take a day and praying no cancellations."

"Genius," she said, impressed.

"Not really. I travel a lot. You learn the ins and outs. And I'm desperate to see you—I can't wait to get there." He paused. "I'm guessing there should be a whole slew of paper airplanes by the time I get there. Probably a fleet."

"You'll have to quarantine when you arrive here, of course. Cooper is in quarantine now, at my parents' house."

"Oh, so he made it home. Good for him."

143

"Yes," she replied, relieved to be talking about her brother. "He got out pretty quickly."

"So . . ." He paused and looked off. She saw the sharp contours of his cheekbones, then suddenly there was his face again, looking at her while he took a bracing swallow of his drink. "A bit more bad news," he said, looking down at his drink.

She waited.

He looked up. He had this way of keeping his head down, then raising his eyes that was so disarming. She felt her heart skip. She knew that look so well. Missed it. He often looked at her that way, or tilted his head sleepily, when they were talking after they'd made love.

"What?"

"Now that I have the formal approval to get into the country, I've been searching for a place to rent."

"What about the house you rented last summer? It was perfect."

"It was. I tried. But it's already rented. In fact, most places are rented. It's crazy. I can't find a decent place on either Isle of Palms or Sullivan's Island."

"It's the pandemic. People are fleeing the cities. Everywhere is rented—for the *whole summer*. And the real estate market is just as wild. A house doesn't stay on the market long at all. My friend who's an agent told me that it used to be someone would fly in and take several days to look at several houses. Now they come in and look at two or three houses and buy one of them immediately. That is, if they don't buy it online, sight unseen."

the summer of lost and found

"That explains it."

"Did you look in Mount Pleasant?"

"Off the island?"

"Yes, but it's not far. Just over the bridge."

Gordon looked down at his drink. "Actually, I was wondering . . . hoping, rather, that there was room in the inn." His smile was quick, almost shy.

Her mind froze and she didn't reply.

"We could live together," he explained.

Linnea sucked in her breath, exhaling slowly while her mind whirred.

The plan had been for him to come to the islands and continue his research project. He'd find a place to live. They'd see each other, some nights she'd sleep over. It would be like the summer before. She was excited to see him again and continue their relationship. She thought she might be in love with him—but she'd *never* said she was moving in with him. That was a big step in their relationship. And she'd had a bad experience with that. Linnea wasn't mentally prepared.

"Here?"

He laughed. "Yes. Since there is really no place else."

"I . . . oh, gosh, Gordon . . ." she stammered. "This is sudden. I didn't plan for this."

"Neither did I. But here we are." When she didn't respond, he said, "We were going to be together anyway. It's just geography."

"Oh, Gordon," she said. "It's so much more than geography."

He hesitated, considering. "Is that a no?"

"I can't," she blurted. "For a lot of reasons. Things have changed here. I have a roommate."

"A roommate? Since when?"

"Anna. You remember her." His face was blank. "Annabelle."

"Yes, of course," he replied. "The redhead. Rotten surfer."

She laughed. "Yes, that's her. We both were furloughed from the aquarium, so we are pooling our resources. The guest room is taken."

"Oh. I see. Fair enough." He paused. "But, Linnea," he said, his voice lowering, "I was rather hoping that we would share a room."

"Oh, of course," she said, feeling tongue-tied. Of course he'd want to stay with her. They were boyfriend and girlfriend. He was traveling across an ocean to be with her. "I want to be with you," she hurried to say. "But what about the pandemic? When you arrive, you'll have to be in quarantine. Like Cooper. You can't do that here." She put her hand to her heated cheek. "Gordon, we have to think this through."

"I have. I could stay at a hotel for two weeks. Quarantine myself per requirements. And then I thought, I rather hoped, we could be together. Isn't that what you'd like?"

"Actually, Gordon . . ." She took a breath. "I'd have to get permission from Cara. And what about Anna? I can't kick her out. She has nowhere to go."

He released a quick smile that quickly fell again. "Have you changed your mind? You don't want me to come?"

He was hurt. She readily saw that. And she couldn't blame him. She felt horrible for not simply exclaiming, *Yes, do come live with me! We'll make it work somehow.* She wanted to take away the disappointment etched across his face. But she felt some inner muzzle keeping her impulsive, eager-to-please self from self-sabotaging.

Still . . . why was she being selfish? Gordon was her boyfriend. He was coming all the way to America to see her, at last. Naturally he wanted to stay with her. And wasn't that the legacy of the beach house? To offer safe haven?

"Of course you can stay here. We'll make it work somehow."

His expression shifted and his smile brightened his eyes.

"I was beginning to think you didn't want me to come."

"I do. I'm just . . . well, scared." She felt herself stumbling. "My visiting your place is one thing. You moving into mine . . . is a big step."

"I understand. You should know, I'm ready for that step."

Linnea sucked in her breath.

"If it doesn't work, if you want your space, I'll find something else. No pressure. I don't want you to feel rushed."

"Okay." Her voice was a whisper.

"Are you okay? Really?"

She nodded. "Yes."

"Then I'm coming to your place?" he confirmed.

"Yes."

There was a pause, each giving the other a moment to say something.

Linnea broke the impasse. "I think we need to sleep. You must be exhausted. It's past midnight there. I know I'm tired." She sighed. "A bit dazed and confused, actually."

Gordon's brow furrowed. "I hope this fellow hasn't got you confused."

She hesitated too long. She saw his face change; a muscle twitched in his cheek.

"He is in your head, isn't he? I can see it. Amazing thing about all this technology. I can see your face."

"Jealous?"

"Absolutely. I'd better get there quick and challenge him to a duel. Paper airplanes at dawn."

She laughed, grateful for his humor. "I don't think that will be necessary. Just come as soon as you can. I miss you."

"Good. I'm glad." His smile now was genuine. "I miss you too. Bye, love."

She hung up the phone and let her hand rest on it for a while, feeling the reverberations rocking through her like aftershocks. What had she done? She fell back on her pillows and stared at the ceiling, her mind rewinding the conversation with Gordon, what she had said. What she had not said.

She had tried to back away from him moving in with her. Linnea counted the reasons she'd offered: a roommate; quarantine problems; the need for Cara's permission. She closed her eyes tight and clenched her fists. She'd told him everything but the one salient truth: she did not want him to move in.

But she'd said yes.

Linnea turned on her side, pulled her covers up over her chilled shoulders, and tucked her knees up, but sleep did not come. In her mind, she wrestled with the unanswered question—why?

# chapter eight

*If a dark cloud is hovering inside the house, get outdoors.*

WHAT WAS UP with Anna?

Linnea stood at the kitchen sink, washing dishes with quick agitated movements. Anna was being a real downer. She stayed in her room, cooked her own food. Rarely spoke. She was more a ghost than a roommate. When she walked into the kitchen, there was a cloud of gloom over her head.

Linnea called out a cheery "Good morning!"

Anna returned a mumbled reply.

Linnea joined her at the table with a piece of paper and a pen, eager to break the ice and begin sharing the house as roommates.

Anna was hunched over her bowl of granola, eating in wolfish gulps. She was still in her navy cotton pajamas and her auburn hair flowed down her shoulders in disarray.

"Now that Hope is gone, it's just you and me."

Anna nodded, but didn't look at her.

Annoyance flared but Linnea pushed on. "I was thinking. Let's make up some menus for next week and a grocery list. You can cook your favorite dishes, and I'll cook mine. It'll be fun. We'll split the cost right down the middle. What would you like to make?"

Anna looked up from her bowl of granola and finished chewing. She swallowed, then her brows furrowed. "That's okay," she said in a monotone, effectively cutting off Linnea's enthusiasm. "I'll just cook my own food. I have my own diet and I'm pretty particular."

"But . . . it will be more economical to cook together."

"Tell you what," Anna said, her expression one of boredom. "We'll split the basics. Toilet paper, laundry supplies, flour, that kind of thing. The rest we can buy for ourselves. I'm used to cooking for myself. Prefer it."

Linnea felt a profound sense of disappointment. "I just thought, given that we're both staying at home . . . together . . . we might make it a bit more enjoyable. Get a bottle of wine from time to time. Share ideas."

Anna just dove into her granola without replying.

Linnea stiffened, anger bubbling at Anna's thinly veiled contrariness. "Well, then, as for the rest . . ." She cleared her throat. "I'll bring you the bills for utilities and all at the beginning of the month.

I should have April's bills coming in any day. In the meantime, I will get staples. If you'd like to check the list, of course you can."

"Hey, don't be mad just because I don't want to cook with you. I hate cooking."

"Okay. I get that. What is it you do like to do? The house needs a thorough cleaning every week, and I hate to tell you, we don't have a maid."

"I'm good with that. Just tell me what to do."

"But, Anna, I don't want to always tell you what to do. I didn't ask you to live here to have to take care of you."

Her face flushed. "I didn't ask you to."

"But you are, by asking me to tell you what to do. Hope is gone. I'm done being a nanny. I want you to take an interest in living here. In the house. Hey, even me. I live here too. Being a roommate means a certain level of concern for the well-being of the person you share space with. We share this house. We live together."

Anna's face clouded and she shook her head. "I'm sorry, but that's never been my experience. I've always lived alone, or with a group of people who barely knew each other. We put our names on our food in the fridge, tried to find time at the stove or the washing machine, and waved at each other as we cooked in the kitchen. Our own food."

That sounded horrible to Linnea. "Was that *college*? We've grown beyond that, I hope." She pursed her lips. "I'm curious . . . who did the dishes?"

Anna snorted a short laugh and twisted her mouth in a grin.

151

"Well, we were all supposed to do our own dishes, but you know guys. They tended to leave them in the sink and say they'd do them later. Ditto with the housekeeping."

"That won't work here," Linnea said simply. "I have a thing about dishes in the sink. Cockroaches. They're real out here on the island. And I don't like a dirty house."

"Cool. No dishes left in the sink. Got it." She scooped out another spoon of granola.

Linnea licked her lips. "Anna, look. This was my grandmother's beloved house. And Cara loves this beach house more than the grand house she's living in now. And so do I. We treasure it. We take care of it." She paused, clenching her hands tight in her lap. "If you don't feel you can embrace that, then . . ." She shrugged. "This is not going to work."

Anna dropped her spoon. It clattered loudly against the bowl. In a swift move, she leaned back against the wood chair, arms clamped together, and swung her head to look out the window a moment, a tic working her jaw. When she faced Linnea again, her eyes were cold.

"I never had any intention of not doing my part. You're dumping this on me because I don't want to share recipes with you."

Linnea opened her mouth to speak, but Anna swung out a hand toward the paper on the table. "Go ahead, write up one of your little schedules for cleaning. I promise I'll follow it. I won't leave dishes in the sink. I'll pay my share of the bills. Okay? But don't ask me to be happy, because right now I'm feeling a little bummed. I've basically lost my job. I've no money in the bank, I'm dependent on you for a place to live, and I have no idea what my future holds. So forgive me if I just don't feel there's anything to be particularly cheery about."

"I lost my job too!" Linnea shouted, her frustration finding voice.

"But you have your family!" Anna's eyes flashed "They have your back."

"I have *your* back. I offered to let you stay here, didn't I?"

"You just threatened to kick me out!"

"Jeez Louise, listen to you," Linnea shot back. "I did *not* threaten to kick you out."

Anna glared at her.

Linnea felt a twinge of shame. "Well, maybe I did. Sort of. I'm sorry. What I mean is, I'm giving you an option."

Anna gave her a skewed look.

Linnea took a breath, not wanting to escalate the argument more. She felt her anger flow away, leaving her deflated. "I'm sorry if you feel threatened, Anna. I didn't mean that."

The tension dissipated. Anna blew out a plume of air. "I'm sorry too. I've been a bitch, I know that. I . . ." She sighed again and shrugged. "I've been pretty depressed."

Understanding brought compassion. "I wondered."

Anna shrugged. "I'm scared. I don't know if I'll ever get my job back, and even if I do, I don't know if it's what I really want to do. For the future."

Linnea leaned forward, curious. She'd thought Anna loved her job working at the sea turtle hospital. "What else do you want to do?"

"That's just it. I don't know. Being stuck at home, I've been forced to take stock. I feel pretty bleak about the future. What's the world going to look like? Will we ever get back to normal? Hell, what is normal anymore? Sometimes I feel I'm a breath away from screaming."

"Oh, Anna. I'm sorry. I didn't know. Well, I knew you weren't happy, but I didn't know why."

"Hey," she said with typical bravado. "It is what it is."

"Is it? I'm worried too. But if we sit around and feel sorry for ourselves, when the pandemic ends—and it will—we won't have anything to show for this time. Maybe you could use this time to explore other options."

"Yeah."

Linnea could see Anna had already shut her out. "Do you want to talk to someone?"

"I'm talking with you."

"No, I mean, a therapist? Someone objective to help you through this?"

"And how am I going to pay for that?" Anna shook her head. "I'll figure it out." She pushed back her chair.

Linnea stopped her by putting a hand on her arm. "Wait, there's something else I have to tell you."

Anna tilted her head. "Oh yeah?"

"Gordon called. He's arriving in a few weeks."

"Yeah. I know."

Linnea cringed. "He'll be staying here."

Anna's brows shot up. "He's moving in *here*?" She looked away, thought a moment, then turned back. "Unbelievable."

"Yeah."

Anna twisted a smile. "So, is he going to chip in too? Dishes, laundry, follow the schedule?"

Linnea lifted her shoulders. "I suppose he will."

"Cool." Anna rose and picked up her bowl, spoon, and coffee cup. "Got it, roomie. No wallowing. Neat and tidy." She turned and went to the sink, where she promptly washed her dishes and set them in the strainer. Then she sponged off the counter, rinsed the sponge, and dried her hands.

"I'll try to find something to help me feel better." Anna stood quietly for a moment, as though she wanted to say more, but only turned and walked out of the kitchen.

A minute later, Linnea heard the bedroom door close.

---

THE LONG-AWAITED WARM weather returned. Despite the sunshine, however, the pandemic worries and fears hovered over the lowcountry, as they did the world. It was strange not to participate in Easter church services, neighborhood egg hunts, or spring breaks. April was the beginning of the peak wedding season, and Charleston and its surrounding plantations and beaches were the top wedding destinations in the county. Yet this year the spring weddings were canceled, shops were closed, restaurants were shuttered, and few people ventured from their homes. Linnea could walk down King Street on one of her rare ventures into the city and see maybe one or two others peeking in the windows, not venturing inside.

Nonetheless, Linnea noticed that the natural world outside her window continued in its normal pattern. She looked out the window and chuckled, as she always did when she saw the Rube Goldberg contraption John had built when he'd installed the new bird feeder. It hung from the kitchen window in such a clever way that no squirrels or varmints could reach it. There was even a trap tray underneath it that somehow opened and closed to contain the dropped seeds. It looked a bit wonky, but it somehow worked.

The feeder was a happening place. All sorts of birds visited for the seed she was careful to keep full in the tray. She usually spied a cherry-red cardinal, or a noisy blue jay, or a bossy mockingbird. Her first instinct was always to call for Hope to come look. Linnea began a journal, writing down the names of the birds she identified to share with Hope. By the month's end, she was surprised how many birds she'd listed: tufted titmice, grackles, finches, chickadees. Plump gray mourning doves with their sweet coos swooped in when the others left. And the ever-present squirrels were comical as they desperately tried to get to the seeds, only to fail again and again. She looked at the long metal arm John had constructed for the bird feeder and smiled. He truly was the master builder.

As she watched a particularly showy painted bunting at the feeder, she thought about what she'd said at the house meeting when Anna had arrived. How she wanted to be able to look back at this time of sheltering in place not as a time of fear and distress, but as a gift of time she would not otherwise have been given. *Time.* That was the salient word. Time to do something different. New.

For her, that meant getting outdoors and paying attention to what was ordinary, and yet supremely exotic. For all that she knew about wildlife such as sea turtles, dolphins, manatees, she had a lot to learn about the wildlife that lived in her own backyard. Because of her time with Hope, learning the names of the extraordinary ordinary creatures that shared this bit of earth with her continued to be her new mission.

She heard a knocking on the kitchen door and left her musings at the bird feeder to open it. She was surprised to see John standing at the threshold. His face, already tanning from his work building the pond, was smiling as he held out a bunch of spring flowers. She tossed the dish towel across her arm and leaned against the doorframe.

"Did you raid your mother's garden?"

"As if she'd let me. All those flowers out there and she won't let me pick any. What's the point?"

He handed her the flowers, a collection of pink and purple cosmos. She took them into her hands and admired them. "They're beautiful, thank you. What's the occasion?"

"Do I need an occasion? I was at the farmers' market—it's open, by the way. Oh, and here," he said, handing her a brown paper bag. "I bought you this loaf of sourdough bread. I remembered you used to buy it all the time in San Francisco."

She took the loaf gratefully, touched that he recalled that detail. "Want to come in?" She stepped back.

He shook his head. "Actually, I want you to come out. It's a beautiful day and I promised Hope I'd come see her. I thought we might walk over together?"

157

Linnea hesitated. It wasn't a date, she chided herself. They were simply going over to see a little girl they both cared about. "Hold on. I'll get Luna."

Luna wasn't thrilled about using a leash for her first walk. She planted her paws on the ground and refused to budge. Rather than drag her, Linnea swooped the puppy into her arms.

"I'd better carry her if we ever hope to get there."

"Sure," John said, trying not to laugh.

They passed the white picket fence that bordered Emmi's garden. She and Flo were working, both wearing large straw hats and gloves.

"Hello!" Linnea called out.

Emmi straightened and, with one hand on the curve of her back, waved with the other and called out a cheery hello. Flo stood unmoving, holding a hoe. She turned her head toward them and removed her large hat, her sparse white hair revealing a pink scalp. She was so thin now her clothes hung from her frame.

Linnea moved closer to the fence and called out, "Hello, Flo!"

The old woman stared at her vacantly.

"Let's go," John said gently, guiding her back to the path. "It's not a good day."

He politely stepped aside so she could walk in front of him along the narrow beach path bordered by dunes. Linnea hoisted Luna higher in her arms and took the lead. The sand was warm and countless tiny black ants scrambled in their chaotic pattern beneath her sandals.

"Poor Flo," Linnea said, shaken.

Linnea had never known the young Florence Prescott, but had

heard the stories over and over from her mother and Cara how Flo was a firecracker. One of a kind.

She'd been one of the first sea turtle volunteers with Lovie on Isle of Palms and Sullivan's Island. Back in the day, they'd tended turtles before the South Carolina Department of Natural Resources began managing the turtle population. They'd made their mistakes, but their hearts were in the right place. Flo had dedicated her life to the sea turtles and to her social work clients. She'd never married, never had children. No nieces or nephews, either.

She'd claimed she liked making her own decisions: "I never want any man telling me what to do." Flo was right proud that she had bought the pretty Victorian-style house on her own merit. It had been in a state of disrepair. Flo spent her vacation time and weekends working on it herself, calling in favors, gradually bringing the old house back to its former beauty. When her father died, Flo took her mother in. Miranda and Flo couldn't have been more different. Miranda was a bohemian artist adored by everyone. As outlandish as Miranda was, Florence was as conservative. Flo's fiery wit and old-school wisdom kept most of the neighborhood—adults and children—in line. Her dearest friend was Lovie Rutledge, and there was nothing she wouldn't do for her.

Or for Emmaline Baker and Caretta Rutledge—Emmi and Cara. She doted on them. The two young girls came together every summer while staying in their families' beach houses a few blocks apart. The girls were inseparable and they both adored Flo, calling her their adopted aunt. The gate between Lovie's and Flo's houses was never closed.

Sweet tea and sugar cookies were always on hand in the kitchens, art lessons were conducted in Miranda's carriage house, and card games were played at night during the steamy summer.

As the years passed, however, Flo had retired, lost her mother, and found herself on hard financial times. That was the time of Emmi's divorce from Tom Peterson. Linnea's grandmother liked to say that good things happened to good people, and Linnea figured that must be true. After the divorce, Emmi had sold her family's beach cottage to Tom. She was proud to say she took the rotter to the cleaners for it. In truth, his guilt let her.

Emmi used the money from her divorce to buy Florence Prescott's Victorian, a house she'd always loved. Not only was it charming, it was smack next door to her best friend's beach house. As a bonus, her buying the house also solved the problem of helping out an aging Flo. That year, Emmi and Cara had made a pact to take care of the old woman they both loved.

Since that time Emmi had lived with Flo in the old Victorian. It had been a good experience for them both. They shared a love of sea turtles, the garden, and the children. But it had also saved them both from the loneliness of living alone. Over the last decade, however, Flo had developed Alzheimer's disease, as her mother had before her. Emmi had managed alone for several years, but recently, Flo's downward slide was accelerating. Emmi and Cara were trying to hold off the day they had to put Flo in a memory center.

"John," Linnea said. "I don't think she recognized me."

"Maybe not."

"How's she doing?"

"Not very well."

"What does that mean?" she asked, turning her head a bit so he could hear.

"She's started to wander again," John said, worry tinging his voice.

"Oh no . . ."

"The other day, Mom discovered the front door open. She nearly had a heart attack. She had to run three blocks before she spied her, walking in the middle of the street. In her nightgown."

"Where was her nurse?"

"The nurse isn't coming any longer, because of Covid-19. She has to stay home with her kids, plus she doesn't want to take public transportation. It's not easy to get to Isle of Palms from North Charleston by bus. I can't say as I blame her."

"Who's helping your mom?"

"You're looking at him."

She stopped abruptly. "You?"

"There's no one else."

Linnea mulled this over as she continued along the crooked beach path, no longer noticing the wildflowers. When she reached the pavement of Ocean Boulevard, she set Luna down and turned to John.

"You're telling me that you're helping your mom take care of Flo?"

"For the time being, yes."

"I don't understand. I thought you were going back to California."

"I was. I am. I just don't know when."

Linnea looked out across the rolling dunes to the ocean. The water sparkled like the proverbial diamonds under the bright, cloudless sky. She wasn't sure how she felt about this news. Part of her was grateful to him for helping take care of Florence Prescott. It couldn't be easy for him to drop everything to be a nursemaid. The other half was worried about him still being next door when Gordon arrived from England.

"So . . . how long do you think? A week? Two?"

John smiled, amused. Outdoors, he wasn't wearing a mask. She saw again how a simple smile could transform a rather handsome face into something remarkable. His green eyes brightened against his tan.

"I'm glad to hear you're so interested in my schedule."

"Well, I . . ."

"I'm here indefinitely," he told her, sparing her embarrassment. "I can work from anywhere, really."

She cracked a wicked smile. "So I was a nanny, and now you're a nurse."

He snorted and looked back to his mother's house. "I don't feel right leaving Mom in the lurch like that." He shrugged. "She's a trooper. But I'm worried about her. Taking care of Flo is beginning to take its toll. She used to be so funny, so cheerful. Now she seems downtrodden, you know? Like she's just making it through each day."

"I'm sorry."

"I love Flo, don't get me wrong. She's been a second mother to me for years. I'm happy to do this for her. Looking at the two of them, I couldn't just pack up and leave. Not when they both need help. And Flo recognizes so few people these days."

"Does she recognize you?"

"Oddly, she does. Favors me, in fact." His smile was quick. "Flo calls for me to help her, rather than Mom. Don't ask me why. It's only been a week since I've come out of quarantine, but she's become quite dependent on me." John shook his head. "She was at my side during the entire construction of the pond. And I mean all the time." He rolled his eyes. "Giving me directions. Telling me I was doing it all wrong. She was a real pain in the ass. But when it was done, a kind of lucidity came to her eyes—that happens every now and then—and she looked straight in my eyes and said in that curt, sure tone of hers, 'Good work, John. I'm proud of you.'" He paused. "Meant a lot."

He began walking again and she kept up the pace, pleased to see Luna so interested in all the new smells that she didn't seem to mind or even realize she was walking on a leash.

"Don't you miss San Francisco?" she asked.

"There are parts I miss, sure," he assured her. "But they're all under lockdown there. All of California has been hit hard with the virus. I'm better off here."

They walked in silence, pausing from time to time to let the puppy linger at some spot of keen interest.

Cara's house loomed ahead, bordering an empty lot that had been placed in conservation many years earlier by Russell Bennett, a friend of Lovie's. Perhaps more than a friend, if rumors she'd heard were true. Linnea would always be grateful to the gentleman from Virginia, whatever his relationship to her grandmother was, for leaving that small bit of beachfront open for sea turtles to nest. And, too, for her to be able to see the ocean, and not someone else's front porch, from her deck.

Linnea's daddy had built Cara's house, and it was without doubt one of the prettiest on Ocean Boulevard. It was more charming than grand, though its size was deceiving to the eye. The large front porch was a signature of her father's. He felt no home was worth the ground it was built on without plenty of porches.

"You're awfully quiet," John said.

"Oh, I'm just thinking about Anna."

"How's Annabelle the Southern belle?" John asked.

"Don't let her hear you say that."

"I couldn't resist. She's a bit . . . well . . . vexatious?"

"That's a fifty-cent word," she said with a wry smile, then turned her head to check on Luna, who'd stopped again, her little legs trembling as she smelled something exotic. Linnea tugged at Luna's leash a bit to get her walking again.

"Anna is depressed," Linnea told him.

"I wondered about that. I can count on one hand the number of smiles I've seen."

"I'm worried about her. She seems so lost. What should I do?"

"Be patient. Offer her support."

"Living with her is beginning to make *me* depressed. It's like there's this cloud inside the house."

"That's not good. Did you talk to her about it?"

"I tried."

"And?"

"She listened. Still, she's pretty much staying in her room."

"Do you want my suggestion?"

She looked at him and raised her brows. "Do I dare ask?"

He shrugged.

"Okay," Linnea said with a light laugh. "What is your suggestion?"

"It's simple. If a dark cloud is hovering inside the house, get outdoors. It'll do you good. Cheer you up. Hope's little garden patch needs tending. I'll be putting koi in the pond this week. Come over and help me. And"—he extended his hand toward the ocean—"in case you've forgotten, there's a whole friggin' beach out there."

She laughed, and he joined in. It felt good to feel that childlike laugh well up inside her again, one that lifted the spirits.

---

LATER, CARA AND David joined them on their trek to the beach. Hope led the way from their back patio along the path to the shore. It turned out to be a perfect day to end the month of April. The sun dazzled in a cloudless sky and the onshore breezes caressed the skin. Isle of Palms was temporarily closed to the public with checkpoints and restricted access to the island due to Covid-19. Starting on April 21, the beach had been declared open for exercise only—running, walking, dog-walking, biking, surfing, and other recreational activities that allowed social distancing. Sunbathing, loitering without moving, and groups of three or more people were prohibited, except for families.

The tide was low, and all along the shoreline, couples walked; some at a brisk pace, others in a relaxed stroll. It seemed to Linnea that people came to escape the confines of walls. To feel the open space, the fresh air, the great expanse of water more now than ever. While David and John talked, Linnea grabbed the private moment to talk with Cara.

"I talked to Gordon last night," she told Cara.

"That's nice," Cara replied. Her white floppy beach hat had a chic orange and white ribbon. Linnea tugged on the bill of her Turtle Team ball cap against the breeze. She was wearing a cutoff T-shirt over yoga pants, which had become somewhat of a uniform these days.

"He's arriving in a few weeks. Somehow, he made it happen."

"I'm happy for you." Cara turned and, searching Linnea's face, said carefully, "You *are* happy about it?"

"Oh yes, of course," she replied, a tad too quickly.

"But . . ."

"But there's a problem."

"There's always a problem with travel these days."

"Not travel," Linnea said. "Housing. Gordon wanted to get the same house he did last summer, but sadly, it's rented for the season. He's checked everywhere and there isn't a place available. The islands are fully rented. You wouldn't know of anyone who'd rent their house? Or has an apartment?"

Cara considered this as she walked a few paces. "Afraid not. Everyone I know has either rented their house or isn't renting at all and moved in themselves to shelter in place here."

"Exactly. So . . ." Linnea sneaked a quick glance at Cara, who was looking straight ahead toward the ocean. "He's asked to move in with me."

Cara swung her head around to look at Linnea. "In the beach house?"

"Yep."

Cara reached out and linked arms with her. Linnea felt a gush of relief at the touch. "Is that what you want?"

"Well, he *is* my boyfriend. Albeit absentee. I might be in love with him. We've been separated for so long . . . I was hoping to find that out this summer."

"But you missed him?" It was a question.

"Oh yes. A lot. We were planning on being a couple this summer. But I didn't plan on living together."

"But he needs a place to stay."

"Right."

"Is this what you want?"

Linnea hesitated.

Cara seized on this. "If you are moving in with him because you feel you *should* do it—don't."

"But you said the beach house is a safe haven. That we should offer it to others."

"True. But Linnea, first of all, your home is supposed to be a safe place for *you*."

"I feel safe with Gordon. . . ."

"Then I ask again, is this what you want to do?"

Linnea nodded, deciding in her own mind. "Yes."

"Okay, then."

"I don't want to overstep my bounds by inviting him to the beach house. It's your house, your rules."

Cara turned to look at her and removed her sunglasses. Linnea felt the power of her aunt's gaze.

"No, Linnea. You live there now. It's your home. It's your rules." She paused and slipped her sunglasses back on. "And your consequences."

# chapter nine

*Sometimes it was the little things that cheered people up.*

May

COOPER COULDN'T PEDAL the old beach cruiser bike fast enough. His head was bent and he pushed like it was a Peloton class. Two weeks in quarantine under his parents' roof and he was about to lose his mind. He had to get out of the house. Twenty-one years of age, and every morning at seven sharp his father called out, "Up and at 'em!"

His mother, God love her, kept shoveling food his way. So much food. Julia had asked him to sit at the dining table, but he'd played the coronavirus card big-time, using it to stay confined in his room. His father was already passing him the blueprints of the house he was building, telling him he needed a good man on the job. How it'd be father and son, working together, building an empire.

Cooper had worked construction during high school summer breaks and knew his way around a hammer. It was hard work, but he'd enjoyed it. He liked being outdoors. Sure, he'd take a job, gratefully. They were hard to come by these days. But working for his father was dancing on the head of a pin. And to be honest, he was pissed that his father had lost the import/export company. *That* was the job Cooper was interested in. He puffed out air. He and his father had never shared the same dreams.

The spring sun beat down mercilessly on his skin. He'd lathered on suntan lotion but the sweat was dripping it off. Man, he was seriously out of shape. He'd been out walking the beach during his quarantine and lifting weights. He'd arrived home from England with skin like the underbelly of a fish. After only two weeks he'd regained the beginnings of a decent tan. He had his grandfather Stratton's coloring, like his aunt Cara—dark hair and skin that tanned after only a day in the sun. That used to drive Linnea insanely jealous; she was more like their father and grandmother Lovie, pale-skinned and blond, lobster red after a day in the sun.

He turned off Palm Boulevard and headed toward the ocean. A few blocks later, he arrived at the familiar yellow beach house. It was perched on a scrubby dune overrun with wildflowers. He pulled off his helmet, wiped sweat from his brow, and took in the cottage where he'd spent so many summers. Unlike his parents' beach house, this one oozed charm. His grandmother used to say there wasn't another place like it, and he believed she was right.

Lovie. He smiled thinking of her. Oh, the times they'd had in this cottage! He remembered sitting on the porch in the late afternoons with all the women who came to Primrose Cottage. A gaggle of geese, his father had called them uncharitably. He tried to remember who all the women were. There was Lovie, of course. And Florence Prescott, the old woman who lived next door. She used to scare him and he never wanted to cross her. His aunt Cara and Emmi Peterson, or Baker now since the divorce. He scanned his brain, but he couldn't remember the names of the turtle team members. They came and went. Oh, yeah, there was Toy Sooner. Only she'd married. He couldn't remember her last name now. And her daughter, Little Lovie, was always tagging along. Then, of course, there was Linnea. Everyone knew she was Lovie's favorite.

That left Cooper the only male. They'd fondly called him Little Fox, as in the fox in the henhouse. He chuckled. What a dork he was. Back then, he'd thought they'd called him that because he could be clever, even sneaky, about grabbing candy and cookies. Only years later did he figure it out.

He walked his bike to the small area under the porch that was used for storage. He spotted Linnea's surfboard, Big Blue, which had once belonged to Brett. Cooper felt a pang at seeing it. He'd adored that man. Brett was his role model of all a man should be—more even than his father. Cooper had been jealous when Cara gave the board to Linnea—not that he blamed his aunt; Linnea was getting into surfing and she was living with Cara at the time. It all made sense. But still. He would've liked something of meaning that had belonged to Brett. Sometimes, he thought, being a male in the Rutledge family, for all the history of primogeniture, felt a bit second-tier.

He brushed aside nostalgia and braced himself for his do-or-die plea to his sister. He rested his bike against the wall, then ran his fingers through his short, thick hair, which was damp with sweat. So was his T-shirt. He pulled it over his head and headed around to the seaward side of the house where he heard the soft beat of Bob Marley playing.

He walked up the steps to the broad expanse of wooden decking that was perched on the dune. Cooper stopped a moment to take in the unobstructed view of dunes, beach, and ocean beyond. Was it any wonder his father had spent years trying to convince Cara to knock down Primrose Cottage and build a grand house on this lot? That empty lot across the street would remain a park in perpetuity, guaranteeing ocean views. The secret of who owned the lot had, so it seemed, gone with his grandmother to the grave. He chuckled. It had turned out his grandmother was the real fox of the bunch.

*What a view*, he thought again.

He walked across the deck to the far corner outside Palmer's bedroom. It was protected from street view by a screen. Linnea was lying on a chaise catching some rays and reading a book. The music switched to another Marley song, and he was about to call out his sister's name when she lifted her head and lowered the book. The name stuck in his mouth and he stopped short. Beneath the wide-brimmed straw hat was a lean, pale-skinned woman with the most beautiful breasts he had seen in a very long time. *What a view*, he thought again.

"Hello?" she asked in an imperious tone as she reached out for her towel and draped it across her exposed chest.

Cooper was by no means shy with women. But this beautiful topless woman left him feeling like the six-year-old boy again.

"Uh, hello. I'm looking for Linnea."

The woman didn't seem embarrassed in the least at having been caught sunbathing. She lifted her chin, pushed up her sunglasses, and said, "She's over at her aunt's house. Who are you?"

Now that she was decently covered, he felt he could walk closer. "I'm Cooper," he replied, trying to sound cool. "Her brother."

"Oh, the guy who came home from Oxford? She told me about you. Sit down."

"Nice things, I hope."

She didn't bother to answer the inane statement. "Do you want something to drink? You look . . ." She cast a look at his sweaty chest and smirked. "Hot."

He swallowed his smile and said, "I could use some water. I know where it is. Want one?"

She held up her own glass and shook her head.

"Be right back."

He ran his hand through his hair again as he headed indoors, feeling like he'd either acted like a fool, or this was the luckiest break he'd had in a long time. Who was this girl? She was nothing like his sister. Thank God that *wasn't* his sister. He shuddered at the thought of seeing Linnea topless. He went to a cabinet, pulled out a thermal mug, added ice from the freezer, and found filtered water in the fridge, same as always. When he returned to the deck, he was sorry to see the girl had slipped on her T-shirt. She'd also moved one of the wicker chairs from the table closer to the chaise.

"I'm Anna," she said as he sat down. "Linnea's roommate."

"I didn't know she had a roommate."

"Well, she does."

Cooper mulled this over. This could jam up his plans to move in. "So, which room are you sleeping in?"

"This one," she said, pointing to Palmer's room. "Are you living with your parents?"

It sounded so lame. Cooper nodded and shrugged. "Yeah. For the time being. Plans were changed."

"Tell me about it."

"When did you move in here?"

"Two weeks ago. I'm just finished my quarantine." She twirled a finger in the air. "Woo-hoo."

"Yeah, me too," he said.

"So, how should we celebrate?" she asked.

Cooper tilted his head. He wasn't sure if that was a come-on, or if he was just wishing it was.

---

CARA WAS DELIGHTED to see Emmi at the door. "Come in," she said cheerily, stepping aside to welcome her best friend into the house.

Emmi hesitated, then said, "How about a walk on the beach?"

Cara understood immediately. People were afraid of Covid-19, and having the virus was akin to having the plague. Even knowing David had recovered, people were afraid they might catch it.

"As it happens, David's out with Hope. They went to Dewees for a playdate with Rory."

"Is that safe?" Emmi asked.

Cara gave Emmi a hard look. She looked thinner, her face drawn. Her hair, usually a vibrant, if slightly unnatural shade of red, had streaks of gray at the roots.

"Yes. We made the decision that the two children could play together. They're family and we are all being very careful. The children need to play."

"But David—"

"If anything, he's the safest one among us now."

"Good," Emmi said with relief. "I'm really glad."

"Thank you for the lasagna, by the way. David devoured it."

"Let's go for that walk."

Cara always felt the years peel away when she walked the beach with Emmi. They'd been friends since the third grade. Childhood friends were tighter than blood. They *chose* to stay together. Since her marriage to David, she hadn't spent as much time with Emmi, then Covid had begun. She felt the distance now.

"I'm *so* glad to see you," she said, wishing she could link arms. "I've missed you."

"What a year," Emmi said with a shake of her head.

"And it's only May. But hey, the turtle season is starting. That's something."

"That's what I want to talk to you about," Emmi said. "Among other things."

"Tell me."

"Cara, I have to ask if you'll take over as project leader of the turtle team this season."

"Me? Why? Are you sick?"

"No, not me. It's Flo."

Cara stopped walking. Emmi stopped too and Cara scanned her face. "What's wrong?"

"Nothing's wrong," Emmi said in a calming tone. "Nothing new, anyway. It's more of the same. Only getting worse."

Cara sighed with relief, and they began walking again.

Emmi said, "Flo's begun wandering again. She's forever trying to go outside, rattling the doors, fiddling with the lock. Rattle, rattle, rattle. I take her out every day to the garden, and she seems content there. Pulling weeds. Watering. She'll speak lucidly from time to time. You know Flo, she likes to be useful. But John had to jury-rig some newfangled lock on the gate so she couldn't escape. But she's clever. Turn your back, and she's gone. Thank God for John. He's installed discreet bars across the window frames of her room, basically childproofed the cabinets and drawers, got a new seat for the toilet. She's getting quite unsteady on her feet." She sighed. "I don't want her to hurt herself."

"You look . . . tired."

"I *am* tired."

Cara winced, feeling guilt. "I'm sorry."

"Oh, Cara, I am too. For Flo. The disease is accelerating. She's having trouble eating solid food. Thank heavens for the Vitamix and avocados. She's increasingly disoriented. Unaware of what's going on around her. She stands and stares into space, or watches the television, only I know she's not really following what's going on. She just sits with this blank face. But if I turn off the television, she startles. So the darn TV drones on and on all day." Her voice hitched. "There are days she doesn't recognize me."

Cara brought her hand to her throat. She hadn't realized how bad things were getting. And she should have known. Guilt washed through her as she took in the obvious signs of exhaustion in Emmi's sagging jaw, her unwashed hair.

"I'll start coming over to help. We'll set up a schedule."

"Thank you," Emmi said fervently. "I think, soon, we'll have to help with her hygiene."

"As in showering?"

"Yes. And other things I can't ask John to do."

"Oh, Emmi." Cara didn't know if she could do that. The indignity of wiping someone's bottom would also wipe away the memories of Flo she wanted to keep. "I don't know that I want to see her like this. You can't get her nurse to come back?"

"Not for love or money."

Cara swallowed hard.

"With John, I think we'll be okay. For this summer," Emmi said. "I've thought it through. I want to give Flo this final summer."

"Emmi, we said that last summer."

"I know," she said with emphasis. "But we've been managing pretty well with her nurse. Making it work." They walked a few more steps. The sand was firm under their feet along the shoreline.

"And now?" Cara pressed. "Without a nurse? With her deteriorating?"

"Let's not go there."

Cara sighed and pumped her fists to pick up the pace. "Emmi, we have to be realistic. The level of care she needs is beyond what either of us is really capable—or even desirous—of doing. We've discussed this before. We found the right place. She's on the waiting list. Perhaps . . . it's time. You've done more than your share of caring for her. It's my turn. I'll cover all the expenses."

They walked awhile at a faster pace, side by side, each considering the situation.

Then Emmi stopped, her breath coming hard. "Cara," she began, then put her hand to her chest to take a deep breath. "Listen to me. This is important. I get what you're saying. If this was any other time, I'd agree with you. But it's not. We're in this crazy pandemic. If we put Flo in the memory care facility now, we won't be able to visit her. They're under lockdown." She narrowed her eyes. "Can you imagine Flo in there, alone? Without us? Without her memories. Not knowing where she is. Afraid."

"No," Cara said breathlessly.

Emmi shook her head. "We can't do it to her. Not until the pandemic is over."

"But, Emmi—"

"This isn't an impulsive decision. I've given it a lot of thought. We'll give it a shot. If we can't . . . if we fail . . . then okay."

"But what will you do when John leaves?"

"John said he'd stay to help." Her face softened. "He's a wonderful boy. He loves Flo too, don't forget. We talked about it seriously. I don't want to interfere with his work. But he was adamant that he can work from here. Honestly, I couldn't do it without him."

Cara felt admiration for John bloom in her chest. "He's a good man. I'll never be able to thank him enough."

"He doesn't want your thanks. But . . ." She smiled. "What you *can* do is take over the turtle team. I'm going to be tied down at the house with Flo. The team needs someone they can count on to show up at every nest. To keep the records. Cara, you've been a project leader before. You know what has to be done. I don't have to teach you. And," she added, elbowing Cara in the ribs, "I know that when I want the job back, you'll give it to me."

Cara laughed and bumped shoulders. "I never could say no to you."

---

LINNEA JUGGLED THE two bags of groceries in her arms as she negotiated the front stairs. It felt like the oat milk in the damp paper bag was about ready to break through. Lifting one knee to balance the bag, she tested the door handle and sighed with relief to find it unlocked.

After a quick twist of the brass handle, she pushed open the door and hurried to the kitchen, where she unceremoniously plopped the bags on the counter with a heavy sigh. She needed to build up her muscles, she thought as she rolled her shoulders.

She heard music coming from Anna's bedroom. "Anna! I'm back!" she called out.

There was no answer. She pulled a latte out of a smaller brown bag, followed by a bag of croissants. Sometimes it was the little things that cheered people up. She put a croissant on a plate and carried her treats from the kitchen down the hall to the bedroom, where music blared out in a pulsing, pounding beat. Balancing the coffee on the plate, she knocked on the door.

"Hey, you! I've got a surprise for you. It's from Paname!"

She heard a gasp, then muffled voices. Linnea's hand lowered and she leaned forward, listening intently. There was definitely someone in there with her. But who? She was tempted to put her ear to the door when she heard a crash, as if something had fallen off the bedside stand. This was followed by a burst of giggling, soprano and baritone. Then came a forced whisper, "Be quiet," that was filled with more mirth than fear.

Linnea felt the paper coffee cup burn her fingers. She was inclined to push open the door and demand to know what was going on. But of course, she knew exactly what was going on. Linnea took a step back, then shook her head in disbelief. Cursing softly, she opened the coffee lid and, blowing on the steaming brew, took a sip as she made a hasty retreat.

The voice she'd heard was her brother's.

---

LINNEA FINISHED THE croissant, carefully licking her fingertips to rid them of butter and flakes. She needed to keep busy, to quell her racing mind. She began preparing chicken salad from the lovely roasted chicken she'd purchased. The meat was still warm to the touch. As she worked, her mind repeatedly assessed how she felt about Anna sleeping with her brother. It was a lot to take in. What was Cooper doing here, anyway? When had they met? Had they been seeing each other on the sly? Linnea snorted. Why didn't they have the decency to take their tryst somewhere neutral? So much for Anna being lonely. She certainly didn't need cheering up!

She took extra care while she chopped the slippery green onions not to cut off her finger. The onions were making her eyes water and she was so agitated, she could barely cut evenly.

"Hey."

Cooper's voice. She took a calming breath, then looked over her shoulder. Could it be more obvious? Cooper had combed his dark hair with his fingers, his skin was flushed, and he had his shirt on inside out. She felt her cheeks flame and turned back to her onions.

"Hello." *Chop. Chop. Chop.*

"I rode over on my bike. Boy, am I out of shape. I'm winded."

"Really? You don't sound winded." She glanced over her shoulder. "By the way, your shirt is inside out."

He lifted his arms to take off his shirt. She couldn't help but notice he was in pretty good shape. He reversed it and put in on correctly this time. "Better?"

She rolled her eyes. He was oblivious.

She finished chopping and tossed the onions into the cut chicken cubes. Then she picked up a towel and began drying her hands. She turned to face Cooper across the room. With his six-foot-two frame, his broad shoulders, his dark hair and eyes, he was handsome in a John Kennedy Jr. kind of way. It was no wonder Anna was attracted to him. Linnea had to face the fact that her kid brother wasn't a boy anymore. Though he seemed a bit sheepdog-like in manner today. Linnea set the towel on the counter and crossed her arms, curious how he was going to play this.

"So, you're done with quarantine?" she asked him.

"Yeah," Cooper said, nodding. He leaned against the opposite counter.

She smiled. "It's nice to see you."

"Long time."

"Yeah." She was waiting it out.

After an awkward pause, he said, "It's been close quarters on Sullivan's. Mom's been hovering. And Dad . . ." He snorted. "He can't wait to get me out to the work site."

"You need a job," she said without emotion. "You're lucky to have one."

"Lucky is not exactly how I see it." Cooper crossed his arms. "There's something I wanted to talk to you about."

*Here it comes,* Linnea thought. She took a breath, hoping she could handle this with grace.

"I can't live at home. I'm going frickin' crazy and it's only been two weeks. Mom's cooking like Gordon Ramsay, shoving food at me. She's trying to personally guarantee I gain the Covid nineteen. And Dad, he's polishing up the brass plate." Cooper spread out his palms like he was reading a sign. *"Rutledge and Son."* He dropped his hands. "I love them. You know I do. But I can't live with them."

She pushed off from the counter. *"That's* what you want to talk about?"

Cooper's eyes widened, and she knew he realized he was skating on thin ice.

She had to turn so he didn't see her face. She reached up for a glass, then went to the fridge for filtered water. As she poured, she tried to sort out her emotions. She didn't know whether to laugh in his face and tell him the jig was up or to get angry at him for sleeping with her roommate. She went for both.

"You're an idiot," she cried, spinning around. "You think I don't know what's going on?"

Cooper's face flushed and he looked at his toes.

"When did you meet Anna?" she demanded.

He looked up and said, his blush deepening, "Today."

"Oh. My. God."

"Hey, it happened." His tone was defensive. "Why are you making such a big deal about it?"

"She's my roommate!"

Cooper breathed in but said nothing.

Linnea threw her hands up. "I don't even know what to say."

Anna walked into the room in black yoga pants and her lime-green sports bra, inside out. "What's going on?"

Linnea speared her with a gaze. "You tell me."

Anna cast a glance at Cooper. He tried not to smile.

"We hooked up," said Anna. "We're not trying to keep it a secret. Do you have a problem with that?"

Linnea's eyes widened. "Yes, I have a problem with that!"

Anna had the grace or good sense to remain quiet.

"Hey, Lin," Cooper said in a conciliatory tone, "I'm sorry if this offends you. We didn't think it would bother you."

"You didn't think at all," Linnea fired back. She felt the last shreds of self-restraint give way and couldn't hold in the flood of words. "I'm doing my best," she shouted, lifting her hands in fury, "my level best, to be half as gracious as Cara was to me when she took me in. And Lovie before her. I opened my house to you"—she glared at Anna—"and let's be honest, you haven't been easy. And now," she said, spearing Cooper with her gaze, "you're asking me to take you in? What do you think this is? The Holiday Inn? I'm fed up! I'm done! You all can just leave me alone."

Anna paled.

Cooper narrowed his eyes.

Linnea bunched her fists and hurried from the room, making a beeline to the rear porch. Outdoors, the breeze whisked her hair as she paced the deck, gulping air, trying to calm down. She felt deflated and, worse, embarrassed for having lost it like that. My God, she was screaming at the top of her lungs. She put her hands to her face. That was the opposite of how she'd wanted to act—calm, gracious, accepting. She felt like a complete, utter failure. She just wanted to run away.

She heard the wood creak behind her and, turning, saw Cooper walking slowly toward her.

"Lin," he called out, his tone tentative.

"Not now," she said, turning away, wiping her eyes.

"Hey, sis, I'm sorry."

"It's okay," she said.

They both knew that wasn't true.

"I know this wasn't cool. I'm sorry for that."

"I'm sorry I shouted like that."

He laughed mirthlessly. "I haven't heard you shout like that since I beheaded all your Barbie dolls."

Linnea snorted. "Yeah, I was pretty mad about that." She sighed and pushed her hair from her face. "I don't know why I got so mad. I mean, yes, you might've given some thought to the whole living situation here. But to be honest, I'm really not freaked by the two of you hooking up."

"Okay." He sounded relieved.

"It's weird," she added, "but that's not why I exploded. I think it was the straw that broke the camel's back. I'm feeling trapped. Cornered. And you know what happens to a cornered animal."

"If you don't want me to move in, I get it."

She shook her head. "No, that's not it. I don't mind if you move in. You're welcome to." She smiled. "I want you to."

Cooper stepped closer, studying her face. "What's really bothering you?"

She sighed and turned to face her brother. He stood still, arms at his sides, ready—eager—to hear what she would say. She and Cooper had always been close growing up. She'd been there for him when he fell apart. And now he was here for her.

Linnea began, "It's like everyone wants a part of me. Not just you," she added quickly.

"Who else?"

"Anna. John."

"What about John?"

"You didn't hear? He's back," she said. "Knocking on my door. I know he'd like to be more than friends."

"I thought that ship had sailed."

"I thought so too." She put up her hands. "Anyway, now Gordon is arriving soon. He wants to move in with me."

"Here? No way."

Linnea looked up at him, surprised by his knee-jerk reaction. "Why do you say that?"

"You hardly know the guy."

"We practically lived together last summer. You weren't here."

"But he had his own place."

"Yep." She conceded that that was the salient point.

He blew out his cheeks. "I don't think you should do it."

Linnea narrowed her gaze. "Why? Don't you like him?"

"I didn't say that."

Linnea knew Cooper was careful with his words. He didn't often speak out against someone, nor was he afraid to share an opinion. "Please. You knew him at Oxford. I want to know what you think."

Cooper rubbed the back of his neck. "He's a decent guy," he began. "But he's . . ." He paused. "Buttoned up."

"I know he's reserved."

"No, it's more than that. It's like he holds back. He doesn't let loose. Keeps folks at arm's length. Once, a bunch of us guys were in the pub and he walked in. I called him over, and he joined us. But he never felt comfortable with us. He doesn't, I don't know, joke around. There's like a barrier he holds between him and others."

Linnea knew that about him. The fact that Gordon had opened up to her made their relationship feel all the more intimate. "Okay. But do you like him?"

"I don't know." He sidestepped.

"It's a yes-or-no question."

"Okay, no," Cooper said plainly. "Like I said, he's a decent guy. But I don't like him."

Linnea puffed out air. "Okay. Thanks." Her head was spinning. She hadn't expected that last answer. Her brother's opinion mattered to her and this deeply unnerved her. To change the subject, she asked, "Hey, I made some cookies. Want some?"

"Chocolate chip?"

"Is there another kind?"

———

COOPER LOST NO time moving in. Anna was settled in Palmer's room, so she apologetically gave Cooper Cara's old room. He'd laughed and said a real man felt confident in pink. The following morning his big black pickup truck pulled into the driveway filled with suitcases, his bicycle and his surfboard.

She'd also received several terse e-mails from her mother.

Linnea. Why on earth would you agree to letting Cooper move in with you without discussing it with us? You know how much we were looking forward to his return.

Linnea. How are you all going to squeeze into that little cottage? And with another girl living there. Across the hall!

I give up. Do what you want. You always do, anyway.

As usual, Linnea thought, it was her getting that flak, not Cooper. She sent her mother one e-mail in reply.

It will be fine. We love you.

The next few days Linnea felt she was walking on eggs. Everyone was trying his or her best to be cool about the living arrangement, but it was going to take time for her to get used to seeing her brother and Anna as a couple.

Linnea made her way to the kitchen, eager for a cup of coffee. She found the Melitta coffee carafe in the sink, the cone still filled with cold coffee grounds. Linnea grumbled to herself as she pulled out the used filter and dumped it in the trash. The pair of them were slobs, there was no other word for it. Their rooms both looked like a hurricane had struck. Baskets filled with clean laundry were topped with dirty items carelessly tossed in. Clothes were discarded and left on the floor where they fell, eventually forming a mountain of shirts, pants, bras, and socks, all wrinkled and interspersed with shoes, books, and papers.

And the bathroom! It gave her anxiety just to think of that room.

Linnea washed the carafe, dried it, and put in a crisp white filter. She didn't want to lose her temper and needed a bracing cup of hot coffee. She went through the motions in the galley kitchen to prepare the drip coffee. This was her favorite morning ritual. Very calming. She'd been teased about her love of coffee, but she couldn't argue. It was true. And she was very particular about her coffee.

Linnea settled on Charleston Coffee Roasters Beach House Blend. She'd tried it for the name, but stayed with it for the flavor. The kettle whistled shrilly, to her, a morning song. It made the kitchen sound like home. She poured the boiling water into the filter and breathed in the breaking scent of coffee as it filled the room. She closed her eyes, relishing the heady smell. While she waited for the coffee to brew, she filled the dog dish with kibble and served it to a patiently waiting Luna.

From down the hall, she heard a door close. Followed by a second door closing. Linnea poured herself a mug of coffee and waited.

"Good morning!" Anna called out in a cheery voice.

Anna certainly was more chipper in the morning lately, Linnea thought as she turned to see her roommate pad across the room in her slippers. She was wearing a thigh-length lavender silk kimono that showed off her long legs. Linnea looked down at her own kimono, its twin, only in pink. Looking again at the lavender kimono, she realized it was *her* kimono.

"Nice kimono."

Anna poured coffee into her mug, then looked down at what she was wearing. "Oh yeah, sorry. My laundry wasn't done, and I needed something to put on. I hope you don't mind. I'll wash it and put it back."

Cooper walked in, wearing his boxer shorts. His hair was smashed to one side of his head. He made his way, barefoot, to the coffeemaker and poured himself a cup. He mumbled something that sounded vaguely like "Good morning," but she couldn't be sure.

Linnea leaned against the counter and eyed the couple, who acted like they barely knew each other, stepping aside, careful not to touch, with polite murmurs of *excuse me* and *do you want a cup?*

Linnea cupped her mug and tried not to giggle. "Did you sleep well?"

Cooper slid a glance toward Anna and hid his smile with his mug.

"Yeah. Great," Anna replied before taking a sip.

"Good." Linnea kept watching them. She couldn't stop. It was like watching a sitcom. She didn't know what was going to happen next. "I found a wonderful book. Kept me turning the pages until the wee hours of the morning."

Anna said, "I heard you talking last night on the phone. Gordon?"

"Yes."

Cooper leaned against the counter. "So, is he moving in?"

190

"Yes."

Cooper lifted his mug as though in a toast. "Your call."

She took a breath. "I'm glad you're okay with it. Because we're going to be cozy here with all four of us," Linnea said, looking first at Anna, then at her brother. "Very cozy."

Cooper rolled his eyes, then said, "I'll take the first shower." He ducked his head and made for the exit.

"Little Fox," Linnea murmured to herself as she watched him sneak off.

The two women sipped coffee in an awkward silence. Finally, Anna spoke.

"I have to admit, I was surprised you agreed to let Gordon move in with you."

"Okay. Let's break that down," Linnea said, straightening. "First, you were surprised about me letting *Gordon* move in? And not about Cooper?"

"Why wouldn't you? He's your brother."

"And your boyfriend."

Anna made a face. "Is he?" she crooned. "My boyfriend?" She shook her head.

"Whatever you call what's going on between you."

"What's going on between you and Gordon?"

"I have no problem saying he is my boyfriend."

"If you say so."

Linnea sipped her coffee, scowling, wondering how much Cooper had told Anna of his feelings about Gordon.

"So," Anna said, pulling out a bowl from the cabinet. "John is out and Gordon is in."

"That's right. Gordon is moving in with me." The words felt strange in her mouth. "It's not a bad thing, is it?" Linnea asked, as much to herself as to Anna.

"How would I know?" Anna poured homemade granola into the bowl. "Really, like Cooper said, it's your call."

Linnea set her coffee mug on the counter and vigorously scratched her head, groaning with frustration. "I'm going to break out in hives before this is over."

"Look," Anna said, turning to face her. "I'm not a professional on love, God knows. But if your body is sending you signals telling you that you don't want him to move in with you, you have to pay attention to that."

"I'm just nervous."

Anna went to the fridge, pulled out the oat milk, then poured some over her cereal. "What I hear you saying is, maybe you're just not that into him."

Linnea looked at her, startled by the casually offered, shocking comment. "But I am. He's wonderful. Kind. Intelligent. Handsome."

"Okay, keep telling yourself that." She smiled. "And who knows? Maybe it's just the timing that has you spooked. The pandemic and everything." She carried the bowl to the table and slid into a chair. "Or, you're just not that into him."

Linnea frowned and grabbed her mug, taking a long swallow of coffee. It was already cold.

Cooper reentered the room, dressed now in a navy sweatshirt over khaki shorts that revealed his tanned, hairy legs and a worn pair of docksiders. His hair was still wet from his shower.

"Uh-oh. This has the feeling of a chick talk. How about I take the dog for a walk?"

"Great," Linnea said. She turned to Luna, whose large brown eyes stared at her adoringly. "Want to go for a walkie?" Immediately the puppy began shaking her rear in excitement. "Go on," she said to the dog, wiggling her fingers toward Cooper. "Her leash is hanging by the door."

They watched Cooper struggle with the wiggly puppy, saying over and over, "Sit. Sit. Sit." At last he secured the leash and, with a wave, left the house.

"A boy and his dog," Anna quipped.

"Yes. Exactly. A *boy*," Linnea said with exaggerated meaning.

"Oh, come on. He's not that young."

"No?" Linnea brought her mug to the table and sat beside Anna. "You don't think a college boy is a little young for you?"

"What's a few years?"

"Five," Linnea said.

"Four," said Anna.

"Whatever."

"It *is* weird," Anna conceded. "Not because he's a few years younger than me. That's no biggie. Trust me, he's a man."

Linnea made a face and put up her hand. "Please, spare me the details."

Anna nodded, silently agreeing there were some lines that could not be crossed. "Right. It's weird because he's your little brother. Neither of us meant for it to happen. It just did." Her long, unpolished nails tapped the table. "We're not taking it seriously. We're chalking it up to being stuck in these weird times. He might not be Mr. Right, but he's Mr. Right Now." She picked up her spoon and wagged it toward Linnea. "Your brother is pretty cool. I like him." She leaned over to nudge Linnea. "And I love his family."

Linnea looked at Anna as she lustily put a spoonful of cereal into her mouth. Anna had lost the dull pallor and the cloud of gloom that had hovered over her when she first moved in. She was still a slob in her room, but she was making efforts to join in cleaning the house and never delayed chipping in her fair share of expenses. *So this was going to be the new normal at the beach house*, she thought.

"Sometimes it's easier not to struggle upstream and simply go with the flow."

Anna reached out with her mug. "I'll drink to that."

They clinked mugs.

Linnea said, "Look, I get it. You and Cooper are both adults. It's awesome if you like each other. As his big sister, I think you should know something, though. Cooper used to party a lot. And he's been quite the ladies' man."

"Okay." Anna had put down her mug and was listening intently.

"But that part of his life is over," Linnea said, stressing her words. "Cooper had a life-changing event at eighteen."

Anna breathed out. "I know. The drug overdose. He told me."

"Oh. Good." Linnea was glad he had. But she had more to say. "He's grown so much since then. Mature beyond his years, you could say." She looked up again and caught Anna's attention. "But he has a soft underbelly. When he cares, he cares a lot. And here's the thing. Take it from one who knows. When you move in with someone, things get serious fast."

She pointed her finger at Anna in a nonthreatening way. "Remember this. If you break his heart, you're not just ruining one relationship." She moved her hand and added a finger to indicate two. "You're ruining two."

# chapter ten

*During these days of isolation, it was all the more important to spend time outdoors, especially when the glowing sun broke through the darkness and filled the sky with pink and golden rays.*

LINNEA'S FAVORITE TIME of the day was the very early morning when the dawn song of nearby birds pierced the night's silence. She'd lie in bed and listen to the first clarion call, a blend of joy and bravery—*I'm alive, this is a new day, and this is my territory.* She could get behind that. After a few strident calls, the song would be returned by another bird, over and over, a simple duet until other neighboring birds joined the chorus. One of the benefits of staying at home was not having to rush out of bed, to dress and dash to work. She could lie there and appreciate the concert of a new day's birth.

At length she rose, yawned, then went to her bathroom and splashed cold water on her face. She slipped into her yoga attire and heard Luna pawing at her crate.

"I see you, baby. Come on," she crooned as she undid the bolt. "Let's go out."

The master bedroom was connected to the deck. It was convenient for her to stroll out with Luna at her heel. She'd created a small fenced area off the deck that Luna could run to, which she happily did.

"Good morning," called out Anna. She came through her bedroom door, also dressed in yoga clothes and carrying her mat.

They had started the routine of meeting on the deck at dawn for sun salutations as a way to bond. Anna was skilled at yoga and had begun teaching Linnea the twelve poses that made up the sun salutation. Linnea felt that during these days of isolation, it was all the more important to spend time outdoors, especially when the glowing sun broke through the darkness and filled the sky with pink and golden rays. She believed the sun's energy could keep her inner darkness at bay.

After yoga, Anna helped Linnea in the kitchen to prepare breakfast. While Linnea made the coffee, Anna poured out her homemade granola into bowls, topped them with fresh berries, and set a carton of oat milk on the table. Linnea still couldn't believe that Anna had convinced her cow's milk–chugging brother to switch to oat milk. While the coffee brewed, she poured Luna's dog kibble into a bowl. The puppy's tail never failed to wag as she trotted after Linnea to the dog dish. Dogs were such dependable critters, she thought.

As usual, the scent of coffee was a lure for Cooper. He padded into the kitchen in a sleepy stupor, murmuring a good morning. There wasn't much talk until all of them had finished their first cup of coffee.

Linnea carried her bowl and mug to the sink and began filling it with soapy water. She looked out the window to see a cherry-red cardinal at the bird feeder, his gray mate waiting her turn. She startled when she saw John walking down the stairs from his loft carrying two suitcases.

He couldn't be leaving! She felt her heart lurch and turned off the faucet. With dripping hands she ran out the back door, ignoring Cooper calling, "What's the matter?"

"John!" she called, hurrying down the stairs, across the gravel driveway. "John!"

He heard her and stopped at the fence gate. "What's the matter?"

She came to a halt before him, breath heaving. "Are you leaving?"

He looked confused, then, looking down, saw the suitcases. He set them down and shook his head. "No, no. I'm leaving the loft, but I'm moving into the main house. I'm not going anywhere."

"Oh," she said. Then again, "Oh, okay." It surprised her how devastated she'd felt thinking he was walking out of her life. Again.

"Did you think I was . . . *leaving* leaving?"

"Well, yes. I mean, you only came for a visit. Your quarantine is over. And"—she pointed to the suitcases—"it seemed obvious."

He smiled a crooked smile. "And you wanted to stop me?"

She held back her grin. "I wanted to say good-bye."

"Ah, okay. Well, sorry. I'm sticking around."

"You've decided, then. You're not going back to California?"

"Not for a while. My mother hasn't asked me for much, so I couldn't refuse. Besides, I can do my job anywhere. But I'm moving into the house to be closer to Flo if they should need me."

"Oh." The loft was empty. An idea began percolating in Linnea's mind. A lifeline! And she was going for it.

"What's your mother going to do with the loft?"

"I don't know. Rent it? It's a seller's market out there. Why? Do you know someone interested? Trying to get rid of the Covid Couple?"

Linnea smirked at the nickname for Anna and Cooper. She shook her head, then pressed her folded hands to her lips. "John, I have an enormous favor to ask you. And I mean big. I'll owe you."

"That sounds interesting. What?"

She took a breath. "Well . . . Gordon is flying in from England."

John's face suddenly grew wary. "Uh-huh."

"He's looked everywhere. I've looked everywhere. There isn't any-place nearby he can rent. So, I was wondering—"

"Oh, no." His brows knitted and she saw a flash of anger in his eyes. "No way."

"John, it would only be for two weeks while he quarantines. He has nowhere else to go."

"Two weeks? Then what?"

"He'll move into my house. Unless . . .," she paused. "He could stay in your loft."

"Your place? There's no room in your house."

"I've been trying to figure it out," she said with frustration.

"I can't believe you're asking me this. You want your boyfriend to stay at *my* house?" He laughed shortly. "I know the world has gone mad, but this is bat-shit crazy."

"John, please. I'm asking you as a friend."

"As a *friend*. Right. I'm in the friend zone. Got it."

She swallowed and straightened her spine. "I thought we were clear on this. I told you I was seeing someone else."

"I thought . . ."

"You thought what?" She held her breath in the sudden silence.

A muscle twitched in his cheek. "Never mind."

There it was, she thought. More proof that John wouldn't, couldn't commit. Her path seemed clear.

"It's simple. Gordon is coming from England to work for the summer, and to see me. He needs a place to rent. Can he rent your loft?"

There was a long silence as John and Linnea stared at each other. She saw the struggle in his eyes. The unspoken words.

"So," John said, "what you're saying is I get to choose between Gordon living with you, or Gordon living in my loft. Sweet."

Linnea put both hands on her head. "I know this is awkward."

"You think?"

"Okay, very awkward," she amended. "I wouldn't ask you if I had any other ideas."

"Here's an idea. How about he can stay at my place and *I* move in with you?"

She offered a wry smile. "Nice try. Please, John. Pretty please."

"Okay, fine. What are *friends* for?" he asked, scowling. Then he bent to pick up the suitcases. The look he gave her told her that she owed him. Big-time. "But he's paying rent." He turned and started walking away. Over his shoulder he shouted, "And it won't be cheap."

---

GRAVEL CRUNCHED AS the hired car pulled into Emmi's driveway. Linnea stood on her driveway, separated by a line of narrow shrubs. She clutched her hands tight as the rear car door opened and she saw Gordon slide out. He was wearing a charcoal-gray suit and carrying a trench coat over his arm, all of which looked wrinkled. Even his hair was longer and disheveled.

"Gordon!" she called out.

He turned quickly, and though she couldn't see his face behind his mask, his eyes crinkled. He raised his arm in greeting. "Linnea! I made it!"

The distance was killing her. He was so close, just across the driveway, not across some ocean. She fought the urge to run to him and feel his arms around her. Seeing him—in the flesh and not on some screen—made him real again. She was glad of the emotions that were bubbling up.

"It's so hard not to come over," she called out.

"I know. But it's wonderful to see you."

The driver approached, carrying two large suitcases. After the business was transacted, Gordon looked over to her again, his arms at his sides. Even from a distance she could feel his yearning to walk to her side.

"I've filled the fridge with beer and wine and cheese," she called out. "There's fruit, and some snacks. I'll bring dinner over on a tray."

"You don't have to wait on me."

"I want to."

"Probably best you don't. I wouldn't want you to get sick on my account. Not after all this waiting. I'll be fine with deliveries. The time will go fast. The hardest part will be knowing you're next door."

"Two weeks."

"Ten days, if current research holds true."

"All the better."

"I could stand at the window. Send you paper airplanes."

She wagged her finger at him. "Don't."

"Then it's back to FaceTime."

"And waves and blown kisses."

"We'll be Romeo and Juliet."

"Do you remember how that ended?"

He laughed. "I'm glad I'm here."

She felt suddenly teary. "I'm glad you're here too," she said, and meant it.

---

ANNA AND LINNEA sat side by side on the sand, their wet suits pulled down to their waists over their swimsuits. The days were getting warmer as May marched on, but the ocean had been brisk. They'd just finished surfing their favorite spot on Isle of Palms. They were taking a break to warm up.

Linnea luxuriated in the feel of the spring sun on her skin. It felt glorious to be stretching her palms down on the warm sand, feeling the kiss of the sun. She reached up to comb her hair with her fingers, letting it fall out in skeins to dry. John and Cooper were still out riding the waves. The surf was unremarkable, but it was enough to get one's metabolism up and create that sense of connection to the sea. No matter the wave, there was contact with the water, the exertion of one stroke after another and balancing on a board, and at last the exhilaration of riding a rushing curl of water home.

She felt her breath slowly return to a steady beat. "It feels so good to be back out on the water," Linnea said, lifting her face skyward.

"Totally," Anna said. She sat up with excitement. "Linnea, you'll never guess."

Linnea turned her head, the tone of voice catching her attention. Anna's face was pinkened from the sea and sun and something else. "What?"

"I got an e-mail this morning from the aquarium. They're calling me back in to work!"

Linnea sat up. "Really?" Hope fluttered in her chest.

"Really. They're taking in a lot of stranded turtles now that the season started. Boat strikes, mostly. I wish those boats would just slow down and give the turtles a chance to get out of the way."

"When do you go back?"

"Tomorrow. They say it's urgent. They need help now."

"Tomorrow? Wow," Linnea said on an exhale.

"Did you get a call?"

"Nope." She tried not to let her disappointment show.

"Oh." Then Anna added with encouragement. "They're still working with a skeleton crew. Hang on."

"I have no choice, do I?" Linnea ran sand through her fingers. After an awkward silence Linnea said, "I miss my job. That was a big part of who I was. Now I feel like I'm in limbo. Waiting to see what happens next. I never thought I'd say I miss getting up in the morning and going to work. But I do."

"If you were at work, you'd be sitting behind a desk. Not sitting here on the beach."

"True." Linnea sighed, not feeing comforted.

"Hey," Anna said. "Why don't you do what you said . . . about finding time to do things you haven't had the time to do."

Linnea turned her head to look at Anna. "You actually listened to me?"

Anna looked sheepish. "Yeah. I always do." She laughed shortly. "Even if I don't show it."

"You seem, I don't know . . . happier."

"I am." Anna smirked. "It's more than the sex," she said.

Linnea laughed.

Anna looked out at the ocean. "I'm sorry I was such a bitch at the beginning," she said. "I was pretty down. And all you were doing was trying to stay positive." She turned to face Linnea. "I admire that about you. Your generosity. I'm not talking about a money kind of thing, but your spirit. I mean it."

Linnea never thought she'd hear those words from Anna. "Thank you," she said simply.

Anna said, "And you know, I never really thanked you properly for letting me move in with you. So . . . thank *you*."

Linnea smiled. "You're welcome."

"And, hey," Anna added with a crooked smile, "I have to admit, it's not too shabby to live on an island."

"I'm glad you moved in. Really. We've become closer, don't you think?"

"Well, there is your brother. We're practically related . . ."

Linnea laughed and jokingly kicked her leg. "You're so bad." She looked out at the surf. "I have to admit, I'm kind of envious you have an open relationship with Cooper. It is what it is. No promises made. No feelings hurt."

"Right," Anna replied, but without a smile.

"I wish it were as clear-cut for me."

"You seem pretty happy Gordon's arrived."

"I am." She saw John take a wave, his arms stretched out. "I just wish I could put my feelings for John away."

"Honey, everyone knows you two have it for each other."

"No!" Linnea swung her head around. "Don't say that."

"When you're in the same room, we're all walking on pins and needles."

"No we aren't."

"Why don't you and John just sit down and talk it out?"

"We don't need to. He has made it clear what he wants out of life. What he and I want are not the same. I'm too old—and wise—to go down that path again. So, we're friends. I must accept that's enough. But . . ." She closed her eyes with fatigue. She'd been going over and over this in her mind. "It's so hard to know someone is not right for you, and still have emotions for him. I wish he'd just go back to California. He's interfering with my feelings for Gordon. I need to give that relationship more time. He's perfect."

"Linnea, first of all, no one is perfect. Think about it. Do you know any relationship that's perfect?"

"Maybe Cara and David."

Anna waved her hand. "They don't count." She laughed. "But even with them, Cara has to still have feelings for her first husband."

"Brett . . ." Linnea said softly.

"You wouldn't be human if you didn't have residual sentiments about John. He was a big part of your life. You loved him. And when you love someone, I don't know if you can ever fully turn it off." She flipped her hands up. "Not that I've ever really loved anyone, so this is all conjecture. Other than my boy toy, of course, but that's another story."

Linnea tried to laugh, appreciating her attempt at humor.

"Life's not perfect. Love's not perfect. Don't be so hard on yourself." Anna looked up sharply, then groaned. "Oh God, look what the ocean spit out."

Linnea followed Anna's gaze and was surprised to see Pandora James walking toward them, swinging her hips in a designer bikini that showed off her body perfectly. Her long brown hair was braided over her shoulder under a big floppy hat. She carried a large designer beach bag and wore her signature enormous sunglasses. Every man she passed turned his head to follow her long-legged gait.

Linnea hadn't seen Pandora since she'd said good-bye at last summer's end, headed for England, and she'd had nothing but one e-mail since January. They'd met the summer before while surfing, then encountered each other again shortly after on Sullivan's Island. Linnea had noticed her fabulous Chanel swimsuit. Pandora had noticed the black garbage bag Linnea was carrying to pick up trash. A friendship was born.

Gordon had strained that relationship. Pandora liked him and had let Linnea know it. But Gordon wanted Linnea.

"When did she get here?" asked Anna.

"I've no idea. Mama was expecting her to check on Mrs. James's house that she decorated, but no one told me anything specific."

Anna harrumphed. "Let the fun times roll."

"Linnea! Annabelle!" Pandora waved as she approached, smiling.

Linnea rose to her feet.

"No hugs, no kisses!" Pandora said, stopping ten feet away. "And please don't ask me to do that elbow thing. It's so banal. Here's an air kiss." She pursed her lips and made a smacking noise.

"When did you get back?"

"Two weeks ago. I went straight into quarantine. I've been dreadfully lonely."

"Why didn't you call?"

"Oh, what would've been the point? I was exhausted and I knew I'd see you when all this virus stuff sorted itself out. It did, and here I am."

"Are you here for long?"

"Plans unknown. I'm waiting to see what Granny James will do.

208

the summer of lost and found

I'm officially here to inspect the house—she sent me first class and expects a thorough report. Your mother did a marvelous job, by the way. I hardly recognized the house! I'm not embarrassed to walk inside anymore. Rave reviews. I know Granny is going to be blissfully happy. She's dying to come, of course, but her doctors won't allow her to travel."

"Mama worked extremely hard on the house. She'll be so pleased."

"Heaven knows the place needed a complete makeover! It could've been on one of the telly shows where people come in and transform a horrid little box into a beautiful home. I was on Team Tear-It-Down, I don't mind telling you. But I confess I was wrong. Your mother is a miracle worker. She always said the house had good bones, whatever that means." She laughed. "Anyway, I'm there now, happy to be back, and I'm *so* happy to see you. I've got a golf cart. We can whiz back and forth between our houses. Won't we have fun?"

"Fun's always a good thing," Linnea said, smiling. Pandora had an energy and confidence that lifted the spirits. "You remember Annabelle, of course. She goes by Anna now." She turned to indicate Anna sitting on the sand.

"Oh. Yes. Hi, Anna." Pandora's tone was flat.

Anna looked away from the ocean. "Hi, Pandora."

Linnea inwardly groaned. There had never been any affection between the two women. Pandora turned again to Linnea. "I, uh, I heard Gordon was here too?"

"Oh, yes," she answered lightly. Pandora's tone made Linnea wonder if she still had a thing for Gordon. "He's here. He pulled every string to get here as early as he could. He's just finishing his quarantine."

"Oh, goody," Pandora replied, smiling. "It will be such fun to see him again. A fellow Brit and all that. Did he rent the same house as last year?"

"No, sadly. Everything was rented."

"Ah, too bad. Where is he staying? I have plenty of room at Granny James's house. He could stay with me."

Linnea realized that Pandora was fishing for information. "He's renting the loft next door at Emmi's house. You remember that sweet carriage house?"

"Oh." She pursed her lips in thought.

"You know, Pandora, you should join our pod."

Pandora tilted her head, perplexed. "What is a pod?"

Anna rose in a huff, brushed the sand off her bottom with quick slaps, then bent to pick up her surfboard. "I'm going to catch a wave."

# chapter eleven

*Joining the pod was more than a promise; it was a bond.*

June

LINNEA WAS MARKING days off the calendar. They seemed to breeze by like a spring wind, even as the days lengthened. The news reported a steady increase of people contracting the coronavirus, causing everyone to double down on their isolation.

Linnea's intimate group of family and friends who made up her quarantine bubble, or pod, was growing. It was time to close ranks. Theirs was a small group comprising four households—Cara, David, and Hope; Julia and Palmer; Linnea, Cooper, and Anna; Emmi, Flo, and John. But with the arrival of Gordon and Pandora, they called a meeting and agreed that these last two would be included.

Gordon was in quarantine up in the loft, and Pandora had just finished her two-week stint of isolation. Both agreed they would abide by the rules and hang out exclusively with the members of the pod and no one else. The agreement was rough water to navigate because everyone had to agree to socialize only with each other and not have interactions with other people. Because of Flo and Hope—the oldest and the youngest, and both compromised—they all understood what was at stake. If someone shopped, or went to work, then social distancing, hand-washing, and masks were nonnegotiable. The effort wasn't for the one individual, but for the good of the group. Joining the pod was more than a promise; it was a bond.

Tonight they were gathering to welcome a new pod in town—a select group of koi fish.

Linnea, Cooper, and Anna headed out together to Emmi's garden, Luna in tow. When they reached the gate, they were greeted with hearty calls of welcome as Emmi rushed over to unlatch the bolt. Linnea smiled at the festive mood on this balmy night. The stars overhead competed with a rising moon for attention. Emmi had set fairy lights around the slate patio and made batches of strawberry daiquiris that definitely were giving folks a buzz.

"Come in and take a seat!" Emmi called, ushering them to the circle of chairs near the pond, which she showed off with glowing pride.

Linnea thought how John had built his mother a real gift. The kidney-shaped pond dominated a corner of the garden, transforming it to a lush wonderland. It was bordered with rocks of different sizes, giving it a natural feel, and surrounded with plants. The pièce de résistance, however, was the waterfall. It had John's signature all over it.

Not satisfied with a mere trickle of water, John had created a waterfall that spilled joyfully over the rocks.

"John, it's a masterpiece," she exclaimed, drawing near.

"You built this?" Cooper asked disbelievingly.

"Yes," Emmi exclaimed with a mother's pride. "John can build anything."

"Will you build one for me?" asked Julia, sidling closer to John. "I need something to jump-start my garden and this might be the very thing."

"Get in line!" Cara called out, and raised her glass.

Everyone was in high spirits, enjoying fully not only the beautiful pond, but the spirit in which a son created such a gift for his mother.

Hope was enchanted with the fish and hovered around the pond, chasing them. John sat nearby, keeping an eye on her and making sure the fish weren't overfed by the eager child. She was meticulously dropping tiny pellets into the water, one by one.

The buzz of conversation was suddenly interrupted by a deep, baritone call from near the pond: *jug-o-rum, jug-o-rum*. Hope froze, arms out, her attention diverted.

"What was that?" she called out.

Cooper laughed and replied, "Either that's a bullfrog or an alligator."

"Here's to the former," Cara called out.

David chuckled and patted Cara's knee. "Don't scare her." Then to Hope he said, "Don't worry. It's not an alligator."

John crooned, "Well, I don't know, David. They do sound alike, you know."

Cara said in a low voice, "Not really. . . ."

Linnea bumped shoulders with John. "Stop, don't scare her."

John turned to Hope. "Have you been near an alligator?"

She shook her head, wide eyes.

"Well, let me tell you, if you ever hear the rumbling of a big bull alligator, you'd never confuse that sound with a frog's. It's so low and loud, you can practically feel the vibrations." He heard the doubtful comments of the group and called out, "I kid you not."

"He's right," David said. "I've heard them on Dewees, and it's powerful."

"That," John told Hope, "is the night call of a male bullfrog. As a matter of fact," he continued, leaning back into his chair, "he's my pet."

Hope drew near, wide-eyed. "He is?"

"Yep. He's taken up residence in this pond, which is okay by me. He does me a favor by eating up all manner of insects. He just sits real still, like this," he said, posing in a stiff-backed manner, his eyes wide open. He was rewarded with Hope's giggle. "He's got these big ol' eyes and just sits there, watching. He doesn't move a muscle. Then, when an insect flies by . . . *zap!*" John shot out his hand and poked Hope's belly. She shrieked and jumped back. "He snaps out his tongue and grabs it."

Hope was all the more enchanted by John. "Can I see him?"

"Well, darlin', we can try. We have to find him first. His big eyes reflect light. The thing to do is get a flashlight—they freeze when you shine light at them."

"Don't touch it, honey," warned Cara. "They'll give you warts."

Emmi laughed and slapped her knee. "Oh, come on, Cara. First of all, that's toads. Second, that's an old wives' tale. Only witches can give you warts."

"Then stay away from Miss Emmi," Cara teased back.

"Don't worry," John said. "Jeremiah is a clean bullfrog."

"Is that his name?"

"Yes," John said with a crooked grin, and let his gaze sweep over the circle of chairs. "Jeremiah was a bullfrog."

Palmer called out, "Was a good friend of mine."

Cooper added in a serious tone, "I never understood a single word he said, but I helped him drink his wine."

Everyone in the group started to groan and laugh. Hope looked confused.

"It's true," John said to Hope. "Jeremiah the bullfrog is famous. Google it if you don't believe me. Go on."

Hope ran across the patio to David, crashing into his knees. "Daddy, will you look up Jeremiah the bullfrog?"

David pulled his phone out from his pocket. "Sure, honey," he replied with a straight face, playing along. "Hold on a minute while I find it."

A minute later the first words of the song "Joy to the World" blared out of his phone.

One by one they all joined in the chorus, belting out the lyrics, clapping hands. Linnea leaned back and looked at the smiling faces. Julia was holding Palmer's hand. Hope leaned against her father. Cooper and

John sat side by side near the pond. Emmi sat beside Cara, who looked at her with eyes shining in the fairy lights.

John truly was a Peter Pan, she thought. Only this time, she appreciated his ability to bring a group together. Linnea couldn't remember the last time they'd gathered around like this on a warm night, singing together. This was a rare moment, and one she hoped they would repeat. The song ended, and Palmer was calling out for David to find another they could sing to, offering suggestions.

"I'll get my guitar," offered Cooper.

"David, find a Beatles song," Emmi directed. "Something we all know the words of."

Then Linnea heard a voice from behind her with a crisp British accent. "Hello. I hope I'm not disturbing you."

The talking stopped as all eyes went to the man in linen trousers and a white shirt. His skin was deeply tanned, and his blue eyes shone in the light as she imagined a bullfrog's might if caught by a flashlight. She felt the vibrations.

"Gordon!" she exclaimed, leaping from her chair, and hurried to his side. "I didn't expect you to come down until tomorrow."

He smiled into her eyes. "It's been two weeks. I've tested negative. And I couldn't wait till tomorrow to see you." He put out his arms.

Linnea hesitated a moment, more out of habit of not giving hugs, then stepped into his embrace.

She turned and, smiling, said to everyone who stared back at them with curiosity, "Y'all remember Gordon Carr."

Most called out a warm welcome, except for Palmer and John. They were polite, but lackluster.

"Will you excuse us?" Linnea asked. "We haven't had a chance to say hello." Then to Anna, "Will you bring Luna home?"

Gordon held out his hand and Linnea grasped it. They walked out from the fairy lights into the soft light of the stars and the moon. Away from the prying eyes. Linnea was aware of every neuron in her hand that was touching his, warm and dry. They didn't speak. The sound of gravel crunching beneath their feet heralded their progress to her home. By the time they reached the deck the sound of the Beatles' "Let It Be" filled the night air, and she smiled to herself, thinking, *Well chosen, David.*

Before they entered the house, Gordon stopped and turned to face her. He cupped her head in his hands and let his gaze sweep her face, his eyes bemused and a soft smile on his face.

"I just want to look at you for a moment," he said in a low voice. "You're really here. I've imagined being here with you so many times, I have to take a moment to let it sink in."

"I know," she said, staring into his eyes. "I don't quite know if I can believe it's really you and not my screen."

His lips moved to a quick smile in response; then his gaze kindled. His smile drifted away. Slowly, with intention, Gordon lowered his head to hers. Linnea closed her eyes and tilted her head in welcome. His lips touched hers, gently at first, tasting her. They pulled back slowly and looked at each other, each knowing that the spark was still there. They'd always had this spontaneous combustion, from their first kiss.

Her arms clung to his neck as she pressed herself against him. She relished the feel of him, his arms around her. She hadn't had sex in so long she'd worried how it would be. But there was no worry now. No negotiation of terms or thoughts of what this all might mean. There was only a thumping, beating, primeval drive. An urgent, pressing message of want and longing.

Still clinging together, lips pressed, they somehow managed to open the door to her bedroom and stumble across the room, clothes falling to the floor en route. With a soft growl in Gordon's throat and a giggle in hers, they collapsed together on the bed.

Which, they both knew, was where they were going to end up.

---

WHEN LINNEA FINALLY awoke, the dawn song had been replaced by the gentle beat of pop rock music coming from the kitchen. Turning her head, she saw Gordon's ruddy face lying on the pillow beside hers, his red-gold hair falling in disarray around his head, his mouth open. A soft snore revealed he was still in a deep sleep.

He'd earned his rest, she thought, smiling smugly. She stretched her arms over her head and yawned like a sated kitten. Blinking, awakening more, she noted that the sun was shining brightly through slits in the plantation shutters. She'd definitely missed yoga this morning, she thought with a silent laugh. Carefully pushing back the sheet from her naked body, she stealthily rose from the bed, not wanting to wake him. She slipped into her pink silk kimono and, tying it at the waist, tiptoed from the room, closing the door gently behind her.

Anna and Cooper were sitting at the round wood table in the kitchen, reading the Charleston *Post and Courier*, doing their usual duet of spooning granola into their mouths. Cooper's tanned back was curved over the table, his elbows resting there. All he had on were his boxers. Anna was once again wearing Linnea's lavender kimono, which Linnea figured was hers now since she'd never returned it. It didn't look like she was wearing anything beneath hers either. Linnea followed the scent of coffee to find a mug and pour herself a cup.

"Sleep well?" asked Cooper without looking up.

Anna snorted a laugh as she ducked her head into the newspaper.

"Ha-ha," Linnea said. Then, bringing her mug to her lips, she added, "Actually, I slept very little."

Cooper made a face and shook his head. "TMI. I'm your brother. Please."

Anna looked over her shoulder and offered an expression of approval. "Help yourself to granola."

Anna offered her homemade granola every day, and nearly every day Linnea politely declined. It was delicious, she'd tried it. But she wasn't a fan of a sweet breakfast, preferring fruit and yogurt, maybe some eggs, all of which she had waiting in the fridge to prepare for Gordon.

"No thanks, I'm waiting for Gordon to wake up. How long did y'all stay out last night?" she asked, coming to join them at the table.

"Not much longer after you left. You kind of took the mood with you," Anna said.

"Yeah," Cooper added, chewing. "John looked really bummed. He sat pounding away the beers in a stony silence. A real downer."

"Be fair. Cara and David had to leave to take Hope to bed," Anna said to Cooper. "That's what really started the exodus."

"Whatever you say," Cooper said. Then he looked over his shoulder toward the bedroom, making sure the coast was clear. "I don't know if you want to hear this," he began in a lowered voice. "You say it's over between you, but I don't think John's feeling the same."

Linnea waved her hand. That was old news for her. "It doesn't matter, does it? I'm with Gordon now." Her tone brooked no discussion.

"Cool," Cooper said, and dove back into his cereal.

The front door opened, and from the living room they heard Julia's voice calling out brightly, "Good morning! It's me. Your mother! I hope you're decent!"

They all bolted upright. Anna practically choked on her cereal and, after a moment's freeze, made a comical dash for the outside.

"She ran out faster than a cockroach when the light turns on," Cooper joked.

Linnea wished she'd done the same. She glanced back to make sure she'd closed her bedroom door.

The scent of her perfume arrived before Julia did. She entered all smiles, wearing a blur of pastels. She was neatly coiffed, her arms laden with several large bags.

From the corner of her eye, Linnea caught sight of Anna streaking across the deck on her way to her room. It was hard not to laugh.

"Mama, what are you doing here?"

"Can't a mother come visit her only two children?" she asked airily. "My children won't come to see me, so I had to come see them. It's after nine," she said, checking her watch. "You two aren't even dressed. I can see what's going on here."

Cooper and Linnea exchanged glances.

"Just because you're not working doesn't mean you should let your lives go to ruin. And you," Julia said, spearing Cooper with a gaze. "Your father is waiting for you to call him. He's holding a job for you."

Cooper's chair scraped the wood floor as he rose. "Yes, ma'am. I know," he said, carrying his dishes to the sink. He left them there and made a beeline for the exit. "I'll go get dressed."

Julia shook her head. "You've got to keep an eye on him," she said to Linnea. "He's doing so well. We don't want him to slip."

Linnea bit her tongue and kept silent. She couldn't even begin to imagine what her conservative mother would say if she knew what was going on in this house with Cooper.

"Is that coffee fresh?" Julia walked to the pot and inhaled. "Smells heavenly." She made herself at home, fixing herself a cup of coffee. She always drank it black, mindful of calories. She took a sip then smiled. "You always make a good cup of coffee," she said with approval.

Linnea didn't think it wise to tell her it was Anna who'd made the coffee this morning because she had slept in.

Julia walked to the pile of bags she'd carried in and pulled out the largest one, bearing the Target logo. "Here, darling. I bought this for you," she said, handing it to her.

"Gosh, what's this?" Linnea pulled a large box from the bag. "An instapot?"

"Yes!" Julia exclaimed, clearly excited by the gift. "Cara told me about them. She's been making soups and stews and absolutely loves it. I bought one for myself and one for you. You can make those beans and lentils you like in no time at all. And they're a wonder with beets."

Linnea looked at the small amount of counter space in the galley kitchen and wondered where she was going to put it. "Thanks, Mama. That was very thoughtful."

"You know how everyone is cooking up a storm these days. When I saw you last night, I thought you looked a bit thin. Are you all right?"

"Me? I'm fine," she said. "It must be the yoga. I'm firming up." Linnea knew she'd lost a little weight from all the stress of the past few weeks, but the yoga excuse would involve a lot less prying.

"Yoga?" Julia brightened at the idea. "You'll have to teach me. Maybe we can do it together."

"Uh, sure."

"How are things with Gordon?"

"Fine," Linnea said, bringing her mug to her lips and taking a sip. She saw her mother's eyes glittering with curiosity.

"Oh, just a minute," Julia said, setting her coffee on the counter. She went to pick up the other bags, which were from Anthropologie. "Be right back."

"Mama, wait," Linnea called, springing to her feet. But her mother was already heading down the hall to the bedrooms. She stopped in front of the seaward room and knocked briskly.

"Cooper? It's me. I have something for you."

Before Linnea could stop her, Julia pushed opened the door. Linnea looked over her mother's shoulders, then groaned silently. Julia's smile fell to an open gasp when she saw Cooper in his boxers tugging a T-shirt over his head and talking to Anna, lying on the bed with her kimono falling open, exposing a breast. The room was littered with Anna's clothing. But the real shock was seeing Cooper's dirty boxers lying on the floor as well. The stunned looks on their faces told Julia all she needed to know. She set down the bags and fled from the room, her cheeks pink against a pale face.

"What the hell?" Cooper said.

Anna fell back against the pillows, her hands over her face.

"Mama, wait!" Linnea called. She stuck her head in the bedroom, shook her head in ominous warning, then closed the door to hurry after her mother. She'd known Julia was going to find out about the Covid Couple sooner or later, but not this way.

She found Julia at the kitchen counter, staring down.

"Mama, it's okay—"

"Why didn't you tell me?" she said, spinning around, her eyes aflame with accusation.

Linnea didn't have time to answer. She saw her mother's eyes widen; turning, she groaned to herself at the sight of Gordon walking in wearing only his boxers. He smiled sleepily, like a cherub unaware of the depths of hell gaping open in the kitchen.

"Good morning," he said, and walked over to kiss the top of Linnea's head. "You wouldn't have tea?"

Cooper rushed into the room dressed in a spanking-new pair of shorts with the tag still hanging from them and a navy T-shirt. He stopped short when he scoped out the coup de grâce of Gordon's appearance. He put his hand over his face and leaned against the doorframe.

Julia drew herself up in an effort to assume some dignity. "I really must go."

Without another word she headed toward the front door, grabbing her purse as she passed.

There was dead silence in the room as Linnea and Cooper drew close and tried to piece together the last fifteen minutes and the repercussions that were sure to follow. Linnea was deeply shaken, Cooper more annoyed. Only Gordon was oblivious as he went about putting water in the teakettle and setting it to the flame. Finished, he turned and caught Linnea's face.

"Something wrong?" he asked.

"You could say that."

"What? Your mother?"

"Of course, my mother. Gordon, you came walking out in your underwear!"

"I didn't know your mother was here," he replied in self-defense.

"Hey, you think that's bad? Mom just got a look at Anna's boobs," said Cooper.

Linnea slumped against the counter with a soft groan.

"You're kidding?" Gordon asked, amused.

"I wish he was," Anna said, walking into the room dressed in khakis and an aquarium T-shirt, her uniform for her job.

"I'll say this for the morning," Cooper said. "It's the first time I've ever seen my mother speechless."

Linnea burst out a short laugh. "This isn't funny."

"What can she do to you?" Anna asked. "You're both adults." Then she raised a brow and looked at Cooper. "Well, one of you."

Cooper returned a cold stare.

Anna went to put her arms around him and kissed his cheek. "I've got to go. I want all the juicy details when I get back." With a wave, she grabbed her purse and departed.

Cooper cast a concerned glance at Linnea, then, shaking his head, left the room as well.

Linnea and Gordon stood in an awkward silence. The romantic mood of the morning had vanished. Linnea felt like she was in high school again, caught making out in the family room. This was her home. Her safe place. Yet it felt anything but that, and she felt again the walls closing in on her.

"I am sorry if I caused your mother any distress," Gordon said. "It wasn't my intention."

"I know, I know," Linnea said, and went to a chair and slid into it, shoulders hunched.

The teakettle began to whistle, a shrill mocking sound. Gordon turned off the flame, poured hot water into his mug, then joined Linnea at the table.

"Anna is right, you know," he said. "You're not a child. We're not doing anything wrong. I don't see why she's upset."

"That's because you're not Southern. She's a Southern mother and I'm her only daughter." She shook her head. "I don't expect you to understand. Trust me, this is not good."

He stepped closer and said sincerely, "Help me to understand."

She waved her hand. "There's the whole cultural thing. I suggest you try reading Faulkner. Or better yet, for my family, Tennessee Williams."

Gordon sat back in his chair, rebuked.

"I'm sorry. That wasn't fair. I'm upset. Because Mama was upset." She paused. "You asked me to explain and I'll try." She paused. "When I went to live with John in California, it was a bad scene. They felt I'd turned my back on them. My father especially. When I returned, tail between my legs, they welcomed me back. But they've been watching my every move. My mother lives in fear I'll end up a spinster."

Gordon reached out to put his hand over hers. "I doubt that will ever happen."

"She's also worried about my reputation. Worried I'll be hurt again." She paused and slid her hand back to her lap. "Worried I'm making wrong decisions."

Gordon looked at his hand alone on the table. "And . . . are you making a wrong decision?"

"About you? No."

"About me moving in with you?"

She looked up at him. "Maybe," she said, speaking honestly.

He pulled his hand back. He didn't appear angry. More hurt.

"Perhaps," he said in his even voice, "this house is a bit crowded." He lifted his gaze to meet hers.

"Perhaps it is."

"I see."

"Gordon, please understand. It's not you."

He laughed shortly.

She cringed, knowing that sounded like the worst cliché. "Listen to me. Not living together doesn't mean we shouldn't be together," Linnea tried to explain. "Yes, my mother for sure finds it improper. I mean"—she had to laugh—"she just found both her kids shacked up here. She must think it's a bordello."

Gordon had to laugh at that too.

"She'll get over it. In time. But then there's the other thing." She paused. "I've been having a hard time with this decision. I admit, I'm gun-shy. The last time I moved in with a man, that didn't turn out very well."

"I'm not John."

"I know that. You're not at all alike. When I say it's me, I mean it. *Me.* I'm not ready for a live-in relationship. And this pandemic isn't helping. My whole life feels applecart upset."

"Apple what?"

"It's an American expression that basically means fucked up."

"Ah. Right." He pursed his lips.

She chewed her lip, not knowing what else to say, giving him time to think.

At length, Gordon asked, his gaze still averted, "This isn't a breakup?"

"No, not at all. At least, I hope not. It's more a step back. It's what we'd planned originally. You were going to come back, rent a house. We'd have another summer to spend together, to get to know each other better. This other . . . it's all too much too soon. Really, don't you agree?"

Gordon shrugged.

"You're not hurt, are you?"

"Disappointed, maybe."

Linnea looked at his hands, scraped from his work on the boat. Noble work. "I'm sorry."

He didn't speak, and Linnea thought of Cooper's comment about how he held part of himself back.

Finally Gordon asked, "Do you think John will rent me his loft a bit longer?"

"Yes. I'm sure he will."

"That could work. We could be near each other, see each other every day, but not officially live together." He lifted his head and sought her gaze. "Would that be all right with you?"

Linnea released a heavy sigh of relief and leaped from her chair into Gordon's lap. He laughed, his arms out in surprise. Then he wrapped them around her, seemingly relieved too that somehow they'd weathered the storm.

OUTSIDE THE STORM clouds were gathering. Cara hurried up the beach path hoping to avoid the first drops of rain. Her backpack of sea turtle supplies and an armful of wooden stakes and the red bucket slowed her progress. Thank goodness the nest was within walking distance. The turtles were coming in steadily now. The islands had ten nests already, a good start. No one had given the turtles the memo about the pandemic.

Hope was sitting on the sofa with David, reading a book. When Cara stepped inside from the patio, Hope leaped from the sofa to run to her.

"Did you see any turtles?" she asked, wrapping her arms around Cara's sandy legs.

"No, no turtles. But we did find eggs."

"Baby turtles?"

"Someday!"

The doorbell rang. Cara looked over at David. "Are you expecting anyone?"

"No." He moved to rise.

Cara put out her hand. "I'm up. I'll get it."

She slipped out of her sand-crusted sandals, swept sand from her nylon pants, and hurried to the front door, smoothing her hair en route. Opening it, she saw Julia, her face flushed and eyes blazing.

"Well, hello! This is a surprise."

Julia didn't smile. "Do you have a minute?"

Cara felt a sudden wariness. Stepping back, she ushered Julia in and led her to the living room, hearing the clicking of her heels on the wood behind her. Julia was smartly dressed in pastel casual pants and top, and her ever-present pearls. Entering the room, Cara noted that David and Hope had disappeared.

"Can I get you some coffee? Water?"

"Coffee if you've got it. Don't go making a fresh pot."

"I have one of those fabulous Italian espresso machines. Makes a cup at a time, freshly ground beans and all. Cappuccino or black?"

"With all that buildup, I'll try the cappuccino."

Thunder cracked overhead, immediately followed by a torrential rain beating against the windows.

"You made it just in time," Cara called out.

"What a day," Julia said, settling herself on the sofa.

A few minutes later Cara returned to the living room balancing two cups of cappuccino in her hands. She offered one to Julia, then sat in a chair opposite her. Outside the palm fronds shook with the wind and dark skies made the morning look like night.

"So . . ." Cara said as an opener. "What's up?"

"I don't know where to begin," Julia said. She took a dainty sip, then set the cup and saucer on the coffee table.

Cara thought the storm outside the window matched the expression on her face. *Bad winds coming,* she told herself.

"I just came from the beach house."

Cara leaned forward to set her coffee cup on the table. She was on full alert.

"What I have to tell you will shock you," Julia began. She dramatically waved her hand, sending the row of bracelets clattering. "You can't imagine how I felt. I had to come here straightaways. You have to know what's happening in that . . . that . . ."

"Please, Julia. Just tell me."

Julia took a calming breath. "Okay. I went to see my children this morning. I had gifts." She paused. "You did know that Cooper moved into the beach house?"

"Yes. Linnea told me."

Julia nodded. "I'm not happy about it. I mean, I haven't seen my son in almost a year and I was looking forward to time with him. Palmer too. But that's neither here nor there," she added. "Anyway, as I said, I brought gifts. An instapot for Linnea, because you told me how wonderful it was, and some clothes for Cooper. For the summer."

Cara started tapping her foot.

"I enter the house, calling out like I always do. Thank goodness I did. Linnea was in the kitchen, and I went back to deliver my gift to Cooper. I open the door to his room, and oh, Cara! I found Cooper in his underwear with that roommate of Linnea's."

"Anna."

"Their clothes were everywhere. *Both* their clothes, if you catch my meaning."

"I'm following you," Cara said, trying not to smile. "I'm sure that was embarrassing."

"Wait. There's more. I walk away, of course. Then in the kitchen I'm talking to Linnea and who comes strolling out in his boxers as free as you please?"

"Let me guess. Gordon."

"You knew?"

"It's not hard to figure that one out."

"It doesn't bother you? That they're all sleeping together?"

"No. Why should it? They're all adults."

"It's your house. It's a bordello."

Cara stifled her laugh, not wanting to shame Julia. "I think you're overreacting. Come on, Julia, you had to know that Linnea and Gordon were sleeping together. And as for Cooper and Anna, that caught me by surprise too. What do you want me to do?"

"Tell Linnea to clear the men out of the house. That's what I would do."

Cara shook her head. "I can't do that. It's Linnea's house now. And I trust her judgment. Julia, the hardest part of getting older is allowing our young to make their own decisions. Even mistakes."

"But Linnea's reputation . . ."

"You have no worries there. She's rock solid. My hat's off to you for raising such a principled young woman." Cara looked at her hands. Sand still clung to her nails. "She's going through a tough time now."

"You mean being laid off?"

"Yes. Partly."

"Oh yes—Gordon coming back. And John being here. I know."

"Honestly? I believe they both are just distractions right now from the real question she's wrestling." She saw worry crinkle Julia's brow and was quick to reassure her. "It's the existential question we all struggled with when we were young. Perhaps we still do, to a lesser degree. She's asking who she is and what she wants out of life."

Dawning washed over Julia's features. "Cooper too."

"All of them. Being young is great, but there are hurdles to get over. Makes being old feel pretty good."

Julia's shoulders lowered as she smiled. "Someone once asked me if I could go back and be young again, would I do it. I said only if I could take what I knew now with me."

Cara thought about the ups and downs of her life. "Girlfriend, me too. No way I'd go back and do it all again. I'm happy right where I am."

Julia sighed and said in a singsong voice, "What's a mother to do?"

"Try to relax. They're both young. You've got a long way to go."

"Look who's talking," Julia said with a laugh. "Hope is only six!"

"God help us."

Julia bent to retrieve her cup. "Thanks for listening."

"Feel better?"

She scrunched her lips and shook her head. "Not really. But calmer. I swanny, I hope I survive to see those two children of mine married and settled."

Cara brought her cup to her lips to swallow any more words she might be tempted to say.

# chapter twelve

*One of the most beautiful surprises coming out of the pandemic
was how a lot of creative people were finding new and
unique ways to use their energies and imagination.*

OUTSIDE THE WEATHER was dreary, all overcast gray skies that didn't show any signs of clearing. Inside, it was just as dreary. The pod, as Linnea now called the group, was hanging out in the living room, slouched on chairs and sofas, drinking wine or beer or their alcohol of choice. She couldn't count the number of wine bottles in the recycling bin these days. She would have been embarrassed to put the bin at the curb except that everyone else's bin was full of wine bottles too.

The ever-present television was on, something she abhorred. Gordon and Cooper were watching some sporting event that was not even in real time. Anna and Pandora were reading, Anna with a real paper-and-spine book, Pandora listening to an audiobook.

"What are we doing here?" Linnea asked nobody in particular. "I can feel my life slipping away, a minute at a time."

Cooper propped his feet on the coffee table, his hands clasped behind his head. "You think this is bad? Remember the weeks spent in the aftermath of hurricanes? The Internet down, electricity off. I was counting the toes on my feet for something to do."

"Look out there," Linnea said, gesturing toward the window. "It's been like that for days. I think I have seasonal affective disorder."

"It's real," Gordon said, and patted the sofa beside him for her to join him. To the others he said, "I came from spending a few weeks on the Cornish coast on a tank of a boat doing research. We were glad to have a gray day, if it wasn't raining. I feel right at home."

Linnea laughed and sat next to him, offering him another beer. She tucked up her legs, then bent to pick up Luna, who was standing on her hind legs, begging with those big brown eyes, to go up on the couch. She placed the dog on her lap and immediately Gordon began stroking her ears.

"Did I tell you my mum has Cavaliers?" he said. "Four of them."

"You didn't. What kind?"

"She likes the whole colors. She has two ruby and a black and tan, and a Blenheim like Luna. They're sweet dogs, but I warn you, they don't take to house-training readily."

"Oh yeah," Anna said, looking up from her book. "I meant to tell you. She left a gift in the bathroom. It's still in there."

Linnea groaned. "I told you to keep the door shut. And why didn't you just pick it up?"

Anna snorted and said, "Not in my job description," and put her nose back in the book.

Gordon patted Linnea's leg in commiseration.

Cooper reached for the remote and began flipping through the channels. "Nobody is playing anything. Sports are all canceled. Even NASCAR. Oh, check this out—Bobby Flay. My day is saved." He smirked.

"Wait, keep it!" Pandora exclaimed, pulling out her earbuds. "I love him. I was thinking," she said, turning to Linnea. "We should start cooking together. Really fun, fabulous meals. What do you say?"

Linnea glanced at Anna and raised her brows. "I absolutely love that idea. Let's do it."

"Fabulous," she said, using what Linnea was figuring out was her current favorite word.

Cooper was still flicking through channels. "What have you all got against Bobby?" Pandora protested.

"I don't know. Maybe because I don't know an oven from a sofa," Anna said. "I happen to love the news. There's so much going on." She turned to Cooper. "Put on CNN."

"No news!" everyone called out at once.

Pandora said, "With all of us gathered under one roof, better to keep politics to ourselves. Especially in an election year."

"Uh, Pan," Gordon said, "I'm pretty sure everyone in this room is on the same side. And I'm not talking Brexit."

Pandora put her hand up. "No, don't tell me. No divisiveness in the pod."

"What else you got?" Linnea asked her brother.

"Man, slim pickings. There are some reruns. How about Wimbledon."

"Ooh, Wimbledon," exclaimed Pandora.

"How about some surfing in Australia?" asked Gordon. "Check ESPN."

Everyone perked up at this suggestion.

"Yeah, surfing," said Pandora, smiling at Gordon.

Linnea groaned inwardly at Pandora's increasingly obvious effort to always take Gordon's side.

Anna rose and said, "I'm going for a refill."

"Slow down. It's only one o'clock," Linnea said.

"It's five o'clock somewhere. Anybody want something?"

The porch door slid open and John came in like a breath of fresh air. His face was lit with excitement as he stepped into the room and clapped his hands.

"Up and at 'em!" he called out.

Cooper groaned and threw a pillow at him.

John caught it in midair and tossed it back. "Seriously, man, all hands on deck! I've got a great idea."

More groans sounded in the group.

"Do you know what this bunch of zombies needs?" When no one answered, he pushed on. "A fort. A man cave. Sorry, I mean a pod cave. And I've found it."

Everyone turned their heads lazily and without enthusiasm.

"Come on, follow me. I'll show you."

No one moved.

"Hey, I said *come on*! Look, it's got to be better than this, right?"

"We're fine," Gordon said, and slipped his arm around Linnea's shoulders.

Cooper clicked off the television, rose, and tossed the remote on the table. "He's right. I've got to get out of here." He put his hand out to Anna. "Let's go, babe."

Pandora rose and reached for Gordon's hand. "Come on, grumpy." Begrudgingly, he took her hand and rose. "Come on, Lin," she added with a bright smile.

Linnea tilted her head, curious about Pandora's brazen grabbing of Gordon's hand.

"Far be it from me to be the spoilsport," she said, and, lifting Luna, followed the group out the porch door. She giggled to herself as they marched in single file across the driveway and through the white picket fence gate into Emmi's yard. They looked like they were playing follow the leader, and leading the troupe was Peter Pan. The boy who wouldn't grow up.

John stopped in front of the carriage house. Linnea had spent many hours upstairs in the loft apartment that summer with John, the amazing place that once was Flo's mother's abode. But in all the years she'd been staying at the beach house next door, she'd never seen the inside of the lower area that had been Miranda's studio.

John waited till they were all gathered; then, in the manner of a master of ceremonies, he lifted the wood bar that bound the two barn-style wood doors together and swung them open, calling out, "Ta-da!"

Everyone took a step forward. The inside resembled a barn, rising past rafters to a high ceiling. Everyone in the group was creative enough to spot a treasure when they saw it. The space was packed to the gills with stuff, but peeking from behind the wooden bedposts, the wicker rockers, the rolled-up oriental carpets, were the gorgeously rendered, vividly colored sea animals swimming in blues and golds in Miranda's mural: whales, dolphins, jellyfish, sea turtles, sharks, and countless colorful fish. Linnea had seen the similar mural in John's loft upstairs, but this one was larger and even more breathtaking.

"Smashing," Pandora said, the first to break the silence. "I feel like I've walked into a discovery of some lost art and treasures. An Egyptian tomb." She strode into the carriage house and let her hand lovingly trail through a thick coating of dust, creating a bright streak on a mahogany dining table.

"It's amazing," Anna said, walking up to a vintage wicker rocking chair. "Whose stuff is this, anyway?"

"Flo's mostly," John said. "And some of it is my mom's. It's been gathering dust in here for years." He was less interested in what was *in* the space than the space itself. "Look how much room there is in here. Once we clear this stuff out, we'll have our very own fort. A place to hang out. Neutral territory. Switzerland."

"Dude, your mom's okay with us all doing this?" asked Cooper, spreading out his hands to indicate the mountain of stuff.

"Okay? She's been begging me to do this for years. What do you say? Y'all go grab something and let's clear it all out!"

"The game is on," exclaimed Gordon.

In good spirits, they all dove in.

Pandora was, as usual, right behind Gordon. "Look at this charmer!" she exclaimed, drawing his attention to a stone statue.

Anna cast Linnea a warning glance about Pandora's advances. Linnea shrugged, and together they marched into the fray.

For the next hour, they carted out objects to the yard. Linnea laughed as from time to time she'd hear someone call out, "Oh, cool!" or "Man, look at this!" or "I haven't seen this since I was a kid!" Boxes of china, wicker furniture, Christmas decorations, an old lawn mower and other assorted tools, various antiques (some good, some not so good), and boxes of *National Geographic* magazines gradually gathered in the yard. It was a motley collection. The damp magazines were the first to go to the corner for trash. Most of the carpets, mildewed beyond repair, were also tossed. Inside the barn, Anna parked herself in front of some boxes of old books.

"It's heartbreaking," she said, separating the books into piles. "Most of these are spotted badly with mold. They have to go." She sighed as she dumped them in the trash bin. "It's like cancer. It spreads to all the good books." Then she gasped. "What the hell?"

Linnea turned her head and called out, "What did you find?"

Anna carefully flipped through the delicate pages to check the copyright. Mouth open, she pointed to it, then looked up, shocked. "Yep. There it is. March 1852. This is a first edition of *Uncle Tom's Cabin; or, Life Among the Lowly!*"

"That's the book against slavery, right?" asked Pandora.

"Back in the day, it was a huge influence when it was published," Linnea added. "It outsold the Bible."

Gordon asked, "But isn't 'Uncle Tom' a racial slur?"

"It's sad, but today it is," Linnea replied, realizing that, being British, he might not understand the history behind the book. "The original character of Tom was inspired by a real man, but time and racism twisted the character until today calling someone an Uncle Tom means he's a sellout to the race."

"But that was so not what Stowe wrote." Anna looked lovingly at the book, closing it and letting her palm rest reverentially upon the tattered cover. "Those of us who love old books live for moments like this. These volumes," she said, "are definitely worth investing in to get them restored."

"May I see it?" asked Gordon. He picked it up and leafed through the pages, then brought the book to his nose. "Yes, definitely mold and mildew. But not too bad. I think you're right, Anna. It can be restored." He looked at Linnea, whose gaze questioned how he knew this. "My parents have a library full of old books," he explained. "They strive for climate control, but they're always checking for mold."

"It's a massive library," Pandora chimed in. "Quite impressive."

Linnea shot Pandora a look. "You've been to Gordon's parents' house?"

Pandora cast a furtive glance toward Gordon. "Yes, once," she said in a casual way. "Ages ago. My parents know his parents. Socially, you know."

Gordon looked at his shoes.

Linnea considered how Pandora's parents, very well connected socially in England, would know the parents of a university professor.

"Anna," Pandora asked, adroitly changing the subject, "how did you get into old books?"

Anna stretched out her leg with a soft groan. Her yoga pants were smeared with dirt and dust, but she looked as happy as a pig in a mud bath. "My mother didn't exactly have a library," she said, casting an amused glance at Gordon. "More like cartons of books she kept piled up in the attic or under beds. We had as many bookshelves as you could squeeze into a rented house or a trailer . . . so, not a lot." She laughed self-deprecatingly. "Mama didn't have one dime to rub against another, but she loves her books. Truth is, she's a hoarder of books. She volunteers for organizations that collect old books— libraries, schools. Her role is to spot the rare one, the find that they could auction off. She taught me everything I know." She laughed mirthlessly with memory. "I've spent many hours at her side, leafing through books. Now I love it too—the history, the feel of the eras right under your fingers, authentic and true. Like this book," she said, reaching up to take hold of *Uncle Tom's Cabin* again. "This is the real deal."

"I don't know about books," Linnea said, opening a box that was filled with bolts of fabric. She lifted several out, revealing vibrant patterns. "But I know fabric. Take a look! Sea turtles, dolphins, jellyfish, like the murals. And here, coral." She picked up bolt after bolt. "These blues and greens are gorgeous cottons."

Linnea's mind spun with possibilities. She could sew almost anything. She especially loved to make her own clothing. This trove of vintage fabric was a gold mine. Suddenly another idea struck. "Hey, Anna, Pandora. We can use this fabric to make face masks. We can donate them to organizations, like the aquarium."

"Great idea," Anna said from her pile of books.

"I don't sew, darling," Pandora said, wiping dust from a small bookcase.

"But you can cut patterns," Linnea teased.

Suddenly Cooper jumped back, dropping the old carton in his hands. He stood spread-eagled. "Holy shit! A rat!"

A flurry followed as most everyone jumped back.

Cooper bolted out of the garage. "It jumped straight out at me, like a bullet. Holy crap."

"What's the matter, haven't you seen a rat before?" asked Anna. She rose to her feet and walked over to inspect the corner the rat had come from.

"Not up close and personal," Cooper said. "I have this rule. I keep to my side and they stay on theirs."

Linnea kept her distance. "Is there another one there?"

"You know what they say, where there's one . . ." Anna replied.

"Okay, game over," Pandora said, raising her hands and heading out.

"Wait a minute, hold on," John called out, waving her back. "It's just a rat. It's not surprising one would be in here. Mice too. But hey, they're not dangerous animals."

"Until you get bit," said Linnea.

"Gordon, you work with wildlife," John said. "Help me out."

"There are always rats around. But you know, I read this article," Gordon said with seriousness. "It was about how now that the restaurants are shut down during the pandemic, rats are looking for new places to forage."

"Thanks for sharing, Einstein," John said with a nod to the ladies.

"What a bunch of babies," Anna said, picking up a broom and heading to the corner. She began vigorously sweeping out the area while the others watched. "Yeah, there's poop here all right. It's a right big ol' nest." She paused and looked over her shoulder. "What are you all waiting for? Grab a broom."

"Oh, no," Pandora demurred. "I didn't sign up for hunting."

"Why not?" Linnea asked. "Isn't that what you do when you go on fox hunts? Chase down animals?"

"We don't . . ."

"Save the debate." John went to the corner of the barn and grabbed two more brooms. "Linnea, Pandora, why don't you start sorting out what's good and what's trash? Gentlemen"—he held out the brooms to Gordon and Cooper—"choose your weapons."

The sun was lowering by the time the barn was cleared out. Several trash bags were lined up at the curb. Linnea put her hands on her hips and took a sweeping look at the group. *Her pod.* They all looked like ragamuffins, covered in dirt and grime, but they were smiling, joking, drinking beers, acting more like a group of friends.

"John, what are you going to do with all this stuff?" Anna asked.

John was carrying one of the last boxes out of the barn. "You can help me with a garage sale later."

"Sell it?" Anna exclaimed. "This is good stuff. I'm going to be first in line."

"I want this," Pandora called, pulling a fox stole from the wardrobe. It was the vintage kind with the fox biting its tail. "It's in remarkable shape." She winked at Linnea. "For my next fox hunt."

"Hands off the vintage clothing," Linnea called out. "I call dibs. Except for that," she conceded to Pandora. "I don't wear fur. Leave the hats too!" She pointed at Pandora, who was trying on a lovely shaped black felt hat with a veil. Pandora stuck her tongue out playfully and tossed the hat at Linnea.

En masse they all began rooting through the items, each finding something he or she wanted.

"Will you look at all you've done!" Emmi exclaimed as she approached. Her red hair was bound up in a bun and she wore a sparkly T-shirt under a jean jacket. "I came to ask if y'all were hungry. I made up a big pot of spaghetti. Now I'm all aflutter." She put her hands on her hips. "Kids, you've done wonders," she exclaimed, walking into the barn and gaping joyfully. "I can see the murals! I haven't seen them since Miranda was alive. She used to paint her big oils in here. What days those were. Cara and I played dress-up in all those clothes." She grew teary-eyed and sniffed. "I don't know how to thank you. I've wanted to get that firetrap cleaned out for ten years."

"You have wonderful treasures," Pandora said, lifting up a painting of an egret.

"Miranda painted that," Emmi said, stepping into the barn. "It's yours if you like it." She turned to address everyone. "All of you, if you find something you like, take it as my thank-you." She put her hands together. "Except, perhaps, the really good antiques. And any silver, of course. And anything else of great value," she added in a lower voice.

"Mom, where did the joggling board come from?" John asked. He walked over to the sixteen-foot narrow plank set between what looked like two rocking sawhorses. It was painted a glossy color called Charleston green, more black than green, faded only a bit by the years.

Emmi came closer to investigate. "This brings back memories," she said wistfully, and reached out to touch the long dark slab of wood. "This was Miranda's. It's been here for as long as I can remember. Flo said she inherited it from the family that built the house. John," she said, her face softening with the memory, "I used to hold you and bounce you up and down on this thing. It was one of the only things that would stop you from crying."

"I'm sorry," Pandora interrupted, "but what is it?" She spread out her hands.

"Legend goes," explained Emmi, "joggling boards started in South Carolina, back in the eighteen hundreds. If I recall correctly, some plantation owner's sister came to visit, and she had bad rheumatism. Their Scottish cousins sent a model of a joggling board and suggested she build one. They claimed that the gentle bouncing would help. So she did. The idea took off, and local carpenters have been making them ever since. They used to be called courting benches." She moved to one side of the board, swiped off a thick layer of dust, and sat down. She bounced up and down a bit. "See? Joggle."

"Ah, as in jiggle joggle," said Pandora.

"John," Emmi called out, waving her son closer. "Sit down on the other end and let's give them a demonstration."

John obliged.

"Okay, now. Start bouncing. Whoa!" Emmi exclaimed. "Gently! You don't mean to knock the other person over. You joggle. See?" she said, gently bouncing up and down.

"It's like a trampoline," Anna said.

"Sort of," said Cooper.

As the board bounced, Emmi and John slid closer together.

Gordon laughed. "I think I see where this experiment is headed. Thus, the courting bench."

John drew close to his mother and kissed her head before hopping off.

"Folks used to say," Emmi continued, "if you had a joggling board on your front porch, you would never have an unwed daughter. Then again, it never worked for Flo." She shrugged. "But the rest of y'all might give it a try."

"I have an idea!" John said.

"Another one?" Linnea teased.

John held out his hand and escorted his mother off the board. Then he hopped up on the board on both feet. The board quivered beneath his weight, but John held out his arms and kept his balance. Then he began joggling, arms stretched out.

"It looks like you're surfing!" exclaimed Linnea.

"Exactly. We can do the Home Break Challenge!" John shouted out. When no one reacted, he said, "Guys, really? You haven't been watching the Instagram Home Break Challenge?"

They all returned blank stares.

He hopped off the board and pulled out his phone. "Where've you been? You've got to see this." After a minute of punching his phone, he held it out.

Linnea and Gordon hovered close, and Cooper leaned over his shoulder.

"It's this challenge set up for stay-at-home surfers for the pandemic. People everywhere are making these rad videos of themselves pretending to surf."

"Oh, that one's hysterical," Cooper said beside John's ear as he drew closer for a look.

"Personal space, man," John said.

"Sorry, dude," Cooper said, backing off.

John handed Cooper the phone while Gordon and Pandora pulled out their own phones and started to watch. John caught Linnea's eye and they smiled, seeing everyone laughing into their phones.

"Okay, here's my idea," John said to the group. "I'm thinking *we* do the challenge. Lowcountry style."

"On a joggling board!" called out Cooper.

"Bingo."

"Cool." Anna was really into the idea. "We need supplies to create the scene."

"Look around," Linnea said. "We're surrounded by supplies."

"We have the perfect backdrop," John said, pointing to the mural.

The beat kicked up as everyone got into the idea. John and Cooper carried the sixteen-foot-long joggling board to set in front of the section of Miranda's murals that displayed a shark with surreal gold teeth.

"Reminds me of a shark I ran into off the coast of Australia," Gordon said.

"Oh yeah, Lin told me you were part of Surfrider International," said John.

Cooper nodded with appreciation. "That's cool."

"We need to come up with a plan," John said. "I was thinking we create a scene like we're surfing on the ocean, right?"

Linnea watched everyone laughing as they pulled out art supplies from Miranda's boxes and chests—paint, brushes, glitter stars, stencils, buttons and bows, and anything one could imagine. It felt to her like decorating a parade float. They each had ideas, shouting out "What if we try . . ." or "Hey, I've got an idea."

Linnea took a moment to stand back and watch the magic unfolding. They'd gone from sitting around moping to this spontaneous combustion of creativity. Perhaps one of the most beautiful surprises coming out of the pandemic was how a lot of creative people were finding new and unique ways to use their energies and imagination.

They took a break for a feast of spaghetti, garlic bread, and lots of chianti, after which Emmi chased them from doing the dishes. "You've done enough for me today," she declared. "Go off and play, children," she called out playfully.

They ran off to grab their wet suits for the video, before congregating again a little later in the barn. The sun had set, and John had turned on the barn lights.

Linnea and Anna walked back from the beach house across the driveway. Anna almost skipped, she was so excited. "This is so fun," she said. "John's such a creative guy."

Linnea felt duty-bound to defend Gordon. "Gordon worked on a lot of the design too."

"Oh, sure, no contest here," Anna said in her blithe fashion. "It's just, well, it was John's idea to begin with. If it wasn't for him, we'd probably all still be lying around the living room. Oh, wow," she exclaimed with awe as they approached the barn.

Linnea was caught up in the moment of wonder. The night was balmy and the barn looked surreal all lit up and with all the glorious murals turning the area into an underwater wonderland. John had found some stand-up photographer lights and set them up near the joggling board, along with table lamps connected to outlets with extension lines.

"The place looks amazing," Linnea said to John.

"I couldn't have done it without my sidekick," John said, pointing to Cooper.

"Good job," Gordon called out as he walked down the stairs from the loft. "It looks like a TV studio."

"I'm ready for my close-up," called out Pandora as she stepped into the barn and removed her robe.

All talking stopped. Everyone else, men and women alike, was clad in a black wet suit. Pandora was wearing a skimpy Balmain black elastic bikini that showed off her curves.

"Uh, we're supposed to be wearing wet suits," Anna deadpanned.

"My wet suit is in my storage at the house," Pandora said, lifting her palms. "At least I found a black swim suit."

"I was watching the videos," Gordon said, "and I saw this one that created a set of waves using fabric." He showed them the video. Two people shook them to make it look like waves. "I thought we might give it a try."

"Great idea, Gordon," said Pandora. She went to the pile of fabrics. "How about this?" she exclaimed, pulling out a bolt of brilliant-blue fabric. "And there's white too. Lin, give me a hand."

Linnea groaned inwardly at seeing her beautiful fabric pulled out of the boxes, but went along. Pandora unfolded the material and found there was more than enough to stretch out the two colors along the length of the joggling board.

"We have to lift it up and down, like waves," Pandora called out. Linnea took the other side and they demonstrated.

Pandora's breasts jiggled enticingly with her effort. "How's it look?" she called out, panting with the effort.

The men stared.

"Looks fantastic," Gordon deadpanned.

"Yeah," echoed Cooper and John.

The fabric fell to the ground. "It's a good workout for my arms," Pandora said, a bit breathless.

Cooper put a Bluetooth speaker on a box and punched his phone; a moment later the song "Wipe Out" blared out.

"The Surfaris!" John called out, and high-fived with him.

"Okay girls," Cooper called out. "Three, two, one, action!"

"Let's do this!" John hopped on the joggling board and, spreading out his arms, bounced on the board, giving a good imitation of being on a surfboard.

Cooper was filming, grinning. "Lookin' good!"

The others cheered him on.

"Linnea!" John called out. "Remember the time we did the tandem longboard?"

She smiled, remembering the long summer they'd spent surfing together, falling in love.

"Get up here, girl!" John reached out.

Feeling Gordon's eyes on her, she reluctantly joined him at the joggling board. Taking her hand, John pulled her up, and after a brief totter on the narrow board, she got her balance. John stood behind her, grasping her hips. Then they began to bounce up and down, joggling. Linnea felt the rise and fall, and even with her arms out, she could barely keep her balance. It was a bit like surfing. It was, in fact, the most fun she'd had in ages.

Below them, Pandora and Anna were lifting the blue and white fabric like two girls twirling a rope. Linnea couldn't stop grinning and joined the whooping and shouting while Cooper filmed the video.

When they were done, everyone was laughing except for Gordon.

He walked up to the board, smiling. "Since we're the only official couple here," he said to Linnea, "let's give it a go."

John released Linnea and jumped off the board. Gordon nimbly climbed up, took a firm hold of Linnea, and once again Cooper punched the play button. This time the Beach Boys were singing "Surfin' Safari." As Cooper rolled the video and the girls shook the fabric, Linnea put on a grin and tried to play the part of the fun surfer girl. But the moment had passed, and it felt forced. She saw John opening the cooler and pulling out a beer; he opened it, tilted his head back, and downed it.

When they were done, Cooper called out, "Got it. We're good!"

"Wait! Give me a chance," Pandora called out, rushing to the board. "Gordon, don't jump down. I need a partner."

Linnea got down while Gordon helped Pandora climb aboard. She looked sexy in her designer bikini next to the handsome man in a wet suit. Knowing Pandora's luck, this video would probably win the challenge.

Linnea took Pandora's place at one end of the fabric and, on cue, the speaker played "Wipe Out" again. As the guitar strum rolled, Anna and Linnea began creating the wave effect again, panting with effort. Anna speared her with a look that clearly said, *What's with her?*

Linnea couldn't help but wonder the same.

# chapter thirteen

*If it's not one thing, it's another.*

TOGETHER THEY FINISHED the barn project, separating the wheat from the chaff. The trash was collected from the street the following morning—in the nick of time. Heavy rains hit the lowcountry again, driving everyone back indoors.

Linnea stood at the kitchen window washing the breakfast dishes and watched Cooper, Gordon, and Anna scurry to their cars in the rain. She listened to the car engines fire up as one by one they drove off— Gordon to the Marine Resources Research Institute on James Island, Anna to the South Carolina Aquarium in Charleston, and Cooper to the building site in Mount Pleasant. She wasn't jealous that they had jobs. She only felt lost that she did not.

After she finished tidying the kitchen, she went to her room, where the stack of fabrics she'd discovered in the barn was now piled on the dresser. She'd washed several bolts and folded them, and now they sat waiting for her imagination to decide what to do.

She wanted to be useful. She was one of the lucky ones in the pandemic. She wasn't sick. She didn't have to worry about being evicted. She had roommates to help with expenses. People who had her back. As Cara had told her when she was laid off, "We pay it forward."

Linnea picked up a pattern with sea turtles, and thought again how it would make for great masks for the aquarium. Ones that made people feel good about wearing them. Smiling, Linnea went in search of her sewing machine.

———————

THAT EVENING, LINNEA sat at the kitchen table putting the dozens of masks she'd sewn into bags. She looked up when the front door swung open and Anna stomped in, hazel eyes blazing, sputtering with rage. Her khaki pants were soaked from the knee down, as were her tennis shoes. A pool of water collected where she stood in the entry.

"What on earth?" asked Linnea.

"Flooding!" Anna shouted.

"Was it bad?"

Flooding was a problem of biblical proportions in Charleston. Linnea knew, as many locals did, to avoid going into the city when it rained.

"Goddamn," Anna swore. She wiped wet hair from her forehead.

"When is this city going to get a grip on the flooding? It doesn't even have to rain to flood anymore." She bent to pull off her shoes and socks with angry movements.

Cooper, hearing her shouts, came in to investigate. "Hey, Anna. You look like the proverbial wet hen."

She shot him a sideways glance. "Thanks."

He laughed and went to the fridge. "The city needs some kind of barrier."

"You mean the wall. I don't know what good that would do," Linnea said. "Most of Charleston is built up from swampland. It's been flooding since the city was built. I think they should consult Holland. They're experts at keeping the water out."

Anna strode in and headed to the sink to wash her hands. "Well, they've got to do something. And soon. I'm so mad I could cry. Trying to get home was a nightmare." She grabbed the towel and dried her hands with agitation. "I took all these side routes to avoid flooded streets and ended up caught on a one-way street that was flooded. Some ass was behind me honking and there was no place to turn around. So I tried to get through."

Cooper, scanning the contents of the fridge, paused to look at Anna. "Oh no."

"Oh yeah," she replied. "I got halfway through and, sure enough, it got deep. The car died."

"Oh no," Linnea sighed in commiseration.

"That saltwater is death for an engine," said Cooper.

"Ya think?" Anna scowled and said, "Hand me a beer, would you?"

Cooper reached in and pulled out a few. Linnea put her hand up to refuse. After handing Anna her beer, he asked, "So where's your car now?"

She took a long swallow. "Sitting in the street, blocking traffic. It has to be towed. There's a long list of us waiting to get our cars towed."

"I'm sorry," Linnea said. "Can it be repaired?"

"I don't know," Anna said morosely. "Even if it could, I doubt I could afford it."

The reality of this shocked Linnea. She knew too well how tight money was. "What are you going to do without a car? You have to get to work."

Anna bent her head. "I don't know."

"I'll drive you."

Linnea turned her head to see Gordon standing at the outer door into the kitchen. He had returned from work and already had a beer in his hand from the loft.

"Hey, come on in."

Gordon smiled and came to gently kiss her. Then, straightening, he focused again on Anna. "I couldn't help but overhear. I drive through the city every morning on my way to James Island. I can drop you off. We'll have to work out how you'll come back. I can pick you up on days I'm not doing fieldwork."

Cooper offered, "I'll pick you up on the other days."

"Thanks, guys. Really." Anna looked at the bottle in her hands. "I don't know how long I'll be working anyway. There are whisperings of another layoff until they can open the doors again. But in the meantime," she said with renewed energy, "I'm going to study up on the flooding situation. There's a lot of controversy about it. What's that saying, revenge is best served cold? Mine will be ocean temperature."

"Watch out, world," Cooper said, clinking bottles with her.

"Great idea," Gordon said with encouragement. "Dig in. Research. Get your own answers."

"Right," she said, a light sparking in her eyes. "That's just what I'm going to do."

---

A WEEK PASSED in a whirl of sunny, hot days, and the turtles were busy laying eggs on the beaches. Linnea slapped the sand from her hands and surveyed the nest. Three wooden stakes held the orange tape that surrounded the nest, protecting it from foot traffic. The mother turtle had laid the nest smack in front of a beach access path, so Linnea had moved the eggs to a safer location high on the dunes. Ninety-two eggs was a decent number. Only time would tell how many hatchlings would emerge in fifty or so days.

Like everything else, the turtle team schedule and duties had changed because of the pandemic. The Department of Natural Resources permitted only two team members to work at a nest, to maintain social distancing. Linnea missed the camaraderie she usually felt with her teammates each morning, the gatherings for coffee at Emmi's or Cara's house. Yet she understood the reasoning. Barb was her teammate this morning, and she'd taken pictures that the team could post for all those who followed the nesting season on the Internet.

It was nearly 8 a.m. and the sun was already bright in the sky. Midweek, the beach was empty save for a few walkers pumping arms. A few peeps played tag with the waves. Linnea turned onto her beach path and headed toward Primrose Cottage. She spotted Emmi and Flo in their garden and veered over to say hello.

"Good morning!" she called out.

Emmi swung her head at the sound, then waved her arm in an arc over her head. "How are things on the beach?" She motioned Linnea closer.

Linnea came up to the gate. Emmi drew close, with Flo right behind her.

"Sorry. We have to keep it locked now because . . ." Emmi jerked her head in Flo's direction.

"I know. John told me."

"Any nests?"

"We had two nests this morning," Linnea told her. "I moved one to the dunes off Second Avenue. Maybe Flo will be able to go out and watch this one."

"Not this year," Emmi reminded her. "No gatherings. We won't even be able to have inventories."

"You're right," Linnea replied with a sigh. "It's such a weird year with all the restrictions."

"We always manage."

Flo surprised them by speaking up. "If it's not one thing, it's another."

Linnea was delighted to hear Flo participate. "That's right, Flo."

Emmi leaned closer. "She's having one of her good days."

Flo stood nearby wearing a broad-rimmed straw hat and garden gloves. Despite her response and faint smile, Flo's eyes stared off vacantly.

"How are you doing, other than turtles?" Emmi asked.

"Good, thanks. Oh, I made masks from the fabric you gave me. I'll bring you over a bunch."

"Thank you, sweet girl. You are a wonder on a sewing machine. Correct me if I'm wrong, but I don't believe your mother sews."

"Oddly, given her love of decorating, no. She loves fabrics and can search for hours, but sewing, not at all."

"Who taught you?"

"I learned to sew in school. I begged Mama for a sewing machine for Christmas freshman year in high school. She bought me a classic Singer and I just took to it."

"I used to knit, back when the boys were little. Might take it up again someday."

"I have the time to sew now," Linnea said.

"What's the matter, honey? You look a bit down."

Linnea set down her turtle team backpack and rolled her shoulders. "I guess I'm feeling a little sorry for myself today. I'm watching everyone else head out to work in the morning. . . . I loved my job at the aquarium. I miss it."

Flo took a step closer. "What do you miss most?"

Linnea was surprised by Flo's question. She looked into the old woman's cloudy blue eyes and saw a spark of clarity. "I love to teach," she answered honestly. "I want to bring people closer to the natural world."

"Then what are you waiting for?" Flo asked pointedly.

"Flo, they laid her off," Emmi tried to explain.

"Call them up. Tell them you want to work," Flo said. "Just do it."

Emmi rolled her eyes apologetically, but Linnea heard wisdom in the old woman's words. She thought of Anna's response to the flood crisis and felt her own blood stir.

"You're right, Flo. Thank you. I will. In fact, I'll do it right now."

---

AN HOUR LATER, Linnea lowered her phone, her eyes wide and her mouth agape. Then she fist-pumped the air. She pushed back from the table and hurried out the door on a beeline for John. She rushed next door and knocked on the kitchen door. John smiled when he opened it.

"Hello, neighbor," he said, drying his hands with a towel.

"John!" Linnea exclaimed, excitement bubbling in her veins. "Do you have a minute?"

"Yeah, good timing. I just finished fixing a leak in the sink. Come in."

Linnea started pacing the room, her mind firing ideas.

John tossed the towel on the counter. "What's got you all fired up?"

"I just got off the phone with Kevin Mills at the aquarium. I wanted to talk to him about volunteering to help the education department. You'll never guess. He said he was going to call me. The education programs are all virtual now. With school closed, their classes were wildly successful. And . . . the aquarium got some grant money. They're developing programs for kids online, and he wants me to be part of it. Habitat, food chains, watersheds—I'm so excited I could burst! This is what I love to do. And for kids! Teach them young, and they're stewards for life."

John studied her face.

Linnea looked at him askance. "What?"

"Nothing. It's just so great to see you excited again. I missed seeing that."

She gave a self-deprecating laugh. "I know."

"When do you start?"

"Immediately. I mean, I got my job back! I'm getting paid." She clasped her palms to her cheeks. "My mind is spinning with ideas. I have so much to learn. That's why I'm here." She dropped her hands and looked at him pleadingly. "I need your help."

His brows rose. "*My* help?"

"It's all online. That's your world. You design programs. I thought maybe you could help me understand how to best help teachers use the curriculum I write. How to make it interactive and fun. Some of the kids will be learning from home, and others will be in small group classes, depending on the school. So it's a challenge."

He took a deep breath, and she thought he was going to refuse, saying he didn't have time. He released his breath with a droll smile. "Yeah, sure, I'd love to help. Sounds like fun."

She felt grateful and a bit selfish. She knew he was working from home *and* helping his mother with Flo. "Are you sure you have time?"

He smiled again. "I'll make time. Want some coffee?"

# chapter fourteen

*I'm just trying to get through the day, you know?*
*Like everyone in this lifeboat called the pandemic.*

July

JOHN AND GORDON had decided it was a perfect day for fishing.

They walked side by side along the side street toward Palm Boulevard. The road was busy, despite the tourism drop. John watched the traffic for an opening between cars so they could cross to the other side, where Hamlin Creek glistened in the morning sun.

"Which one is it?" Gordon asked, gesturing toward the docks that bordered Hamlin Creek. There were at least a dozen, protruding from the slim strip of earth alongside Palm Boulevard into the creek. Some were weatherworn, some newer. A few had large boats designed for speed on lifted docks. A few were covered.

They walked along the gravel side of Palm Boulevard to the third dock.

"This is it," John said, pointing to one of the oldest docks. It was a step away from dilapidated, missing a few wood slats and leaning to the side. Vines crept up the pilings near the shore. At the end of the dock, a pelican perched serenely on the railing. It watched them approach with a proprietary air before spreading its long wings and taking off.

"Do you own this dock?" Gordon asked.

"I wish. This dock is owned by an old friend of my mother's," John said. "Clay used to be the mayor of the city and has always been very generous whenever I wanted to use his dock. He's like that with all his neighbors. Time was, he brought my mother and Cara tomatoes from his garden. Life used to be like that around here. Now, sadly, there are a lot more rentals." They stepped onto the dock, each of them wearing rubber-soled shoes. "Mind your step."

It was a precarious walk along the crooked boardwalk, which was missing almost as many slats of wood as it had kept. At the end, an old fishing boat dating back to the 1970s floated in the water. John thought it looked like an old boot—worn and used, but one you could still walk around in dependably.

"I called Clay. He left out a few poles for us," John said.

Gordon, dressed in tan nylon fishing pants and a brown T-shirt, lifted one of the poles lying on the dock and inspected it. He turned to John and said teasingly. "I think this was one Hemingway used."

John laughed, looking down at his own olive-green fishing pants. They were both dressed for a day on the water with ball caps, sunscreen, and wicking shirts.

"Yeah, well, Clay's getting up there. I'm sure he has his own rods that he keeps aside. These are freebies, so you know what they say about beggars and choosers."

"Check this out," Gordon said, lifting the rod to show the hook dangling from the line. "There's a petrified worm on this rusty hook."

John struggled to keep a straight face. "Wow, look at that."

"You really spare no expense. I didn't know you were a *serious* fisherman. When was this used last? The Civil War?"

"Going fishing was your idea, Einstein."

"I wanted to thank you for allowing me to rent your loft. For an exorbitant price. I thought a bit of male bonding was in order."

"Sure. We both know Linnea ordered us to go out." He scratched his head. "Look, I know this isn't first class, but we'll be fine. There's a hook. You put bait on the hook. The fish bites the hook. How hard could it be?"

"So, what you're telling me is that you don't know how to fish either."

"You mean you don't?" John asked. "I thought all Brits fished."

"I thought all lowcountry men fished," Gordon fired back.

John looked out at the water and shrugged. "I was always more of a surfer."

"Now that we're done with stereotypes, let's say we figure this out."

John picked up one of the poles. He had to admit, it was in pretty bad shape. "I didn't know fishing poles could rust."

"Most of it is the salt," Gordon said with enviable knowledge. He squeezed a hook between his thumb and index finger. He didn't look at all surprised when it cracked in half. "Perfect. Do you have a spare?"

"A spare?"

"You did bring hooks?"

"You didn't?"

"I don't suppose you brought bait, either." Gordon bent to open the cooler.

"Nope. All beers in there. I took care of packing the serious provisions."

"Fantastic." Gordon looked annoyed. "One of us has to go to Harris Teeter. They've got bait and hooks there."

"I nominate you," John said, tossing Gordon his car keys.

Gordon caught them on the fly. "You idiot. They could've fallen into the creek."

"I trusted you. The first rule of fishing. Trust your partner. My car's in the driveway. I'll be on the end of the dock, tipping a cold one. Drive safe."

Gordon looked fed up with the whole expedition. "Very well. At least grab the poles. Would you do that? Please?"

John grabbed both poles with one hand. "All done. Thanks."

John watched Gordon walk back down the precarious dock and felt a twinge of guilt. Sure, he wanted to stick it to him. Gordon was lording his man-of-the-house presence at the beach house, never missing a chance to put an arm around Linnea or, his personal favorite, kiss the top of her head whenever John walked into a room. John tipped back the bottle and took a long swallow. He couldn't deny it was killing him. He couldn't sleep at night, knowing that guy was in bed with Linnea. There wasn't enough alcohol to quench that burn.

Let the Brit be a gofer, he thought sourly, drinking again. Still, it didn't sit right, treating him like this. If he weren't with Linnea, John might even like the guy.

From around the corner house across the street, John spotted someone approaching. Squinting, he recognized Cooper, wearing nylon shorts and a T-shirt. In one arm he carried three brand-new fishing rods, still with price tags flapping in the breeze. From his other hand dangled a small Coleman cooler that bumped against his thigh as he walked at a lazy pace.

"Yo," Cooper called out.

Gordon stopped walking to turn in Cooper's direction. He raised his hands in the air. "We've been saved!" He waited while Cooper watched the traffic, then sprinted across Palm Boulevard. Gordon slapped Cooper's shoulder, clearly glad to have been saved from a trip to the store. He reached out to grab the cooler. The two men sauntered back to the dock, then navigated the treacherous boards to the end where John sat shaking his head and grinning.

"Who invited this guy?" John said to Gordon.

"Not me," Gordon said, clearly in a better mood. He set the cooler on the dock. "He just kind of *shows up*. Like a paper airplane that floats into a room."

John's eyes darted toward Gordon.

"It's a God-given talent," Cooper said, resting the rods against a piling. "Right place at the right time."

"Maybe you can make little origami bait out of some old newspaper," Gordon said to John, continuing the dig. "I hear fish love to hit on those."

"You guys are still at each other's throats, I see," Cooper said. He spied the poles in John's hand. "Nice. You steal those from a Civil War museum?"

"Right?" Gordon said, laughing.

"Whatever," John said. "What's in the cooler? We've got beer."

Cooper smiled. "Ten bucks says neither of you geniuses remembered to bring bait."

John and Gordon stared back with blank eyes.

"I knew it. You guys think of beer, and I bring essentially *everything* needed to fish. Rods . . . patience . . ."

"We didn't even invite you," John said.

"Yeah? Well, my sister said I had to come babysit you guys. Looks like she was right. You wouldn't even be able to fish if I hadn't shown up. Come on, Romeos. Let's go."

John looked around the dock, scratching his head. They were both being put properly in place by the kid. There were fish bloodstains from an incalculable number of catches deeply entrenched in the wood. Old hooks with a few inches of fishing line still attached littered the dock, some with encrusted bait on the end.

"Maybe we should chip in for Merry Maids," John joked. "Seriously. Fifty bucks and they'd have this place spotless."

"Clay likes things just the way they are," Cooper said in a warning tone. "No one says anything against him in my presence. Just sayin'."

"Only kidding," John said. "I know he's the best. Clay's from a different era. Like this here dock." To Gordon he said, "Isle of Palms and Sullivan's used to be sleepy islands. People knew each other. They were good neighbors and didn't worry if their dock was gentrified." He pointed to the white house across the street. "I'll bet he's up there now, watching us, wishing he were here. I wish he was too. Clay's getting up there in age and lying low. The virus would almost certainly kill him."

"I learned most of what I know about fishing from Clay," Cooper said. "He was always right here, ready to give me pointers on how to catch red drum, or gig for flounder. They broke the mold when they created him." He looked back at the house and a flicker of sadness crossed his features. "Let's go fishing."

It was clear that Cooper knew his way around a boat. John was chagrined to see that Gordon did as well. They moved quickly, in tandem, bringing in the gear, standing aside without being asked as they worked on the fuel line, checked the engine, and untied the hitch.

"All aboard," Cooper called out.

The water slapped lightly at the hull of the boat, a gentle smacking noise that was hypnotic. The small, tattered American flag secured above the pilothouse flapped in the wind. The hull of the boat was weathered, like everything else, in need of a scraping and paint job. Clay was long past the days when he cared about barnacles and paint.

"Nice call with the choice of beer," Gordon called out when he took a sip. "Were they out of battery acid?"

"Hey, I didn't know what you liked," John said over his shoulder. "I

271

thought this was a safe middle-ground kind of thing. I guessed you were a mai tai or daiquiri kind of guy but figured there wouldn't be a blender on this tub. Make do."

"I'm more of an IPA guy," Gordon replied soberly. "Though we Brits prefer ours warm. And for your edification, a mai tai is *not* a blended drink."

"Good God!" Cooper shouted over his shoulder from the wheel. "Are we fishing or negotiating terms for World War Three? Gordon, untie the line. John, just—just sit down. Get out of my line of sight."

John sat, noting Gordon's twitching lips.

With the engine purring, Cooper expertly guided the seventeen-foot boat away from the dock.

"Nice boat," Gordon said, taking it in. "It's a smaller model of a classic design. If I'm not mistaken, it has hydraulic steering and no autopilot."

"Right you are," said Cooper.

John narrowed his eyes, wondering if all that was just to show him up.

"Clay may be a bit lacking in housekeeping," Gordon said with appreciation, "but he knows his boats and follows the safety guidelines to the letter."

"Speaking of which, put on those life vests," Cooper instructed. "At least until we get out on the water. They've got cops all over the place and I don't feel like getting a citation."

The engine gurgled quietly as Cooper guided the boat along Hamlin Creek. No other boats were on the waterway, a sign of the times. But the ever-present seagulls called out their mocking song, dipping low close to the boat's stern, looking for a handout.

"Do we want to fish the Intracoastal or go out with the big boys?" Cooper asked, turning away from the wheel.

"Big boys," John and Gordon blurted simultaneously.

"Yeah, right," Cooper replied with a sorry shake of his head. "No way we're going out that far." He glanced up at the sky. "It's going to be one of those days," he muttered more to himself.

John wiped his brow, feeling the humidity and trying to remember if he'd packed extra suntan lotion. It was going to be a scorcher—already near eighty degrees, and it wasn't even nine in the morning.

"If we're lucky," Cooper called back over the roar of the engine, "we'll catch some redfish, sheepshead, maybe trout, though it's late in the season. And maybe shark."

"Thanks, but no thanks," Gordon said. "I get enough shark when I surf."

"Oh yeah? What's the biggest shark you've ever seen?" John asked. He knew he was starting it, the mine's-bigger-than-yours stories.

Gordon didn't skip a beat. "I've surfed all over the world, but my favorite spot is off the coast of Australia. I have a lot of mates there and it's a good time. And the waves." He half-smiled. "Not the little skimmers you have here." He paused to take a drink.

Cooper barked out a laugh while John simmered.

"Anyway, I was out on my board, minding my own business, waiting for a wave. We were all a good distance apart. I remember looking out, thinking about the serenity of the moment. All was so quiet.

Peaceful. And then, out of nowhere, I catch sight of this bloody huge gray shadow under the water. Sixteen, seventeen feet, at least. It all happened so fast. Suddenly there was this head. A great white. The pink gums were pulled back. The teeth." He shook his head. "Monstrous. I drew back. It was instinctive. Then he comes crashing down on the board, literally flipping me high into the air. Except, I'm still tied to the board. I hit the water, and the next thing I know he's diving and taking me with him. I was trying to pull myself free of the band when the shark must've let go because the board came rocketing up to the surface, dragging me up with it. I surfaced, choking, and ripped off the leash. My buddy came paddling toward me and I climbed on his back. Somehow we managed to catch a wave." He laughed. "It was a miracle we both stayed on the board." He paused, remembering. "I'm lucky—I know that."

"Well, shit," said Cooper.

Gordon looked out at the water, then turned to John. "I've stared into the eyes of a lot of animals—whales, dolphins, sea turtles, seals. There's a connection there that's beautiful. But looking into the eye of a shark . . ." He paused again, and shook his head. "It's like looking into the eye of a dead man."

There was a long silence.

"That's . . . wow," John said, backing down. He'd never been to the Australian coast. Hell, the farthest away he'd ever surfed was off the coast of California. There was no contest.

Cooper shook his head. "I didn't know we were getting into *Jaws* stories." He laughed. "Dude, we need a bigger boat."

Laughing, Gordon raised his hand, and John tossed him a beer, which he snared with one hand.

"You?" John asked Cooper.

"No thanks. I'm driving."

With the life vest covering most of his chest, Cooper reminded John of back when the kid used to beg his dad to let him take the wheel. *They raised him right*, he thought, tossing Cooper a cold water.

"He old enough?" Gordon asked teasingly.

"Old enough to know better, still young enough not to care," John said smiling.

"Since neither of you seems to be in control of your faculties, I've decided we're fishing the creek," Cooper said. "I don't like the look of that front coming in, and I'm not going to end up a headline on CNN."

"Safe, smart. I like the way you think," Gordon said, raising his beer.

Cooper cut the engine, and immediately the boat began to drift sideways. John eyed the thick marsh on either side of the waterway, some fifty yards from shore to shore.

"Throw out the anchor," Cooper called.

Gordon was quick to his feet, and the anchor hit the briny water with a splash.

"Sun's getting hot," John said, wiping his brow with the back of his hand.

"Slow down on the beer, bro," Cooper advised. "There's water in the cooler. You don't want to get dehydrated."

"Climate change is real," said Gordon. "Over the last century, the average surface temperature of the earth has increased about one degree Fahrenheit. Now, I realize one degree doesn't seem like much." He paused to put down the bait box. "But to the world, it's potentially catastrophic. And just to cheer things up," he added, picking up one of the fishing rods, "in keeping with all the other treats this year has had to offer, 2020 is on course to be the hottest year since records began."

"What about those guys who say we're still in an ice age?" asked Cooper. "That this is normal?"

"Idiots," Gordon said. "The facts are clear. The warming trend over the last fifty years is twice that for the past one hundred years. The oceans are warming. Glaciers are melting and sea levels are rising."

Cooper frowned and wiped his brow. "What does that mean for us?"

"It means we're screwed."

"And we called Anna the Debby Downer," John said.

"I'm not without hope," Gordon said matter-of-factly. "My entire career is based on finding solutions for the future. I work with dedicated men and women in all areas of environmental protection. Wildlife, habitat, air, sea, sky, atmosphere, the coral reefs, clean technology, you name it. They are relentless. But despite all we learn, there are those who ignore the facts. And others who are simply too lazy to pay attention. To my mind, it's not enough to watch others do the hard work with admiration. Hope is a thing that must be earned."

John listened to Gordon, who had earned the right to hope, and felt a begrudging admiration for him. He set his beer down and reached into the cooler for a water.

"You've convinced me," Cooper said good-naturedly. He lifted his fishing box and began explaining what he was doing. "I'm tying this eight-inch piece of leader between the snap swivel here and one of the hooks."

John watched in awe. The kid knew what he was doing.

"Got to make sure the leaders are short enough, so the hooks don't get tangled," Cooper said. "Seen some guys use beads or spinners on here to attract the fish. But we're going old-school."

"In truth, I fly-fish," Gordon confessed. "It's very different."

"Yeah," Cooper said. "I've always wanted to try that. But you," he continued, working the hooks, "you go way out on the big boats when you do your research, don't you?"

"Yes, but when I'm out on the ocean, I'm not deep-sea fishing," he said with humor. "We're out capturing seals and dolphins for research. But when you put it like that, for both, the goal is catch and release."

"I've read some of your papers. Linnea gave them to me. You're doing important work out there," Cooper said. "Saving all this"—his arm stretched out over the water—"for the rest of us. For my part, thank you."

"No thanks necessary," Gordon said modestly. "We're all on the same side. The farther out you go in the ocean, the clearer it is that plastic has become the scourge of the planet. I've seen whales, dolphins, porpoises caught up in discarded fishing nets. It often results in animals starving or drowning. Ah, but the whales," he said with feeling. "They're strong and can sometimes break free of ropes. But they can also end up towing nets behind them for months. It's a horrible death. Shameful. They're some of the oldest, most majestic creatures on the planet. It does something to you."

John took another swallow of water. This fishing trip was not meant for him to start admiring Gordon. Quite the opposite. He thought of the vintage poles that he'd staged on the dock as a joke. The joke had fallen flat. He'd never appreciated the wildlife research Gordon was involved in, all over the world. He was doing good on a grand scale. While John . . . He felt embarrassed now. He could see Linnea's attraction to him all too clearly. Hell, *he* was starting to like the guy.

John smiled in a lame attempt to be more amiable. He clapped his hands. "Okay. Let's get this show on the road. What are we using for bait, captain, my captain?"

"We have some in the cooler, but I thought we'd try catching our own," Cooper said. Grabbing a white cast net from below the captain's chair, he checked the small weights tied to the bottom of the net.

"Big fish like to eat little fish," Gordon said to John. "Just a fun fact for you."

"Cast net. Got it," John said with a roll of his eyes. "It requires skill to throw, a little like a cowboy uses a lasso. Americans are good at that."

Gordon was fascinated with the new technique, soaking it all in. John gave them room while he watched Cooper teaching Gordon how to cast a net and thought Cooper was proving himself to be a shining example of a lowcountry boy in his prime. Cooper coiled up the line and grabbed the throat of the net. First, he jostled it, making sure the weights were not tangled. Then, with the grace of an athlete, he shot out his right arm and released the net. It unfolded slowly, like a chrysanthemum opening, over the water, widening into a large circle and landing with a delicate splash.

"Bravo," Gordon exclaimed.

"You make it look easy," John said.

"It's not," Cooper replied. "You can make a real mess of this if you don't know what you're doing." He let the net sink to the bottom, then steadily pulled the rope back in, jerking it to tuck the net into a bag. Soon after, the net resurfaced holding a dozen small shad.

John whooped and brought over the drop bucket. "To think we were going to use worms. Rookie move, right?" he said.

Cooper cast the net again and drew it back in while Gordon baited the hooks. In the spirit of brotherhood, John went to his backpack and pulled out a few cigars. He handed one to Gordon, who sat comfortably with his feet on the rail, cradling a beer. He took the cigar, nodded with appreciation, and placed it, unlit, in his mouth.

"Cooper, you want one of these beauties?"

"No thanks," Cooper said, picking up his rod and already casting his line, intent on getting some fishing in. "I've given up cancer for Lent." He cast again, closer to the reeds. "Just a matter of time, boys, till I reel in the big one."

"Okay, junior," John said, preparing to cast. "You're on."

Gordon reeled in his line, then moved closer to John. John looked at him, curious.

Gordon spoke in a low voice. "I've got to tell you, to clear the air, I wasn't psyched when you came back here to Isle of Palms. And that you were living next door to Linnea. I was half a world away, could only see my girlfriend through a screen, and she let it slip you were here."

John focused on reeling in his line. "Nah, man—there's no secret. We're not doing anything wrong. I just want to try to repair our friendship."

Gordon turned his head to check on Cooper, who was doing what he could to look preoccupied with his fishing.

"Don't worry," John said. "He can't hear us."

"He *can* hear us," Gordon said. "He's just got enough grace to appear to not listen in."

"Look, man," John said begrudgingly. "What do you want me to say? We were together a year ago. We fucking lived together. Then I screwed up and let her go. What else do you want to know?"

Gordon looked at him impassively. "Do you still love her?"

John wasn't about to tell this guy how he felt about Linnea. "I don't know."

"Does she . . . have feelings for you?"

"How the hell am I supposed to know?" When Gordon continued staring at him, John said brusquely, "No. Not really. Maybe a little. I don't know. I mean, we're friends again. I think."

Gordon smirked. "How well do you really know her?"

"Trust me. I know her."

"What's her favorite color?"

"Pink."

"Wrong." Gordon smiled. "It's green."

"You're both wrong," Cooper said. "It's blue."

"I thought you weren't listening," John said, then turned to Gordon. "Okay, smartass. Does she like rom-coms or action films?"

"Both."

"Damn."

Gordon cast his line again, a little too close to Cooper's.

"What did I say about crossing lines?" Cooper called.

Gordon winced. "Feels great being corrected by a ten-year-old."

"I can hear you. And I'm twenty-one," Cooper retorted.

Gordon leaned closer to John. "Listen, this whole thing is kind of embarrassing. I feel like we're competing and, frankly, I've traveled halfway around the world chasing this woman. And now, you show up. And you say . . . *maybe* you're still in love with her."

John narrowed his eyes. "What's your point?"

"My point is, you've had your chance. You let her go."

John snorted and shook his head.

"Why would you think she'd give you another chance? She told me what you did when you broke up. Harsh. Why do you think you even *deserve* another chance?"

John felt a rush of shame and couldn't argue back. He didn't feel funny anymore. He felt like the fool he was. "I don't think I do deserve it."

Gordon didn't reply.

"Hey," Cooper interrupted. "She's a woman and she's entitled to change her mind."

"Just fish," Gordon snapped. "This has nothing to do with you."

"I beg to differ," Cooper said with his first flare of temper. "It has a great deal to do with me. I'm her brother. I give a damn about her. You two can float away like sea foam, but I'll still be her brother. And I'm not going to let you two play Lancelot and Arthur around her. You won't hurt her, got it? Neither of you. Not on my watch."

"All right," John said, his palms up in surrender. "Maybe I deserve that. But don't either of you pretend to know what goes on in someone else's relationship. It's never cut-and-dried. You have to be in it to know it."

"It's a two-way street," Gordon agreed.

"It takes two to tango," Cooper said with exasperation. "What the hell? Those are quotes from, like, Clark Gable, Humphrey Bogart movies. Cliché central."

"Hey," John said to Gordon, "I'm impressed he knows who Humphrey Bogart is."

"I'm a film guy," Cooper shot back. "And, if you don't mind my saying, I don't know what she sees in either one of you."

"Right," Gordon said, tossing up his hands. "I can't even make a paper airplane."

"What?" Cooper stared at him in bewilderment.

"It's called ingenuity, numbnuts," John said, facing off to Gordon. "You might be Jacques Cousteau out in the deep, but I'm a multi-faceted guy. I can do a lot of things. Paper crafts are just one thing."

"Paper crafts?" said Gordon with disbelief. "Did you just say *paper crafts*?" He looked to Cooper.

Cooper shrugged. "What can I say? The man has some skills."

"Skills are how a man romances a woman," Gordon said. "Not paper crafts."

"Seriously," Cooper said, turning away with a wave of disgust, "you guys are turning me off love. I didn't think it was possible. Yup. You've just turned me off of love. Nice job."

"Enough games," Gordon said irritably. He was clearly reaching the end of his long rope. "Let's be straight. Are you still in love with her? Is that what this be-a-good-neighbor bit is all about?"

"This *what*?"

"You coming home and being there to fix things, help her out. You sticking around. *Always* around."

"Me giving you my place to live in . . ."

Gordon's expression changed. "Thank you for that." Then he tilted his head. "I think. Or is that one more way you're trying to make yourself the good guy in this scenario?"

"You know," Cooper said, chuckling, "if this was a film, the heroine would have to choose between Hugh Grant, which is you"—he pointed to Gordon—"and Ryan Gosling, which is you."

"Why are you saying I'm Hugh Grant?" Gordon asked. "Because I'm British? Well, if you want to pick someone who is British, then how about . . . Liam Neeson."

"He's Irish." Cooper smiled.

"Hugh Jackman, then."

"Australian," John jabbed.

"I know," Gordon said. "Benedict Cumberbatch."

John looked at Cooper and they smirked. "Okay, sure."

"Never mind," Gordon said. "This is a ridiculous game. Don't you two ever take life seriously?"

"All right. Look," John said in a serious tone. "I'm just trying to get through the day, you know? Like everyone in this lifeboat called the pandemic. Maybe I do care about her still. Maybe I know I messed up. Maybe it's just a lot of maybes right now. So, why don't we all just fish or cut bait."

Gordon's line suddenly dropped hard, the tip pulled into the water.

"Bloody hell!" he said loudly, suddenly alert. "I got a hit." He beamed as his line whirred.

"Let it out," Cooper instructed, stepping closer. "Let the line out. Let it wrestle a bit, get the hook in there good."

"Don't pull too hard, you'll pull the hook out," John suggested.

"What the hell do you know about fishing?" Gordon snapped.

"Okay, bring it in . . . slowly. Slowly." Cooper was at Gordon's side, encouraging him.

"This bloke is strong." Joy and concern were mingled on Gordon's face.

John moved closer. "Can I help?"

"Yes. Get away," Gordon snapped.

John put his hands up and backed away.

He sat and watched as the battle raged for another few minutes. The sun was hot, the boat was rocking, and he was feeling sick. He wanted this morning to be over.

Cooper was calling out encouragement, telling Gordon to "give him line," when, in a great moment of anticlimax, the line broke. The boat rocked in aftershock.

"Bollocks!" Gordon shouted, catching his balance.

Out on the water, the line floated pitifully on the surface, the fish long gone. The three men watched the ripple in the water, all that was left of the battle.

"It's all right," Cooper said, bending over the side of the boat to reel in the lost line. "It happens."

"Yeah," John said, and looked up from the water. "Sometimes they just get away."

# chapter fifteen

*Only one thing matters in life. Family.*

WHILE THE GUYS were fishing, the women were organizing their new clubroom with the remnant furniture, lamps, and other miscellany from the goods they'd kept. The joggling board remained against the side wall beneath the shark. Though they hadn't won the Instagram challenge—John had declared that they were robbed—photographs of them surfing the joggling board had been framed and put on the wall behind the board.

Pandora, Anna, and Linnea grunted under the weight of the large, ruined oriental rug but finally got it spread out in the center of the room. Though the magenta and blue still looked vibrant, the carpet was laced with holes.

"What a shame," Pandora said, looking at it. "This carpet must have been magnificent in its day."

"Shitty mice," said Anna. "They chewed the fibers with their sharp little teeth to build their nests."

"I'm just thankful we didn't find any mice—or rats," said Linnea. They had rented a machine from the hardware store and washed this carpet and three others they'd found in similar shape. "Let's get the table."

Together, they moved the large mahogany dining table into the middle of the room, then added a second, smaller table to its end to create a length of over twelve feet that would accommodate the entire pod. They'd also discovered a mismatched assortment of chairs—some wrought iron, some wood with embroidered seats. These were set around the table. Linnea had laid claim to the two vintage wicker rocking chairs but agreed to temporarily put them in the barn to create a reading corner beside small tables and lamps. Miranda's large armoire placed against the wall was still crammed full of art supplies, and now board games as well. Gordon had purchased a refrigerator as his contribution. John bought two large rotating fans that when strategically placed kept the air circulating. Cooper and Anna had gone to the Goodwill and found a sofa that would last the season.

Linnea put her hands on her hips and thought that, all in all, their pod/fort was coming along nicely.

Pandora took a long breath, then plucked the blue rubber gloves from her hands. "I'm knackered. We've been at this for hours. The boys are out fishing. What's wrong with this picture? I quit."

"You can't quit yet," Anna protested. "We're almost done."

"I am done, my hardworking friend. Your kin may have been laborers, but mine were not. These hands were not meant for manual work. Look at my nails!" she cried. "They're ruined. And I can't even get a bloody manicure these days. I hate this damned pandemic."

"If you're done with your hissy fit," Linnea said, walking to the fridge, "let's all take a break. I just had a brilliant idea I'd like to share with you. Go on," she prodded when no one moved. "Sit down at our beautiful table and I'll grab some bubble water."

"Put vodka in mine, please," Pandora called out.

"I will if you buy some."

As Pandora and Anna obliged, Linnea opened the fridge with Luna at her heels. Whenever a fridge opened, the puppy was hopeful. Linnea had begged people to stop feeding her treats, to no avail. Luna was becoming as bad a beggar as the worst dolphin at a dock. With her large, melting brown eyes, no one could refuse her.

"Sorry, girl, there's nothing in here you'd like," she said, scooping up three bottles of sparkling water. "*Your* water is right there," she said, bending to point out the water. Luna was not interested.

On the way to the table, Linnea grabbed a few pens and a yellow legal pad from the rocker where she'd been sitting earlier while putting together her to-do list. After distributing the bottles of water, she took a seat at the table. Luna begged to come in her lap, but after a firm "no" she settled with a snort at Linnea's feet.

Pandora and Anna opened their waters.

"What's on your mind?" Anna asked.

"We need a party," Linnea announced.

Pandora brightened. "A party? Now, that's an idea."

"What's a party?" Anna asked. "It's been so long."

"I know, right?" Pandora said, and the two women clinked bottles.

"What kind of party?" asked Anna before taking a sip.

"Does it matter?" asked Pandora. "Alcohol and party favors. I'm in."

"Well," Linnea said with exaggeration, pressing on, "the Fourth of July is coming up. I was thinking, let's have a good old-fashioned Southern barbecue to welcome our English friends. We can only invite the pod, of course, but that will be enough to fill our grand table."

"There's that box of china," Pandora said, getting into the spirit.

"Let's use paper," Anna countered. "No one wants to do all those dishes. Plus, duh, there's no kitchen. We'd have to schlep dishes across to the house."

Pandora's face fell. "I hate paper plates."

"Why would anyone hate paper plates? Use them, dump them, no headache and no extra work," said Anna. Then, in a lower voice, "If we could only do that with men."

Pandora's mouth twisted to a grin and she eyed Anna with new appreciation.

"Sorry, but no paper plates. It's a waste of paper," Linnea said firmly. "We'll use the china and do it proper. Nathalie Dupree, the quintessential Southern chef, gave my mother a nugget of great information for parties. She said to keep a cooler of soapy water in the kitchen, and you just dump all those dishes and pots in there to soak. We'll do that." She raised her bottle of water. "We're having a party!"

Her enthusiasm was infectious. Before they'd finished their bottles of bubble water, they'd begun long lists of family favorite recipes to prepare, because everyone knew a good barbecue wasn't worth its salt without an impressive spread of home-cooked side dishes.

Linnea was in her element, as bubbly as the water as she came up with ideas, her pen scribbling across the paper. "I'm going to fix the cornbread. It's an old family recipe. My grandmama Lovie used to make it and it's as light as a feather."

"My mama makes a mean sauce," Anna said.

"Mustard or sweet?"

"Sweet."

"Good. You're on."

Pandora felt out of her league. "I don't really cook much. And I don't have family recipes to share. But I can order anything you like. I'm a master at making reservations. Got my PhD in ordering online."

Anna laughed, and Linnea realized the two women were bonding for the first time over humor. At her expense.

"Pan, why don't you supply the wine and beer?" suggested Linnea.

"Brilliant," Pandora said, grinning. "That's something I know a lot about. Why don't you let Gordon and me do the drinks? We'll stock the bar in the fort too. Do it up right."

Anna shot Linnea a look that said *careful*. Linnea brushed it aside and said, "Perfect. There's an ABC store next to the bridge."

"Oh, darling, I *know*."

---

JULY FOURTH ARRIVED, and the island was on full alert. Independence Day was considered the biggest holiday of the Charleston beaches. American flags fluttered from lampposts. Despite the growing pandemic, the island was expecting the holiday to be among the biggest—if not *the* biggest—on record. So many people had been cooped up for so long, many were without jobs, and many more thought it was safe to go to the beach with the family because they were outdoors in the fresh air and sun. Others just didn't care about the pandemic and were headed out to the beach no matter what anyone said.

"Did you see the Connector?" Cooper asked, walking into the cottage from an ice run. "The cars are backed up for miles. It's like a parking lot out there. And there's no place to park when they get here! It's crazy."

"So much for social distancing," commented Anna, opening up the cooler for the ice.

"Everyone's got a right to have a good time at the beach," Cooper said. "I mean, if you didn't live here, you'd probably be out there right now."

Anna straightened. "What's that supposed to mean?"

"Nothing. Just sometimes you come down hard on people. You can't get angry at people just because they do something you don't like. Lighten up."

Linnea pinched her lips and stirred a bit more Duke's mayonnaise into her potato salad. "No one go out on that beach today, hear? It's wall-to-wall people, and I don't see many masks. As far as I'm concerned, that breaks the rules of the pod. Let everyone know."

"I feel for the police, is all," Anna said, still chafing from Cooper's remark. "They have their work cut out for them, bless their hearts."

"The beach crowd seemed like a well-mannered, friendly group from what I saw," Cooper said.

"If we keep to ourselves, we'll not have to worry about the virus. Cooper, did you wash your hands?"

Cooper set down the bags of ice and went immediately to the sink.

———

BY MIDAFTERNOON THE men were banished from the barn. They'd been sitting at the table, drinking beer and playing poker while the fans whirred in an attempt to beat the heat of the hottest month of the year. In short order the women turned on music and began dancing and laughing as they set about the task of decorating the barn for the party.

Pandora hung the many renditions of American and British flags they'd all painted the day before using the art supplies. Everyone had enjoyed the project, no one more than Hope, who had felt so proud that she was painting with the grown-ups. They covered the tables with white paper tablecloths and set out the cobalt-trimmed white china. With a nod to ease, red-white-and-blue paper napkins and small American flags gave the table a patriotic flair. Isle of Palms had been the first city in the state to forbid plastic utensils, but they'd relinquished the restrictions during the pandemic. Nonetheless, Linnea and Gordon had both insisted they should use and wash tableware.

Anna and Linnea twisted red, white, and blue crepe paper. A short while later, the men returned, curious and offering to help. Emmi happily handed the men strings of twinkling lights and set Gordon and John to work hanging them from the rafters. They worked in tandem, and Linnea noted the odd peace that seemed to have fallen between the men since the fishing trip. She supposed male bonding was a real thing after all.

By six, the sun was still high but the table was set and the guests gathered. Cara and David arrived carrying a bounty of freshly baked fruit pies from the farmers' market. Pandora ran up to help carry the pies in, sniffing as she walked, declaring that she'd been dying for American pie ever since she'd arrived stateside.

"I love, love, love pie," Pandora exclaimed in her dramatic fashion, carrying two of the fruit pies to the long side table that was already groaning under the weight of the food. "Who cares about all that meat?" she asked, lovingly laying the pies beside the cookies. "Just leave me with these two beauties."

Julia and Palmer arrived soon after. Palmer's arms looked strained under a large wooden dough bowl wrapped in tinfoil. "Let me through!" he called out, struggling under the weight of the large bowl. He pushed past offers to help and made it to the serving table and set his burden down with a gasp.

"Wait till you see," Julia exclaimed, coming up behind him. With a grand flourish, she took off the foil to reveal the wooden bowl brimming full of shrimp, corn, potatoes, and sausage.

"Frogmore stew!" Cooper shouted with a fist pump.

Hope looked up at Julia in horror. "You cooked Jeremiah?"

It took a moment for the adults to register what the little girl meant. Already her lower lip was beginning to tremble.

Cooper, the first to realize, shook his head. "No, no, little one. Not Jeremiah. Not any frog. There are absolutely *no* frogs in that stew. Zero." He made a zero with his fingers. "None."

Julia finally caught on. "Oh, child, no," she answered. "Frogmore stew is named after a small fishing village on St. Helena Island. It's called Frogmore. Some people call this a lowcountry boil, or Beaufort stew. But I swear, not a single frog lost its life in this dish." She looked at her son. "I made it special for you. Even if there's no frog in it," she said, accepting his kiss on the cheek.

The sprinklers were swirling in the garden and the fans were whirring in the barn. The scent of baby back ribs and hamburgers wafted in the air as David and John carried the barbecue to the serving table. Anna ladled her family's recipe of red barbecue sauce into bowls with utmost care, proud of her contribution. Gordon served as bartender, making margaritas in the blender. Wine, beer, and Gordon's favorite IPA were nestled in ice in the cooler.

At last the feast was ready. The table was overflowing with the Frogmore stew, crisp ribs and juicy burgers, steaming corn on the cob, all manner of greens and cold salads, hot biscuits sitting under cloth napkins, and, of course, the four pies.

Emmi and Cara hovered over the tables like mother hens, clucking directions, attending to every detail, refilling bowls as needed, feeling like the matriarchs they were. They were cracking jokes and bumping hips behind the table, serving up dishes, high on a friend-ship that had lasted decades and ripened with age.

Cara's gaze surveyed the room, filled with the people she loved most in the world. Everyone was seated around the long table, their plates overflowing. She felt a stirring emotion run through her think-ing of her mother, as she always did at family gatherings.

Lovie had been known as a consummate hostess in Charleston back when the family lived on Tradd Street. Cara remembered lurk-ing in the background with Palmer, watching the grand parties her parents had hosted in the old days when waiters dressed in black car-ried trays weighed down with appetizers and flutes of champagne. She'd watched her mother glide through the rooms, a tiny doll in her pearls and blond hair pulled up in a French twist, chatting with guests, all while keeping a firm eye on the staff. Mama had made the extravagant events that her husband, Stratton Rutledge, demanded appear effortless.

Julia had followed suit for Palmer when she'd stepped into the Rutledge name and house. She'd been every bit as elegant a hostess as Lovie.

But times had changed. Lovie had passed, and Palmer had lost his fortune. Those grand fêtes, even the great house on Tradd Street, were now but memories of the past. Cara caught sight of Linnea leaning toward Gordon as they chatted. She was wearing one of Lovie's vin-tage shirtwaist dresses and her double strand of pearls. She reminded Cara so much of her mother it took Cara's breath away.

Yet she knew that she and Linnea were cut from a different piece of cloth. They both knew the rules of etiquette, but neither of them cared so much about such things as china, silver, and formality. This gathering of family, in a decorated barn festooned with handcrafted art, surrounded by family and friends, was the kind of party they preferred. And on second thought, Cara thought, her mother had too. Hadn't she fought all through her marriage to keep the beach house and the casual lifestyle she enjoyed here?

Tapping her wineglass with a spoon, Cara signaled she'd like to make a toast. As everyone quieted and gazes turned toward her, she rose, glass in hand.

"Let me start by saying thank you to all who worked so hard to prepare this wonderful feast. And to all you young people who worked so hard to gift us with such a beautiful place in which to eat it!"

"Hear hear!"

"Honestly, I can't remember stepping foot in this barn since Miranda passed, God bless her soul."

"To Miranda!"

"And to Flo!" called out Emmi.

"Where is Flo?" asked Linnea. "She should be here too."

Emmi shook her head. "Oh no, honey. This would be too much for her. She's eating a plate in her room, happy as a clam. I'll go check on her after we eat."

Cara returned to her toast. "Mama . . . Lovie . . . would have loved this night. She would've basked in the glory of seeing family and friends celebrating what was a favorite holiday of hers. In fact, her last party was a Fourth of July feast much like this one. Many of you were there. Even you, John," she added with a wry smile. "Though if I recall, you were a handsome young teenage buck and you and your brother breezed through the food line so fast you might not remember."

Amid the laughter, she heard John call out, "I remember!"

"If there is one lesson I learned from Lovie," Cara continued, "and there were many, it is that above all, only one thing matters in life. Family. Who your people are, as she used to say. And by that she didn't mean lineage or exclusivity. Nor wealth or position. But instead, what Lovie meant is what is visible right here in this barn tonight. We've weathered a lot since the pandemic began. We've been frustrated, upset, and challenged. But we've also been brought together in a way none of us could have foreseen. We are weathering yet another storm together, with, if you don't mind me saying so, compassion, camaraderie, ingenuity, commitment, friendship, yes, fun too. And most of all, love.

"So tonight I raise my glass to all of you wonderfully unique individuals from different parts of the world. You who make up this pod. To our new family."

Everyone cheered and raised their glasses, calling out "To the family! To the pod!"

"Mama," Cara said softly, looking up at the sky. "I miss you."

---

LINNEA SIPPED AND looked over her wineglass at her friends and family around the table, eating, drinking, and talking. She couldn't remember a better party. It may have been her idea, but it wasn't her success. They'd all worked hard to make the feast special.

Her gaze caught the pinkened skin on the faces from all the sun. The candles were dripping wax in the summer breeze. The flowers in the odd assortment of vases were wilting in the humidity of a Southern night. She wiped a bead of sweat from her brow and hoped the pending storm would hold off as predicted. Around the room, everyone seemed to be enjoying the night as the fans circulated the air.

She noted that David was deep in conversation with Cooper. He'd told her that David's drone business was booming in London. Who knew? she wondered. Cooper was studying international business. Maybe a job there was in Cooper's future.

Beside her, Gordon and Pandora were head-bent in some discussion that had Gordon gesturing with his hands. Linnea smiled, thinking how he got so caught up in his work. He was always eager to share with someone his latest research. He'd found an eager listener in Pandora. Perhaps too eager, she thought, observing how Pandora hung on his every word. Linnea wondered, too, why she didn't feel all that concerned.

Speaking of flirting, sitting in the rocking chairs in the corner she spied Palmer and Julia leaning close as though to catch every word. If she hadn't known who they were, she'd have guessed her parents were a couple just hooking up. It made her happy to see them happy.

She looked at Julia, dressed in white jeans and a chic navy-and-white-striped shirt, and didn't think she'd ever seen her mother more beautiful, or more comfortable in her own skin. Julia's work at the James house was not only lucrative for her business but had firmly placed her new company on the local stage. Linnea recalled her conversation with

Julia last summer. Julia had had little confidence in herself, yet claimed she didn't want to be known only as someone's daughter, wife, or mother. *Well, Mama,* Linnea thought with pride. *You did it. You are Julia Rutledge of Rutledge House Interiors.* And perhaps, her inner satisfaction was the glow that her father found so attractive.

Her attention was diverted by Emmi as she rang an old school bell.

"Okay y'all! Let's have dessert!"

———————

PANDORA, LINNEA, CARA, and Anna were packing up the china and wrapping up the last of the food and dividing it up to go to different homes. John and Gordon were carrying out pots of coffee and tea when Emmi hurried from her house, her face pale with worry.

"Has anyone seen Flo?"

Immediately, all conversation stopped, chairs were pushed back from the table, and everyone started running around the enclave of houses calling out Flo's name.

"You're not to blame," Cara told a frantic Emmi, putting a comforting arm around her shoulders. "No one is. She's wandered off before and we've always found her. We'll find her now."

"She's not at my place," Linnea called out, returning at a sprint from the beach house.

John put his hands in his back pockets, his face worried. "She's nowhere in the house."

"When was the last time anyone saw her?" David asked.

"I checked on her right before we sat down for dinner. She was sound asleep," Emmi said.

"That was over hours ago," Cara said. "She could be anywhere."

"Should we call the police?" asked Emmi, worry making her voice wobble.

"We've gone through this before," Cara said, interjecting a note of calm. "She walks, so I don't believe we have to worry about her going in the ocean."

"But it's getting dark," Emmi argued. "She won't be easy to find."

John said, "Let's break into pairs and start searching for her. We'll meet back here in half an hour. The sun should be setting by then." Looking up he added, "And the rain should be coming in soon after. If we don't find her by then, I say we bring in the police."

Pairing off and arming themselves with flashlights, they all took off. Palmer and Julia headed toward Palm Boulevard. Cara and David took Hope with them to fetch the golf cart and search Ocean Boulevard. The young couples headed for the beach.

"Gordon," said John. "Why don't you and Pandora head toward Front Beach. You know that area well."

Gordon opened his mouth to protest but then tightened his lips and nodded.

"Okay," Linnea said. "John, that leaves you and me. We'll head toward Breach Inlet." To Gordon she said, "See you back at the house in thirty."

The wind was picking up, scattering sand and sending the final stragglers on the beach packing up their gear and heading to home or to their cars. The crowd had thinned but there were long lines of cars jockeying for space in the exit lanes off the island.

"I hope we find her before that storm hits," Linnea said, picking up the pace.

"We'll find her," John reassured her. "How many old women are out here in a brewing storm for a stroll?"

A gust of wind laced with biting drops of rain slapped her face. She caught her breath at the sudden shift in weather. Overhead all trace of the sky had been replaced by clouds tinged an eerie green. The ocean was tumultuous, whipping up steely-colored waves that crashed against the shoreline.

Suddenly everything was aquiver. The wind picked up to swirl around Linnea in a strange mixture of warm and cool, humid and icy. The young stalks of sea oats rattled like castanets. It felt like a tornado.

"It's really blowing up a storm and its coming on fast," John said, and turned her way to be heard over the wind. "You okay?"

"I'm fine. Let's keep going. Flo!" she called out at the top of her lungs. Her voice was lost in the roar of the surf.

They kept walking at a fast clip toward Breach Inlet, where even on good days the treacherous water swirled with deadly undercurrents. The quickly changing tides often fooled tourists into thinking it was safe to wander far out on the sand at low tide, not aware how fast the tides could roll back in. Every year there were rescues in Breach Inlet, not all of them successful. Tonight it swirled like a Mixmaster. Linnea silently prayed, *Please, God, don't let her wander into the water.*

"John, look," she said. She pointed to what looked like a dark gray wall in the air, straight ahead. "What is that? Rain?"

"Yeah," he said, sounding as amazed as she was. "I've never seen anything like it."

In another few steps, Linnea couldn't believe they were walking right into a wall of rain. It was like stepping from one universe into another. The rain was pelting, cold and stinging on their bare skin. Neither had brought a rain jacket or an umbrella. Linnea shielded her eyes with her hand as they picked up the pace. They called Flo's name over and over, to no avail.

The island curved southward toward the Hunley Bridge. Overhead, the sky had darkened to the deep purple of a bruise. Few house lights pierced the black, and fewer headlights flickered on the bridge. It was so dark, they were losing their bearings. John stopped and, using his flashlight, checked his watch.

"It's been a half hour," he said. "We should head back. We can't see anything anyway. We'd better call the police."

"Wait," Linnea said. "Let's check under the bridge first."

"She won't be there. She may already be home."

"Listen, when I do my turtle walks, we have to check every inch of the designated walk. I can't tell you how many times we get a call from some tourist that they found tracks in some remote spot that was skipped. It pays to be thorough."

"Okay. Let's check it out."

John set the pace through the cold rain. They were both thoroughly drenched by the time they reached the bridge. Once they'd ducked underneath, they were spared the beating of the rain, but Linnea shivered nonetheless. The blackness was blinding and the humidity was close in the confined space. The light from John's flashlight snaked along the rippled sand, illuminating a narrow path for them to follow.

"John!" Linnea gasped as she pointed.

There seemed to be someone huddled against the cement wall of the bridge covered with bold green and red graffiti. Drawing closer, Linnea cried out, "It's Flo."

She was wearing her nightgown, a flimsy blue sheath of cotton that clung to her trembling frame, so thin now that she looked like a child. Her knees were close up to her chest. Her wispy white hair was plastered against her head. When the light hit her face, Flo's blue eyes revealed her terror and utter confusion. She lifted a pale, bony hand to shelter her eyes from the penetrating beam of light. Linnea spotted what looked like a discarded chunk of soggy sandwich clutched in her hand.

When they moved toward her, Flo crouched back and put both hands over her head, crying out, "No! No! Leave me alone!"

John signaled Linnea to back off.

She froze, her heart beating hard in her chest.

"Call my mother," John said in a clipped voice. "Tell her we've found her. To bring a car. And to hurry."

She did as he ordered, pulling out her phone and punching in the number. While the phone rang, she watched John approach Flo slowly, speaking in a low, calm voice. He set the flashlight down so it wouldn't startle her. Flo shrank farther back against the wet wall, her hand held out as pieces of wilted lettuce and stale meat fell from the soggy bread.

"Hello?" Emmi's voice was curt and shrill.

"We found her."

"Thank God," Emmi said, her voice breaking. Linnea heard Emmi shout out, "They found her! Linnea and John found her!"

In a few short sentences, Linnea gave directions to where they were. "We'll meet you in the parking lot at Breach Inlet. And, Emmi, bring a blanket."

She tucked her phone back in her pocket and took a few steps closer to John and Flo. He'd succeeded in calming her down. She was no longer screaming, but she still trembled visibly from the cold.

"Well, hey there, Flo," John crooned, smiling. He was crouched to walk hunchbacked under the curve of the bridge's foundation. "It's me. John. You remember my handsome face?"

Flo lowered her hand and peered into his face. Her head tilted, the light casting shadows on the sharp cheekbones of her thin face.

"Brett?" she said in a weak, tremulous voice.

Linnea brought her hand to cover her mouth. Brett. Flo thought John was Brett Beauchamps, Cara's first husband.

Brett had been Flo's knight in shining armor, as he had been Lovie's before her. He was always on call for the old woman living alone, to run an errand, fix a broken pipe, lift anything heavy, and to bring home a pound of shrimp from the dock when asked. It dawned on Linnea: *that* was why Flo had always asked for John, preferring him to help her over Emmi. In her dementia, Flo had mistaken John for Brett.

Linnea watched John reach out and gently remove the soggy sandwich from Flo's hand, tossing it behind him into the darkness. He began speaking so softly Linnea couldn't make out the words, but she watched him reach out once again, and this time Flo let him take hold of her hand. He gently guided the old woman away from the graffiti-covered wall.

Tears filled Linnea's eyes as she kept a light on the pair. John was very much like Brett, she thought. Both were tall and broad-shouldered, and their hair was tawny brown. But they didn't look alike. It was more their gentlemanly manner that was similar, their kindness, and their lowcountry charm that gave them an ease in the landscape they were born and raised in. Flo, for all that she'd lost in her mental faculties, saw the truth clearly.

Linnea had loved her uncle Brett. He'd been her teacher when she'd come as a child to Isle of Palms in the summers with Cooper to spend weeks in the sun and surf. And later he'd been her mentor, when Linnea was a teenager and worked summers on his tour boats that cruised the Intracoastal. Brett had shared with her his love of all things wild, not just the popular dolphins and sea turtles. He'd revealed to her the beauty of the cordgrass waving in the last rays of sunlight on any given day; the history and medical importance of horseshoe crabs, calling them our living dinosaurs; the humor in a fiddler crab waving his one oversize claw to impress a mate.

John lifted Flo into his arms as gently and easily as he would a child. Linnea realized she probably weighed as little. She followed with the light as he carried Flo out from the shelter of the bridge, smiling down at her with kindly affection. The rain had mercifully slowed to a drizzly mist and the worst of the wind had already blown offshore.

Suddenly Flo looked out toward the sea, and a beautiful smile transformed her face. She arched in John's arms and reached out to wave enthusiastically. Linnea turned, but there was nothing there but the pitch black of sea and sky.

"Hello! Hello, Lovie!" Flo called out. Her face was filled with childlike joy as she waved.

John's and Linnea's gazes met, first with worry, then with wonder as they realized they were witnessing something neither of them could understand.

Other voices called out, this time coming from behind them along the beach path. "Linnea? John?"

"Over here!" Linnea called out, and ran to the edge of the bridge. She waved her flashlight to guide them. Figures made their way down the beach path from the parking lot in single file. David was first, carrying a large lantern that lit up the area. He was followed closely by Cara carrying blankets, and then Emmi.

Flo saw them and clutched John in fear, burying her head in his shoulder.

"It's okay, Flo," he said softly. "Look. It's Emmi. And Cara. They've come to take you home."

# chapter sixteen

*Every day is meant to be lived. Fully. With our eyes wide open.*
*Our senses on full alert. Not wasted. Or squandered in doubt or self-pity.*

THE FAST-MOVING STORM had left the coast drenched. The sand was deep and soft and difficult for walking as John carried Florence up the steep incline over the dunes to the parking lot. Emmi and Cara guided Flo into the backseat of David's Range Rover. Her eyes had closed and her head fell on Emmi's shoulder.

Linnea and John, wrapped in blankets, stood quietly watching. From this distance, Linnea couldn't tell if Flo was resting, had fallen asleep, or passed out. The old woman was still trembling, even under her blanket. Linnea whipped off her blanket and handed it to Cara.

"Cover her with this one too. She's still cold."

Cara's eyes gleamed with gratitude. "Darling girl," she murmured as she took it and placed it over Flo.

"There's room for one more," David called from the front seat.

"You take it," John told Linnea.

"I'm not going without you."

"You go ahead," John called out to David. "It's only a few blocks. Get Flo home. We'll walk."

The big car pulled away from the curb and Linnea watched the red taillights disappear into the mist. John moved his blanket so that it covered both their heads. Under the blanket it smelled of wet wool, which was oddly comforting. They walked hip to hip, her arm around his waist, in lockstep.

"Thank God we found her," John said. "If you hadn't insisted, we'd still be looking."

"She doesn't look well," she said.

"No."

Linnea turned her head to look at him. "John, that sandwich," she said with disgust just remembering it. "My God, do you think she ate it?"

"Yeah. I could smell it on her breath."

"Oh God," Linnea moaned. "It looked rotten."

"I'm more worried about contagion."

"Covid? You don't think she'll catch it?"

"It's possible. She was out with all those people, not wearing a mask," he said, his fatigue cutting his voice. "She's so fragile . . . she weighed next to nothing. When I think of Florence Prescott, I think of this strong, invincible woman. She'd challenge Peter at the Pearly Gates." He wiped his nose. "I held her in my arms like she was a child."

A car passed them on the road, splashing them with water. They were so wet already, neither of them cared.

Linnea had to ask. "Did you hear her calling Lovie?"

John walked a few steps. "Yeah."

"She was *waving* to her. Like she was seeing her."

"I saw it myself, or I wouldn't have believed it."

"Do you . . . do you think she really saw her?"

"I don't know . . ." he said with sincerity.

After the night they'd had, walking together under the shelter of the blanket, hip to hip, step in step, there was a raw honesty in the air.

"She seemed so happy. Like . . . like she was letting her know she was coming." Linnea turned her head. "Do you think it's possible that Lovie was coming for her?"

John sighed and shook his head. "I don't know what to say. Maybe. Yeah."

"I think she was," Linnea confessed. "You know," she added, "Cara has seen Lovie a couple of times."

"Her *ghost*?"

"Yes," she replied fervently. "And you know Cara's not the kind of woman who'd make that up. She swears by it. And my father saw her too."

"*That* I find hard to believe."

"Which is why I believe it. If Cara and Daddy saw Lovie . . ."

"This is giving me the creeps," John said as they turned down the street toward the beach house.

"Not me," Linnea said. "It makes me feel less afraid. Hopeful. To think that Lovie came to Flo when she needed her." She looked up at him. "Don't you find that comforting? It gives me hope."

John walked a few paces before replying. "Do you want to know how it makes me feel?"

"Of course."

"No. Forget it."

There was something in his voice. A breaking point. "John, tell me," she urged.

They'd reached the corner before Linnea's house. John stopped walking and dropped his arm, letting the blanket slip from their heads. The fine mist seemed to glisten under the light from the lamppost. She looked at him, his clothes as soaked as hers. His hair clinging wet to his head. But the light in John's eyes burned like a flame.

"All this talk of life and death," he began. "Ghosts . . ." He ran his hand through his hair, pushing the locks from his forehead. "A damn pandemic is haunting us every bit as much as any ghost. It's the god-damn Grim Reaper. None of us knows if it's going to get us. We could all die tomorrow."

"That's bleak."

"Is it? Not for a lot of people right now. Not for Flo."

Linnea cringed. "We should go."

"Wait." John sighed. "I don't mean to be grim. Just the opposite. What I mean to say is . . ." He took a breath. "That every day is meant to be lived. Fully. With our eyes wide open. Our senses on full alert. Not wasted. Or squandered in doubt or self-pity."

There was a long silence while they stared into each other's eyes.

"You asked how all this makes me feel," he continued. "It makes me feel shocked straight. Even afraid."

"Afraid of what?"

"Afraid I'm going to die without you knowing that I still love you."

Linnea's lips slipped open in a silent gasp. She stared into John's eyes, two intense green flames, and couldn't feel the cold.

He took a step toward her and held her against his chest, so tight her breasts crushed against him. She knew the smell of him, the taste of him. She felt desire welling as he cupped her cheeks and lowered to a kiss . . .

"No!" she cried, pushing back from him, her breath coming hard.

John stared back, his eyes glazed.

"I won't do this again!" she cried.

"Linnea, I—"

"I don't trust you when you say you love me. You have no right to tell me that now," she shouted at him. "It's too late."

He took a step toward her, his hand outstretched. She slapped it away. Unlike Flo's, *her* memory was still sharp.

"You broke my heart!"

He moved his hand to his head and raked his hair, momentarily stunned. "I'm sorry. I was a fool. Please . . ."

"No." Tears flowed down her cheeks, mingling with the rain.

"I can only say this once," he told her, wiping his face with both hands. For a moment he stood with his palms covering his face. Then he dropped them, and he looked at her, his gaze boring into hers.

"I've always loved you. That was never the issue. I was afraid. I didn't think I was ready. But when you left, you took everything good with you. Any chance for happiness walked out that door with you. For a year I tried to get you to listen to me, but you wouldn't answer my calls. My e-mails. My texts. I even wrote you a letter. When I didn't hear from you, I didn't give up. I thought, okay. You needed time. Linnea, I never gave up hope. But this spring, when it came on a year, I couldn't wait any longer."

He paused and made a sound of exasperation. "I didn't come here for some conference! I came here for you. I knew I'd run out of time. I had to be here, to tell you how I felt, before some other guy realized how amazing you are and swept you off your feet." He paused. "And I was right."

"What did you think would happen?" she asked, daring him to answer.

"Not the goddamn virus, that's for sure. I could not believe my rotten luck. I was stuck in that carriage house able to see you from the window, but not talk to you. But then came hope in the form of a little girl. And a paper airplane. She made a connection possible. A tenuous beginning based on us being friends again. I grabbed hold of that. I knew you felt something for me." His smile was sad. "You've never been very good at hiding your feelings."

"I do have feelings for you," she cried. "And I wish they'd stop."

"Why?"

"Because you're never going to want the same things I want." Her voice broke.

"I do," he said, taking a step closer.

Linnea took a step away.

John put up his hands, as though steadying a wild horse about to bolt. "I'm ready," he said. "Linnea, I swear, I'm full-on ready to take it all on. I want to commit to you. Commit it all. My love. My life. Every day I have left on earth, I want to spend with you."

Linnea put her hand over her mouth and shook her head.

"Don't choose him, Linnea." He pounded his fist over his heart. "Choose *me*."

Linnea stared at John, at the water dripping down his face, his green eyes catching the light from the streetlamp. John's eyes were wet, and she couldn't tell if it was the mist or tears.

"I can't," she choked out.

She turned on her heel and hurried across the street toward the warm lights spilling out of her beach house. Behind her she heard John call, "Linnea!"

———

LINNEA RAN UP the front stairs into the house, tears flowing, soaked to the skin. She pushed open the door and stood gathering her wits, dripping on the floor. Anna and Cooper looked up from the sofa. Gordon rushed from his chair to her side. He took hold of her hands.

"Your hands are like ice."

Cooper was at her side. "Is it Flo?"

Linnea tried to catch her breath. "She . . . she's home."

"Thank God," said Cooper.

"She's not well."

Gordon held her close. She knew he misunderstood her tears. He thought she was broken up about Flo.

"It's all right," he said, kissing the top of her head. "Flo's in good hands now. She's safe. That's all we can do for the moment. But you—let's get you into some dry clothes."

Pandora stepped from the kitchen. "I'll make you a cup of hot tea."

The door burst open again, and John rushed in. Like Linnea, his hair was dripping water and his clothes were drenched, and he was dragging a wet wool blanket at his feet.

Pandora rushed back into the room carrying a teakettle.

John stood wide-legged, breathing heavily, and looked around the room, momentarily fazed by seeing the group staring at him in curiosity. Then he focused on Linnea, in Gordon's arms, and a spark of jealousy flared in his eyes. He dropped the blanket, took a step forward, and grabbed Linnea's hand, pulling her from Gordon's arms.

"We're not finished yet," he told Linnea.

Gordon pushed John's chest, shoving him a few steps back. "Don't touch her."

"Fuck this." John came charging at Gordon like a bull, hitting him in the chest and pushing him clear across the front hall, crashing into the small Hepplewhite table and sending the mirror on the wall crashing to the floor. The women screamed and they all retreated a step as Gordon and John kept throwing punches.

"Stop it!" Linnea shouted.

The two men threw punches and, gripping each other, crashed

316

into the back of the sofa, falling over it and tumbling, locked together, as they wrestled each other to the floor. The coffee table wobbled, tossing all the glassware to the floor. The sound of crashing glass and the screams of the women brought Cooper into the fray. The two men were back on their feet, circling, when Cooper stepped between them, arms out, only to catch a punch in the chin from John. Anna screamed again as Cooper spun and crashed to the floor.

Gordon and John stopped fighting and stood panting, staring at Cooper.

"I'm sorry, man," John gasped. "Never meant . . ." He bent over, grasping his knees.

Gordon wobbled back, then stood wide-legged, eyes on Cooper.

Linnea ran to her brother and crouched beside Anna to check on him. He had raised himself to a sitting position and was rubbing his jaw. He was going to have a nasty bruise.

"Are you okay?"

"Yeah, I'm fine," Cooper said, sounding more embarrassed than hurt.

"You tosser," Gordon said to John.

John's fists formed again, but this time Linnea's voice was heard.

"Stop it, both of you," she shouted at the top of her lungs.

She looked at both men. John's hair was plastered against his face, his T-shirt torn, blood dripping from his lip. Gordon stood a few feet away; he was going to have a black eye and his collared shirt was ripped open, missing buttons.

"Go home. Both of you." Her shoulders slumped and she felt she was ready to slide to the floor. "I don't want to see either of you. Please. Just leave."

When neither of them moved, Pandora stepped forward and clapped her hands. "Okay, fellows. You heard the lady. Everybody out."

Linnea walked to her bedroom and quietly closed the door.

---

A HOT SHOWER had never felt so comforting. Linnea stood under the steady stream of water, relishing the warmth. She spread lavender soap over her body, washing away the musty smell of the blanket and the haunting sight of Flo looking like some mad homeless woman. She emerged cleaner, calmer, but beyond exhausted. Wrapping her hair in a towel, she slipped into a nightgown and a thick terry robe. She went to sit on the bed with Luna in her lap, stroking her soft fur while staring out at the dark night.

A soft knock sounded on the door. She closed her eyes and released a long sigh. "Please just go away."

"Linnea? It's me. Pandora. I've brought you a nice hot cup of tea. It's just what you need."

"Are you alone?"

"Yes."

"Come in."

Pandora walked in carefully balancing a tray in her hands. She kicked the door shut behind her. Luna rose and growled at the intruder.

"Hush, Luna," said Linnea. "It's Pan." She held Luna back so Pandora could set the tea tray on the bed.

"I didn't know what kind you liked, so there's hot water and a selection. And some honey and lemon."

"Thank you."

Pandora went to sit on the opposite side of the bed. Luna came trotting to her side, sniffing, allowing Pandora to pet her.

"Are they gone?" asked Linnea, tearing open the packet of chamomile tea.

"Oh, yes. Anna and Cooper cleaned up the broken glass. That mirror is a goner, I'm afraid."

"Oh no," Linnea said. "Cara won't be happy."

"I think you have bigger things to worry about than a mirror."

"Not tonight."

"Yes, tonight," Pandora persisted.

Linnea looked at her questioningly. She was exhausted. Worried about Flo. She didn't have the bandwidth.

"You had to know this was going to happen."

Linnea let her head fall back against the pillows. "You think I wanted them to fight?"

"Linnea, you've been dangling those two men in the air for the past few months! Leading them both on."

"Wait a minute," Linnea said, feeling her anger rise. Luna, hearing her tone, hurried back to her side of the bed. "I have not."

"Linnea, I'm your friend and I'm going to spell things out for you. I should've told you before."

Linnea looked at her warily.

"It's about Gordon."

Linnea set her jaw. "You take a pretty strong interest in him."

"I do," Pandora admitted. "That shouldn't come as a surprise. I liked him last summer. I've had a thing for him for years, as a matter of fact. You stole him from me, remember?"

"Oh, please! I didn't steal him from you. He was never yours to begin with."

"You never gave us the chance. You swooped in and made him fall in love with you."

"You can't make someone fall in love with you. It happens."

"Look, Linnea, I've tried to be a good friend. Better than you were to me. I didn't come on to him—"

"What?" Linnea said incredulously. "You've been hanging all over him. Flirting. 'Gordon let's do this, Gordon let's go there.'"

A flush crept up Pandora's cheeks. "Yes, I admit it. I've been going after him. Why not?" Her eyes flashed. "You're dangling him like a cat playing with some mouse."

"I'm not playing with his affection. We're still trying to figure things out. He came here to see if we could make it work. What's the rush? I'm hoping he'll stay on beyond the summer. Maybe take a teaching job here. Any place would jump at the chance to have him. We just need time to see where this is going."

"Hold on," Pandora said, sitting back with a look of wonder on her face. "Do you think, for a moment, that Gordon would even consider moving to the United States? Permanently?"

"I know he loves Oxford. But it's possible."

Pandora looked at the ceiling, her lips tight together, and it seemed she was going through some kind of personal struggle. When she looked at Linnea again, her eyes were hard with decision. "You really don't have any idea, do you?"

Linnea's face went still. "About what?"

"Darling, there's no possible way in the world that Gordon could leave England. His family is there. He has an *important* family."

"I have an important family. An old one that means something in Charleston. That doesn't mean I wouldn't move. I went to California."

Pandora rolled her eyes. "I promised him I wouldn't tell you."

"Tell me what?"

Pandora ground her teeth.

"You have to tell me now."

Pandora blurted out, "Gordon's father is a peer of the realm."

Linnea felt her stomach fall. "What?"

"He's the only son of a viscount. When his father dies, he will be Lord Gordon Carr of Rochester."

Linnea couldn't speak.

"Granted," Pandora said, "his family doesn't have much money. And the house isn't all that grand. But the man will someday in the not too distant future inherit the title and all the responsibilities that title brings. Gordon will have to live in England. In Rochester, to be precise. Where his ancestral lands are. Do you understand what this means? Your dream of him moving to the United States is just that. A dream."

"What I understand," Linnea said, "suddenly and with great clarity, is *why* you're in hot pursuit. You don't want Gordon. You want his title."

"That might have been true last summer," Pandora admitted. "But the more I spent time with you both, the more I realized how much I really like him. Everything about him. Maybe even love him. It drives me crazy to know you aren't sure you want him, when I . . . I want him so badly."

Linnea was stunned by her honesty. "Why didn't you talk to me about it?"

"What would I say? 'I want your boyfriend'?" She shook her head. "I couldn't." Pandora looked at her hands. "Full transparency. I tried to kiss him. Just once. I knew he felt something for me. But he wouldn't. He said he cared too much about you to do that." She scowled at Linnea's shocked expression. "Don't look at me like that. You kissed him when you knew I liked him."

"You weren't dating him. And he told me he thought of you like a sister."

Pandora flushed.

"Thanks for telling me about Gordon. All of it," Linnea said after a moment.

"I've wanted to tell you, so many times."

"Why didn't you?"

"I swore to Gordon I wouldn't. But after tonight . . . I told you to help you make up your mind. Because you have to, Lin."

Linnea leaned back against the pillows with a soft groan.

"Will you tell Gordon?" Pandora asked.

"I have to talk with him about all this."

"It will make things easier for all of us."

"I know."

Pandora pulled herself together and rose from the bed. "I'll leave the tea and be going."

"Yes. Good night. Thanks for the tea."

She closed her eyes and heard Pandora's footfalls cross the room, the door softly closing behind her.

———

LATER THAT EVENING, Anna sprawled out on Linnea's bed, her head perched on her palm. Across the room, Cooper sat on the cushioned chair, hands on his knees. Linnea leaned against a pile of pillows with Luna in her lap.

"A viscount?" Anna asked.

"His only heir."

"I . . . I don't know what a viscount is."

"He's royalty," she replied. "I admit, I had to look it up myself. A viscount is above a baron and below an earl."

"What the hell?" said Cooper. "All this time and he didn't tell us."

"No," said Linnea.

"It sure explains a lot," Anna said.

"What do you mean?" asked Linnea.

"Why Pandora has the hots for him. She wants his title!"

"She says not."

Anna snorted. "Yeah. Sure. Come on, Lin. She's so status-conscious. Honey, he's got the ultimate brand. Of course she wants his title."

"He should marry her," Cooper said.

"What?"

"It makes sense. He's got the title, she's got the money. If this was the Victorian age, he wouldn't have a choice. His family would pressure him to marry her."

"What are you going to do?" asked Anna.

"Talk to him," Linnea said.

"Does it make a difference?"

"His being a viscount? No," she answered. "Surprisingly, it doesn't. Him not being able to move here?" Linnea pursed her lips. "That's harder for me to answer."

Cooper crossed his legs. "Would you move there? If you do, I'm coming with you."

She tried to laugh, but it came out more of a snort. She shook her head in mock dismay. "Love's breaking up that old gang of mine."

"Speaking of which . . ." Cooper said. "I'm giving you my notice. I'm headed up to Columbia in two weeks. Some guys found a house and asked me to move in. Senior year, baby!"

Linnea was stunned. "You mean, they're going to open for classes? What about Covid?"

"There'll be required masks, testing, social distancing. Some classes are offered online. It's not great, but it's happening. Classes start August twentieth, but I'll need to get there early to settle into the house, get books, and, yeah, get tested for Covid. It all takes time." He spread out his hands. "Thanks for letting me stay."

"Of course." She petted Luna in her lap. "I have to say, I didn't expect this. I thought you'd take classes online and stay here."

"Nope." He looked at Anna.

"Uh, Linnea . . ." Anna said.

"What?" Linnea asked with suspicion.

Anna tried not to smile. "I'm giving my notice too."

Linnea sat up, sending the puppy sliding from her lap. "You're joking, right?"

Anna shook her head. "I'm moving to Columbia too." She grinned, eyes sparkling. "I'm going back to school. I'm doing it. I'm going into politics. I want to get things done. I'm getting my master's in political science. I got my application in just in time, and I was accepted."

"But . . ."

"Tuition? Yeah, I thought that would be the big problem, but it wasn't. I got a student loan," she said with glee. "I can't believe it, but, Lin, it all came together. And I have Gordon to thank for it. He put the idea in my head."

Cooper slapped his knee. "What about me?"

Anna smiled at him. "And mostly Cooper. He really pushed me to apply to the program. You know me, I didn't think I'd get in. Dragged my heels."

"Bitching and complaining . . ." added Cooper.

"But I got in. Then he pushed me to get the loan. To believe in myself."

Linnea saw the excitement in her eyes, her joy, and felt her own bubble up. "That's great. Really wonderful. I'm speechless. I just . . . wonder why you didn't tell me?"

"I didn't tell anyone until it was settled," Anna said. "I was going to announce it tonight at the party, but then . . ." She shrugged.

"Yeah . . ." said Linnea. Then a piece of the puzzle settled in her mind. "Wait a minute. You're moving in with Cooper, aren't you?"

"Busted," said Cooper.

"But . . ." Linnea was flabbergasted. "What was all that about a summer fling?" She made quotation marks in the air: "*It's nothing serious*." She dropped her hands. "The Covid Couple?"

Anna laughed and blew a kiss to Cooper. "Hey, Covid's still on-going."

"You're not mad?" asked Cooper. "With us cutting out on you?"

"Oh, Cooper. Anna," she said, reaching out to take hold of Anna's hand. "How could I be mad? In the midst of a pandemic, with all the ups and downs, the disappointments and frustrations, you found something of meaning. You're changing your lives. I'm so proud of you both." She smiled and wasn't embarrassed for the tears. "And it's so wonderful to hear some good news." Then she laughed and fist-pumped the air. "Go Gamecocks!"

# chapter seventeen

*Follow your instincts.*

THE FOLLOWING MORNING, Linnea woke to voices outdoors. She glanced at the clock and gasped to see it was nearly nine o'clock. She bolted from her bed, stunned that she'd slept so late. She'd talked with Cooper and Anna until ten, then couldn't sleep for wrestling with thoughts about Gordon and what she would say to him.

She slipped into yoga pants and a Turtle Team T-shirt and hurried outdoors. The storm left its mark on the lowcountry. Torrents of rain had been dumped in a short period of time in conjunction with the king tide, a supertide that occurs when the moon is closest to the earth. The end of her driveway was a large puddle and plants drooped with the weight of water.

In Emmi's driveway she spied Cara, Emmi, and John standing in a semicircle. They looked as tired and worn out as she was sure she did. Cara's and Emmi's faces were flushed, as though in an argument. As she drew near, she glanced at John, sorry to see his bottom lip was swollen.

"What's going on?" she asked Cara as she drew near.

"Good morning, Sweet-tea," Cara said. "Flo spiked a fever. She's refusing to eat or drink. I'm afraid it's bad." Cara turned to Emmi. "She has to go to the hospital."

Emmi locked her jaw, shook her head, and crossed her arms. "No way. If she goes to the hospital, she's never coming back."

"Good Lord, Emmi," Cara said with barely disguised frustration. "I went along with you as long as I could. Enough now. The woman's barely conscious. We're not equipped to deal with this. At her age, in her state . . . Emmi, she could die."

"Then she can die at home."

Linnea startled. "Emmi, no."

Cara went poker-faced. "And if she can't breathe? She starts choking? Are you prepared to watch her suffer?"

"Mom . . ." said John.

The sound of an ambulance pierced the air.

Emmi's eyes flashed as she confronted Cara. "You called the ambulance?"

"No, I did," said John.

Emmi turned on him. "Who gave you the authority?"

"Flo did."

Emmi's shoulders sagged as she tried to make sense of what he'd said. "Wait. What? When? She wasn't conscious. Or lucid."

"Yes. She was." John paused. "I was taking my turn sitting with her. It was early, just before dawn. She opened her eyes, and she knew it was me. She looked right at me and said, 'John, I want you to take me to the hospital.' When I asked her if she was sure, she said she was. She said she didn't want to die in this house. She said . . ." He swallowed hard, trying to form the words. "She said she only wanted good memories in this house."

Emmi stepped into John's arms as Cara put her hand over her mouth and turned her back, trying to hold back her choking sobs.

———————

A SHORT TIME later, Cara held Emmi's hand as they watched two paramedics in full protective gear carry Flo's stretcher into the ambulance. At the hospital, Flo went directly into intensive care. For three days, all three houses were shrouded in the silence of waiting. Cara cooked meals, watered plants, allowed Hope to watch far too much television. Emmi didn't call. She didn't respond to Cara's messages. Not because she was angry, but because she couldn't. Cara knew it was especially hard on her to think of Flo in the hospital, sick and alone, not aware where she was.

Then the news came.

Cara heard an insistent knocking on the door. She opened it to see Emmi, her face grief-stricken, her eyes rimmed red. Cara didn't have to ask. Flo was not coming back to Isle of Palms.

Emmi walked into Cara's arms and the two women hugged and wept openly.

"We never got to say good-bye," Emmi wailed.

"We did say good-bye."

"No," Emmi said harshly, pulling back. "No, we didn't. Calling out a good-bye at the ambulance, watching the doors shut and the van drive away . . . that's not saying good-bye."

"We all knew that family wasn't allowed into the hospitals."

"But the reality of it is still hard," Emmi said in a broken voice. "Knowing that at the end of her life Flo might've been scared and we couldn't be there. After all the time I spent with her, not to be there when she most needed me." She choked back a sob. "I'm sorry, but that feels to me like I failed her."

"Oh, Em, no. She knew that we loved her," Cara said, trying to be strong for Emmi.

She settled Emmi on the sofa and prepared two mugs of steaming tea with milk and honey. It was a hot July day outdoors, but inside both women needed the comfort of something warm and sweet.

They pulled out old photographs and recalled memories of happier days when they were young with Lovie and Flo.

"We ran back and forth, back and forth between Flo's and your mother's beach houses. Nonstop."

"Most of the time we ran from turtle duty," Cara said teasingly.

Emmi laughed. "Remember how we giggled as we rode our bikes away when they called?"

Cara nodded. "They took two ragamuffins and taught them, kicking and screaming all the way, not merely the rules but the art of tending turtle nests."

Emmi smiled. "They weren't fools. They were training us to take their places."

"Think," Cara said. "They're together now."

"Yes." Emmi drew in a long breath. "This is what we needed now. Nothing cheers up a soul like good memories."

"That's what Flo wanted us to have."

After a long silence, Emmi set her mug on the table. "I've been thinking, I need some time away. I feel a bit lost with Flo gone. Like I've lost my footing in soft sand."

"I'm sorry you had to take on the major effort of Flo's care. I know we said we'd share the duties, but living with her, you've borne the brunt of it. It had to be such a burden."

"No, Cara. I've never seen it as a burden. Living with Flo, taking care of her the past few years, it was my privilege. I wouldn't have given up a moment of it. But I need to get away."

Cara looked at Emmi, and wondered how she had ever been so fortunate as to find Emmaline Baker in her crazy, whirlwind life. Despite the many miles that had sometimes separated them, regardless of the years when they didn't speak or the differences in life philosophies, political views, even their fashion style, Emmi had always been her best friend.

She was concerned about the new lines she saw on Emmi's face. Her skin was as pale as the milk in her tea. It was rare these days to see her signature wide smile. Most disturbing, however, was that Emmi looked worn out. Vulnerable. She had been so busy taking care of others, she hadn't given a thought to herself.

"Where will you go?" Cara asked.

"I'm not sure. Not far. I don't have many choices with the pandemic. I was thinking it'd be nice to rent a place at Pawleys Island. I've always liked it there. I have people I know I can ask. We'll see."

"Will John be around? I'd be happy to check on your house. Feed the koi."

Emmi sighed. "Maybe. Everything's up in the air with those kids. Don't ask me about the bruises on his face, much less what John's going to do. There's nothing holding him here. I'd hoped he'd work something out with Linnea." She shrugged. "I guess it was just wishful thinking on my part."

"Those two . . . or should I say three?" Cara finished her tea and set the mug on the table. "I don't want to meddle. I'm just here to help if they ask. They're good kids. I have faith in them." She patted Emmi's hand. "Best we stay out of it. No matter how much we may wish to step in."

"All the more reason for me to go away for a while."

"When do you want to go?"

"Soon. After we spread Flo's ashes." She reached for Cara's hand. "God give me strength."

---

IT WAS A balmy night on the beach. The moon was ghostly, barely visible in the rolling clouds. Linnea and Cara sat side by side on towels beside a turtle nest that was due to hatch. They both welcomed the opportunity to escape the confines of the indoors to the fresh, freeing air of the seaside to clear their minds.

"I'd forgotten how much I love to sit on the beach at night," Cara said in a low voice. "I'm spoiled living here. Sometimes I take all this beauty for granted. It's out here all the time. It's a funny game the mind plays on you. Sometimes I walk through the living room and don't even look out the windows."

"I know. I do it too. We get so caught up in what we're doing, we don't stop to look around and take stock." Linnea breathed deep. "Oh, that air," she said in a soft groan of pleasure. "It feels like silk."

Cara leaned back on her arms. "I think we both really needed this. My heart feels battered and my mind . . . let's just say I'm on overload."

"Me too."

It was nearly midnight. They'd been sitting at the nest since 9 p.m. and the turtles had yet to emerge. A group of hatchlings sat at the top of the nest, their dark flippers and beaks poking out of the sand, forming a circle that always made Linnea think of a chocolate chip cookie. She and Cara couldn't leave the nest now. Not on such a dark night when the moon and stars were blanketed by clouds. The hatchlings might be drawn to the streetlights rather than the natural light over the sea. Especially not when the emergence was imminent.

"Cara?"

Linnea felt a chill, even on a sultry night. The velvety darkness cloaked her in a security that gave voice to even her most private thoughts.

Cara turned her head to peer at her through the darkness.

"I guess this isn't the best time to ask for your advice. . . ."

"Why? Are you in need of some?"

"Badly."

Cara straightened and slapped the sand from her palms. "Ask away."

"If you came here to relax . . ."

"I came here to take my mind off Flo. This is just what the doctor ordered."

Linnea brought her knees up and rested her chin on her arms as she stared out into the vast sea. "I'm falling apart." She heard her voice break and struggled to tamp down her emotions.

"Oh no . . ."

Linnea took a breath to be able to speak. "I've spent the summer trying to pay it forward. Like you said. I've tried to be supportive, helpful. Especially now, when the whole world is in crisis. But in the process, I've managed to hurt two men I care a great deal about. I've failed. " She wiped her eyes. "Utterly. And I'm so sad. All the time. I feel so . . ." Her voice broke. "Lost."

"Oh, Linnea," Cara said, her voice tinged with compassion. "When I told you about the legacy of the beach house, I meant for you to understand that it is *your* sanctuary too. I admit, I was worried when you kept inviting people to stay with you."

"I was trying to pay it forward," she repeated.

"And you did." Cara chuckled. "You didn't fail. Don't you see? You succeeded."

"How?"

"The beach house became like the mushroom in the children's story. Remember the one?"

Linnea squinted. "I don't think so."

"It's one of Hope's favorites. All these animals seek shelter from the rain under a mushroom barely big enough for one. The rain kept coming down and the animals kept arriving. Somehow, they all managed to find shelter. When the sun comes out the following morning, they discover what happens to a mushroom in the rain. It grows!" Cara smiled. "It's such a sweet story. Your care and love is the rain, Linnea. As it was your grandmother's. Love grows. That is the magic of the beach house."

She reached out to smooth a lock of Linnea's hair that was falling across her face and tucked it behind her ear. Linnea closed her eyes at the gentle touch, feeling it deeply.

"Sometimes, though, a woman gives too much. When things start to fall apart, when you begin to feel angry, when you make mistakes, it's time to stop and take stock." She laughed. "Control is an illusion. I learned that lesson."

"I guess I still have to learn that one," Linnea said.

She felt something scratching at her hand. Startled, she softly shrieked and looked down. A hatchling was trying to climb over her fingers. "Oh my God, Cara! The hatchlings. They're coming!"

Oh so carefully, Linnea and Cara rose to their feet, lest they step on one of the dozens of hatchlings scrambling past them. Even as she moved slowly. Linnea felt her excitement bubble.

"I'll stay by the nest. You guide them to the sea," Cara called out.

Linnea flicked on her red flashlight and made her way gingerly ahead of the squadron of tiny brown hatchlings marching toward the ocean. In the dim light they looked more like moving pebbles covering the beach. Some were circling around and heading back to the dune. There were too many of them for her to use her feet as blockades.

"They're turning!" she called to Cara.

"Be the moon!"

Linnea hurried to the surf and, thankful she was wearing sandals, stepped into the sea. The water was bathwater warm and as dark as ink. She hated being in the ocean at night; it was hunting time for sharks. She'd seen more than her share of sharks in shallow water. Still, the hatchlings were disoriented and duty called. Higher by the dune, she saw the narrow beam of red light of Cara's flashlight as she walked with the red bucket, scooping up hatchlings to bring them closer to the water and safety. The perils of a dark sky with bright streetlights were a deadly combination.

*Be the moon*, she thought.

Linnea walked deeper into the sea, stopping at her knees. Then she flicked her flashlight to white light and let it shine across the waterline to compete with the bright lights of the streetlamps and houses. She watched as the hatchlings turned once again toward the white light, toward the sea. Cara reached the shoreline and, lowering to her knees, tilted the bucket and released the hatchlings. They raced off in their comical fashion, flippers scrambling, forward toward the bright light and home.

Then it was over.

Linnea slowly returned to shore, her heels deep in the undersea sand, the warm water swirling around her thighs . . . her calves . . . her ankles. She stepped out of the sea as the last hatchling's dive instinct kicked in. A winsome smile crossed her lips as the tiny creature caught an outgoing wave, flippers stroking hard. Then, in an instant, it disappeared.

She felt akin to that young turtle, seeking its destiny in the swirling, dark waters. Moving forward, always onward, toward . . . what?

Cara and Linnea turned in tandem and slowly walked back to the nest. They knelt in the cool sand and in a companionable silence, began scooping sand and filling in the gaping hole. When the nest was closed, Cara smoothed out the surface then placed an *X* on the top so the turtle team would know that the nest had emerged.

Finished, Cara sat back on her haunches and took a deep breath. There was a unique stillness in the wee hours of the morning. Solitude was keenly felt.

"This never gets old," Cara said.

"Never," agreed Linnea.

Cara slid to her side to sit comfortably, appearing not ready, even unwilling, to let go of this serenity. Linnea felt it, too. After so much turmoil, she felt no urgency to pack up and head indoors. The night air welcomed them with gentle breezes, the velvety darkness blanketed them, and the gentle lapping of the waves in the distance was a crooning lullaby.

She thought again of the turtle.

"When the hatchling enters the sea, do you think it wonders what tomorrow will bring?" she asked. "Does it fear the darkness? What propels that young creature to stroke so determinedly, even eagerly, into the unknown?"

Cara didn't reply for a while. As she sat in silence, Linnea began to wonder if she would, or if she'd even heard her. Linnea joined her in looking out into the sky so dark she could barely make out the outline of sea and surf. Then she heard Cara's voice.

"Long ago, on a night much like this," Cara began "my mother told me a story. I, too, was feeling unsure. About a lot of things." She laughed shortly. "About a man. Should I stay or should I go? Should I marry or live on my own? Should I, should I, should I?"

She paused and Linnea thought about her own litany of *should I* questions running through her mind.

"Mama told me to remember the turtle," Cara continued. "'They're ancient dinosaurs. They've been around for over one hundred million years, and they survived all those years because they follow their instincts.'" Cara turned to look at Linnea. "Mama looked at me and said, 'Follow your instincts.'"

"Yes, but . . . How will I know what is my instinct and what is some rambling fear or worry?"

"My darling girl, have courage! When the hatchling runs into the sea it is following its instinct, without fear or doubt. Onward! Perhaps it's time to stop asking the questions and simply listen. When the answer reveals itself, you will feel peace in the knowing."

Cara moved to face Linnea. "I understand your doubts. I had my bags packed, a ticket in my hand, plans made, and yet I felt conflicted about my decision. Doubt niggled me. Then the night before I was to leave I stood at the precipice of a dune and looked out at a scene unfolding before me—hatchlings racing to the sea, my family guiding them, Brett standing at the surf—and I knew."

Cara reached out to place her hand on Linnea's arm and gave it a gentle squeeze. "So now I'm telling you. Follow your instincts. Listen to your intuition. Trust yourself. That is where you'll find your truest advice."

# chapter eighteen

*I can't say yes to you until I say yes to myself.*

LINNEA SLOWLY CAME to terms with her grief over Flo's passing. Since the night of the fight, she'd avoided talking to Gordon or John. Keeping to herself, taking long walks on the beach, looking at old photographs in a week's peaceful solitude helped return her to an equilibrium that had been missing for the past several weeks . . . even months.

But she knew she couldn't dodge the conversation any longer. This morning she'd called Gordon and asked him to come over for tea. She boiled a kettle, set a tray, and carried it outside to the deck. She noticed how dry the earth of her potted plants had become. The leaves were beginning to look a little yellow.

A noise from behind brought her attention to the steps. She exhaled, seeing Gordon step onto the deck. In his hands he carried a bouquet of pink roses. The skin around his eye had turned that faint yellow of a healing bruise. She was sorry to see it.

She shook her head as he drew near. "Look at you," she said with sympathy.

"You should see the other guy."

Linnea laughed congenially, grateful he still had his sense of humor. He handed her the flowers and she accepted them, bringing them to her nose. There was no scent.

"Pink roses are said to mean *I'm sorry*," he told her.

She looked up at him over the blush colored roses. The bloom of her love for Gordon had passed. She knew that now, and it gave her courage and compassion. "I'm the one who should say I'm sorry."

"Why? You did nothing wrong."

"But I did. I've come to understand quite a few things in the past several days." Linnea extended her arm toward the pergola. "Do you want to sit down?"

Gordon followed her to the wicker table. Before she sat, she asked, "Tea?"

He put up his hand and gave a quick shake of his head. It was a simple gesture, yet refined. Linnea realized that she had always noticed his effortless elegance; now, knowing his lineage, she understood so much more. She couldn't see him without thinking of his title.

"I heard you've moved out of the loft?"

"Yes. I couldn't stay there."

"No. Of course. And where . . . ?"

"I'm staying at Pandora's. She offered."

A wry smile passed her lips. "Of course she did."

He looked at his hands.

She felt a new strain between them. His nervousness. In contrast, her calm.

"Gordon, I'm sorry. I see now that I've put you . . . and John . . . in an indefensible position this summer. I didn't mean to. Honestly. I was just taking it day by day, like everyone else. Please believe me, I was so happy when you arrived. I have feelings for you. Very strong feelings." She paused. "What I didn't expect was that I still had feelings for John." She glanced at him. He was still looking at his hands.

Gordon looked up and said, "When I arrived, did you know then?"

She shook her head. "I was more annoyed by my feelings for him. I honestly didn't expect it to be an issue between us. We tried to be friends. And when I felt stronger feelings, I fought them. Truly, I did. But clearly, I failed. I apologize for that."

Gordon's silence spoke volumes.

"And maybe now," she said, "you owe me an apology as well."

His brows rose. "Me? What have I done?"

"You tell me, Lord Carr, Viscount of Rochester."

Understanding flooded his face. He opened his mouth to speak, then closed it again. After a minute he asked, "Pandora told you?"

"She didn't tell you she had?"

He frowned. "No."

"Don't be mad at her. She was right to tell me. Gordon, *you* should have told me. Why didn't you?"

He put out his hands. "I didn't want to tell you precisely because you didn't know."

"I don't understand."

"I was surprised Pandora hadn't told you back when we met. That's when I swore her to secrecy. That sort of thing never gets hidden in the UK. One's title follows one everywhere, clouding relationships, making people act false around you. It gets very old, I promise you. Then you came in like a breath of fresh air and took me for who I was. You were fascinated with my *work*. Not my title. Linnea, I fell in love with you. And I lived in fear that you would find out and it would change everything."

"I did find out. And it does change everything."

His face stilled. "Why?"

"You're a viscount. Gordon, I didn't even know what that was."

He laughed and reached out to take her hand. "But that's exactly why I love you. And I'm not a lord, by the way. My father is still alive. I'm a mere mister."

"And the only son."

"Linnea, it's not all glamour like the movies make it out to be. My family is struggling to hang on to the property for taxes and expenses. We're barely able to sustain the house."

"You should marry Pandora. She's rich. And I think she rather fancies a title."

He shook his head ruefully. "Pandora."

"She's definitely into you. Maybe even loves you."

"If this was the nineteenth century, I would have no choice. I like to think I have a choice in the twenty-first. Linnea, I don't love Pandora. I love you. I thought you loved me."

"I do."

"You have to choose, Linnea."

There it was. He was asking her to decide. As John had done.

"Gordon, no matter who I choose, someone is going to get hurt."

"I'll make it easier for you," Gordon said, laying out his cards. "England is my home. I must return. And I want you to come with me."

She felt a crack in her heart. He'd put it all on the line. It was like Gordon to see things clearly, and to be able to restrain his emotions when needed. Her eager-to-please self leaned toward saying yes.

And yet, her body coiled in resistance. She felt her skin itch. Her heart rate accelerate.

"You're asking me to make my mind up right now?"

His forehead creased. "I suppose I am. Do we really need more time?" he asked, leaning toward her. He spread out his palms like a player showing his hand. "My project here is ending. And"—his eyes brightened—"I just received an exceptional opportunity in England. I haven't been able to discuss it with you. I want to." He paused to fold his hands together, as though to rein the conversation back to the decision at hand. "I love you, and I hope you'll come with me."

This time, Linnea didn't hear his words of love. She heard his demand couched in them. Going with Gordon now meant that his career would take precedence over hers. The worth of his title would supersede her own name. Linnea's spine stiffened as her vulnerability slipped off like a coat removed. Gordon had told her what he wanted. And his feelings were fair. But it was also fair for her to have her own needs.

She scratched her arm, smiling inwardly. Her body was screaming at her what her mind had refused to hear. *Follow your instincts.*

"I'm sorry, Gordon. I can't do that."

He blinked and sat up. "You're saying no."

"I'm saying you are a wonderful man. A man I care deeply for. But I can't go to England with you."

"What if I gave it all up? Stayed in America? If Harry could do it, so can I."

"Dear Harry," she said with a mirthless laugh. "I can't ask you to do that."

"It's more than the title, isn't it?" he asked. "It's John."

She shook her head. "It's more than John. I've been telling you this all summer, but you didn't listen." She shrugged. "Nor, did I, not seriously." She spoke slowly, enunciating each word: "I am not ready to make that commitment."

She laughed shortly. "It's taken this crazy, mixed-up, difficult, oddly wonderful summer to fully understand it myself. Years back, when I went to California, I lost myself. I returned home broken. I've worked really hard since then in my career and with family to find myself again. Actually," she said, "it's more than that. I'm just beginning to grasp hold of what it is *I* need." She offered a wan smile, hoping he'd understand. "So you see, I can't say yes to you until I say yes to myself. I'm a work in progress. And I have to continue that work here. In the lowcountry."

Gordon sat for a moment, gazing at the sky. Then he looked at her with sadness lurking in his eyes. He leaned toward her, and she raised her face to kiss him. But he went higher and kissed the top of her head.

"I wish you great happiness, Linnea." He rose, then looked at the bunch of roses on the table. "I suppose I should have given you chrysanthemums." His gaze was tender, his smile brief. "They mean *good-bye*."

# chapter nineteen

*Hindsight is twenty-twenty.*
*Yet in this year of 2020, there is no hindsight to be had!*

THEY GATHERED AT the small dune where years earlier they had scattered Lovie's ashes. The dune was directly across from the beach house, a spot on the beach where many memories had been forged. As Lovie liked to say, only the good ones. Cara, Hope, and David, Emmi and John, Palmer and Julia, Anna and Cooper, and, standing alone with her dog, Linnea formed a semicircle on the dune, each carrying a rose from Flo's bushes.

Dawn held special meaning for this group. For Emmi, Cara, Linnea, and especially Flo, it was the early hour of beach walking when the sun broke the shroud of night and the strident calls of birds sang out with hope.

Emmi lowered to her knees and, using a large whelk shell, dug a hole twenty-four inches deep in the sand, the same depth and circumference as a sea turtle nest. When she was done, Cara stepped forward holding the nondescript black box that carried the ashes of the woman they'd known as Florence Prescott. Cara kissed the box, then handed it to Emmi.

Emmi was calm as she pried open the box and, without words, tilted it to let the ashes fall down into the nest-like hole. When the last of the ashes were poured, Emmi moved aside as, one by one, each member of the group tossed her or his rose into the trench.

Linnea was the last. She took a shuddering breath and released the flower, whispering, "Good-bye dear Flo." Then she too stepped back to join the circle. She watched as Emmi and Cara knelt side by side in the sand to fill in the hole as they would a turtle nest, handful after handful, patting the sand firm when finished. Emmi placed the large seashell, one that Flo had used to dig her nests as a "Turtle Lady," atop the grave.

Linnea knew that Flo wasn't in that hole in the sand. She remembered vividly that frightening night when Flo was in John's arms and looked out at the sea, her face lit up with joy, and waved to Lovie. Linnea absolutely believed that her grandmother had come to guide Flo to the other side. She could feel both of them here now, on this dune with the people they'd loved. And she knew in her heart she would always find them whenever she looked out at the restless sea, or at the clicking sea oats on the dunes, or at every hatchling that eagerly raced home to the sea.

When the two women finished, they rose and embraced each other. Then, needing the touch of sympathy, they risked hugging each other, not knowing when they'd have this luxury again.

There were few words left to say. Linnea watched them depart in single file along the narrow beach path. These were the people who made up the heart of her world. Each one of them had in his or her own way pointed her in the direction of her own path. She knew she'd still be afraid of failure. That she was flawed and would make many more mistakes. But it was their individual examples of day-to-day bravery that encouraged her to keep trying, to not give up, to be authentic. To be like the turtle and follow her instincts.

Each of these people was on his or her own path too, she thought. Emmi was on her way to Pawleys Island. Anna and Cooper were leaving soon for the university. Palmer and Julia would begin a new house project somewhere. David and Cara bookended Hope, who would be their chief focus for several more years to come. Only John remained at her side. Linnea turned to look at him now.

He was wearing a black shirt and black jeans. She let her gaze wander over his strong nose, dark brows, and ruddy skin. He stood solid with his legs spread and his arms crossed, watching the exodus. He, as much as or more than anyone else, had rocked her world. He'd made her feel the exaltation of love and the heartbreak of abandonment. He'd also revealed sincere regret and humility and the desire to change. His declaration of commitment had, she knew, taken courage.

"Where are you headed off to?" she asked him.

He turned to face her, squinting in the light from the rising sun. "I haven't figured that out yet."

She mulled that over. "Me neither."

He cracked a begrudging smile. "Gordon settled up and left."

"I know."

"I guess it's over between you?"

"I guess."

John rocked on his heels. "What have you decided?"

She looked up into his green eyes and shrugged with a freedom she hadn't felt in a long time. "I've decided not to decide."

He blew out his cheeks. "Okay."

She laughed at his confusion. She understood it all too well. "It was Flo who made it clear to me."

"Flo? Really?"

"Yep. She told me something very wise. *If it's not one thing, it's another.*"

"Lord help me," John said, looking skyward. "She must've said that at least once every day."

She laughed again. "But did you listen? I know I didn't. All summer long I worried about if and when I'd get my job back. Then it was whether Anna was depressed or Cooper horny or my mother mad. Or if Daddy would get his house built. If David would get well. If Hope would ever go home again. Where Gordon would live and, of course, if you were going back to California. Every time I thought I had a plan figured out, something else would come up and blow the plan into ether. Now, I confess," she said, scratching behind her ear, "it took me a while to understand what Flo was trying to tell me. But it finally sank in. I *can't* make a plan or a decision right now. None of us can. We're in the middle of a pandemic! We have to know when to zig and when to zag to avoid the calamity that's heading toward us every day. The key word for us is pivot."

Linnea turned to face him, her intent to be heard. "*Hindsight is twenty-twenty*. Yet in this year of 2020, there is no hindsight to be had! *All* of us are trying to make the best of this year like no other. We don't know what the future will bring. It's like you said, every day is precious. So let's be happy just living in the here and now. Let's try not to get sick." She laughed. "That's enough adventure for me. That's all the decision I can make right now. There's a freedom in that. The pressure is off. I'm going to take it one day at a time. And you know what?"

John shook his head.

"Today, I'm glad you're here."

His face broke into a wide grin. "I am too."

Linnea looked out across the empty beach. Not even a dog frolicked at the shoreline. The tide had swept away all sign of trespass. Nary a footprint scarred the smoothness. Linnea felt a sudden urge to make her mark.

"Want to take a walk?" She stuck out her hand.

John grasped her hand, and they began walking down from the dune to where the sand was soft under their feet. Luna trotted happily at her side, nose in the air. Linnea looked over her shoulder. The sea oats waved on the dune where a seashell sat on a small mound. The only marks along the beach were her footprints and John's, side by side, in the sand.

Looking forward again, she smiled and lifted her face to the rising sun.

# acknowledgments

EVERY BOOK I write is a journey. Yet the writing of *The Summer of Lost and Found* was, like the year 2020 it was written in, an experience like no other. For the past twenty years I have written books in a process that I had designed to help me create themes I developed from the species or environmental issues I chose as the novel's backdrop. That process included intuition in the choice of species, academic research, extensive interviews with experts in the field, and finally, hands-on work experience with the animals. From that research and experience, I derived my story. By the time I wrote the first word, I knew my themes, plot, characters, setting, and often, the end.

Not so with this book. I figured that since all my stories center around a woman's life—I write family sagas—what could be more interesting to write about than the changes and challenges families faced with forced isolation, togetherness, and economic strain? I wanted to write about this phenomenon we were living in—not about the Covid-19 illness, but family dynamics. And how better than with a family I knew so well—the Rutledge family of the Beach House series.

I wrote this novel in real time—and what a roller-coaster journey it has been! I let go of a process that worked for me and went boldly into the story. I write from structure and yes, I did begin with an outline. The problem came, however, when living through the weeks and months of the pandemic year, my perspective kept changing and I threw out my outline. I was introducing the next generation in the series and recognized that the problems of 2020 were different for the older generation than the younger. After the original shock and fear of a global shutdown, we went through the five stages of grief: denial, anger, bargaining, depression, and acceptance. Our defense strategies shifted to coping strategies.

What I wanted to say in April was different in July and changed again in November. Rewrite followed rewrite. I pulled my hair out, cursed the characters, the story, swore I would never do this again. It was a long, arduous process. By the year's end, I read my novel for the last time, tweaked the final words, and smiled with satisfaction. My story was told. I'd sharpened and shared my perspective of 2020 through the voices of my characters, especially the two Rutledge women of two generations: Cara and Linnea.

I realize, too, that like so many other aspects of my life in 2020, I could not have written this novel alone.

I must begin my acknowledgments with those women I spent the pandemic with as we sheltered in place at my house in the mountains: Marguerite Martino, Ruth Cryns, and Lauren Rutledge. To the Women of Windover—thank you for the early morning sessions with birdsong, poetry, coffee, and hope. And to my mountain girlfriend Cindy Boyle, thank you for brainstorm sessions and messages of encouragement. Tweet-tweet!

# acknowledgments

My heartfelt thanks to Sally Murphy for reading and editing early drafts of the novel, making sure all the science and nature facts were correct. And she's fabulous at copyedits, too. Kelly Thorvalson, thank you again for sharing your expertise on the world of conservation and sea turtles. You both are an inspiration to so many.

Love and gratitude go to Gretta Kruesi for helping me introduce the next generation of young, spirited, realistic, and likeable characters. And to James Cryns for giving the men in my novel more bite and laugh-out-loud wit. Thank you both for your ideas, outlines, and edits that helped me deliver a new freshness.

Much love and thanks to Mary Kay Andrews, Kristin Harmel, Kristy Woodson Harvey, Patti Callahan Henry, and Meg Walker, (always alphabetical!) my writing friends and sisters, for hanging in there with me, sparking the writing sprints each morning, and generally encouraging us all to move en masse forward with our novels sans fear or distractions. We also surprised even ourselves in 2020 with the creation of the incredible Friends and Fiction online program that seemed both serendipitous and destiny, and that brought to us a legion of new experiences and online friends.

I began this book with a new editor as well. Sincere and heartfelt thanks to Hannah Braaten for taking on the seventh book in a series with fresh eyes and ideas, for check-in phone calls, and for infinite patience as this story took shape. And to my superb copy editor, Joal Hetherington, who may know my backlist better than I do. I am indebted to you both for your skill and sensitivity.

What can I say to the rest of my Gallery team—you who have

shown such kindness, and have been stalwart supporters of my novels and me? I am deeply grateful to Jennifer Bergstrom, Jennifer Long, Jennifer Robinson, Aimee Bell, Sally Marvin, Eliza Hansen, Michelle Podberezniak, Bianca Salvant, Lisa Litwack, Andrew Nguyen, and everyone at Gallery who helps brings my words to readers.

A special, sincere gratitude to my agent, Faye Bender. Heartfelt thanks for your calm during this turbulent year and your expert guidance of the ship.

This book is being shepherded by a home team like no other. What stars shined on me as I gathered the best of the best: Angela May, Kathie Bennett, Laura Rossi, and Molly Waring. And to Claire Dwyer for your style and guidance. I cannot thank you enough for your brilliance, your enthusiasm, and your genuine support of my work and me.

I am blessed to have a team of supporters—my ARTists—who shine like the stars they are. Thank you for all your support, for sharing your ideas and suggestions, and most of all, your love.

There are so many people who came forward this year to help me with inspiration, talent, and support. Please know how grateful I am: Polly Buxton, Danielle Fabrega, Erin Kienzle, Alli Steinke, Judy Drew Fairchild, Lisa Minnick, Max Glenn, Danielle Noe, Lowell Grosse of Charleston Coffee Roasters, Loma Wang, Thomas McElwee, Jeff Plotner, Ben Ross of Brackish Bow Ties, Wendy Ellis, Sue Tynan, and Christiana Harsch.

As always, I end with the one person who begins and ends every day, Markus. Here is to living real time with you.